Also By Christopher C. Tubbs

THE SCARLETT FOX SERIES

Scarlett

A Kind of Freedom

Legacy

DECOY SHIPS

Kingfisher

Warley

CHRISTOPHER C. TUBBS

Warley

THE DECOY SHIPS
BOOK TWO

LUME BOOKS
A JOFFE BOOKS COMPANY

LUME BOOKS
A JOFFE BOOKS COMPANY

Lume Books, London
A Joffe Books Company
www.lumebooks.co.uk

First published in Great Britain in 2024 by Lume Books

We love to hear from our readers!
Please email any feedback you have to: feedback@joffebooks.com

Cover design by Imogen Buchanan
Cover images © IanDagnall Computing / Alamy Stock Photo

ISBN: 978-1-83901-582-3

No Stranger to the Sea

Tom Batrick sat in his mother's cottage in Poole in the county of Dorset, England, and pondered his future. He had recently returned from Nova Scotia in Canada where he had spent the last ten years on the privateer *Rover*, under Captain Alexander Godfrey, working his way up to first mate. She had been a lucky ship and had made him enough money to go home and buy the cottage. He was now thirty years old, qualified as a captain and married to Mary, whom he had met in Canada. She sat with his mother knitting him a jumper.

"Will you take the offer to sail with Aaron Clerk?" Mary asked.

Tom had known Aaron since they were children and his friend had offered him the first mate position on his ship, the *Rose of Poole*. It was a fat-bellied cargo ship which hauled Purbeck marble from the mines along the coast to London and Calais.

"I will, if I don't hear from the Company."

He had applied to the East India Company for a position on one of their big East Indiamen. His letter had been well written and given his experience to date, he was hoping for captain but would settle for first mate if that was all that was offered.

"He won't wait forever," his mother, Anne, said.

"I can wait for a while. I have plenty of money put by."

His mother shook her head. Tom had always been a patient boy; he had built his first boat when he was twelve years old. Begging wood from the boatyards, he had made a skiff. Then, getting scraps of sailcloth from the sailmakers, he had stitched together a sail. The boat had sailed well, and he had spent most of his spare time outside school in the harbour carrying people to and from ships anchored farther out, to make some money.

When he was seventeen, he bought passage to Canada, telling his mother he would make his fortune. He had sent money back regularly and letters whenever he could. There he had met Captain Godfrey and taken a berth on his ship. In the following years, he had sailed and fought in the Caribbean and in the Gulf of Mexico. His education had been furthered, his reading, writing and arithmetic improved and he learned to navigate and worked his way up to first mate. Then Godfrey retired and Tom decided to go home. He had saved his money and was quite well-off.

A month passed before the long-awaited letter arrived. Tom took it from the messenger and carried it to his chair by the fire, then sat looking at it for a long moment before slitting it open with his sailor's knife.

To Mr Thomas Batrick

The directors of the Honourable East India Company do desire that you present yourself to them at East India House, Leadenhall Street, London on the 27th of June in the year of our Lord 1793 at ten o'clock of the morning.

Please be prepared to go to sea immediately your ship has completed refitting.

Yours faithfully

"Well, that doesn't tell me much," he muttered.

"What do it say?" Anne asked.

"I have to go to London to join a ship. They don't tell me anything else but that."

"Nothing?" Mary said.

"No position, what the ship is, nothing. Just 'go to East India House and meet the directors'."

"That's odd. When do we have to be there?"

"By the twenty-seventh."

"But that's only a fortnight away. We had better get sorted and book ourselves onto the mail coach."

"No need, we can get there by sea. There are plenty of ships carrying cargo to London. That will only take a few days."

He found a ship easily enough: one carrying a cargo of salted fish. Mary wasn't that impressed with it.

"It stinks—and *we* will stink when we get there."

"We will have a couple of days, love. We will want to buy new clothes anyway—I can't present myself in my working rig, can I?"

She had to agree, since his wardrobe was limited to sailor's woollens and sea boots, in the main. Hers was also outdated and worn, so some new clothes would be welcome.

The trip took three days and was a sight more comfortable than the coach would have been. The food wasn't bad, and they got the skipper's cabin to themselves. They smelled London before they saw it, as they sailed up the Thames.

"Bugger me! What is that stink?" Tom asked the skipper.

"That, my boy, is the smell of civilisation. The shit and sweat of a million people. Look at the river."

Turds, dead animals and even the occasional body floated by.

"Jesus, nothing much can be living in that."

"Not much. Mind, it's coming up to high tide so it's not flowing out. When the tide turns, it will wash out to sea."

They sailed into the Upper Pool of London and tied up next to another ship.

"Blimey, there must be seven or eight hundred ships in here," Tom said.

"Yes, and we will just have to sit and wait our turn. I will put you and your missus ashore by boat."

Hackney carriages waited in a rank near the docks, and they asked the cabby to take them to a good pub near East India House. They were taken to a pub called the Grapes, which had rooms and was not far from Leadenhall Street, in Limehouse. It was clean and sold food as well as a reasonably good beer. There were shops nearby, but the landlord told them if they wanted quality clothes, they needed to head into the city.

Rather than walk through the filth that seemed to cover the roads and pavements, they hired a coach and driver to take them around. That's when they found out how noisy a city like London could be; the roads were cobbled. There were horses everywhere, pulling carts or carriages—with iron-rimmed wheels that set up a cacophony of sound far louder than anything they were used to—and depositing shit all over the road.

The driver took them to a shop that sold men's clothes for the middle classes. He told them, in a thick London accent, "Some of them shops only 'ave stuff for the dandies. You know, upper-class idiots wiv more money than sense."

The tailor was a small, thin man with chalk-covered fingers and a measuring cord around his neck.

"How can I help you, sir?" he said, with a decidedly foreign accent.

"I need clothes suitable for working on an East Indiaman."

"In what position, sir?"

"There's the rub. I don't know yet. Could be captain or first mate."

"Let's be safe and go for captain." The man smiled.

"What is your name?" Mary asked.

"Eli Issacs, madam."

That explained the accent—he was probably from eastern Europe.

"May I suggest moleskin breeches? Moleskin is a hardwearing material, suitable for both social activities and life aboard a ship. Will sir be fighting?"

England was at war with the French.

"I may have to."

"Then silk shirts as well as cotton. Good wool coats with silver or pinchbeck buttons and cravats. Oh, and one must not forget the hat."

He was measured, and ready-made clothes were brought forward for fitting. Adjustments were made while they waited, and they left a pound poorer but equipped with enough clothes to see Tom through the next year or two.

Then it was Mary's turn. A suitable dress shop was found, and dresses, bonnets and gloves procured. Another pound left his purse. Next was a cobbler, where they stocked up on shoes for her and boots for him.

When the twenty-seventh came, Tom was suitably suited and booted and arrived at East India House on time. He was shown straight up to a boardroom, where six very wealthy men sat around a large oval table. He bowed as he entered the room.

"Captain Batrick, please take a seat."

It's captain, then! Inside, he exulted.

"We are the directors of the East India Company, and are responsible for its profitable running and the safety of our ships," the man at the head of the table said. "I am Francis Baring, this is Mr Darrell, Mr Hunter, Mr Lushington, Mr Mesurier and Mr Inglis."

Baring was apparently the one who did the talking.

"Gentlemen," Tom said, with a sitting bow.

"We have read your letter and researched your credentials and find you a suitable candidate to captain a special ship that is currently being built at a shipyard in Blackwall. At this point, I must ask that you give us your word that you will tell no one of what is said in this room. Do I have it?"

Tom was intrigued.

"I give you my word of honour. I will hold everything secret."

"Excellent: it's for your own good as well as ours."

"The ship will be called the *Warley*," Mr Hunter said. "She is fourteen hundred and sixty tons burthen; one hundred and seventy-six feet; five inches along the deck; and has a beam of forty-three feet nine inches, while being one hundred and forty-four feet at the keel. She will carry thirty-four eighteen-pound cannons, and twelve six-pound."

Bugger, that's a warship!

"She will be completed in a month. We expect her to set sail upon her first mission, with a fully-trained crew, next year. You will also be given a letter of marque."

"I am expected to fight her, then?"

"Indeed. She will look like any other Indiaman; but your job is to lure in the French and any pirates and teach them not to toy with the East India Company."

"A *disguised* warship. Interesting," Tom muttered to himself, then spoke louder. "How many men will she have?"

"A hundred," Hunter said.

Tom did some calculations in his head.

"Sir, a navy ship of that armament would carry two hundred and fifty men. If I am to fight both sides—"

"How do you calculate the complement?" Baring asked.

"She has seventeen eighteen-pounders to a side. They take ten men to operate, that's one hundred and seventy men plus three men to a six-pounder. That gives us one hundred and eighty-eight men, plus another thirty to sail the ship. Which is a total of two hundred and eighteen."

"I am reliably informed that you can fight an eighteen with eight men," Hunter said. "That gives one hundred and thirty-six men to fire a broadside. You can have one hundred and fifty men and twenty soldiers."

The entire board nodded. *End of argument,* Tom realised.

The *Warley*

He met Mary outside, where she waited in the carriage.

"Are those your papers?" she said, looking at the oiled-cloth packet he carried.

"Yes. My commission as a captain and …"

"Captain!" She squealed, and threw her arms around him. The coach driver grinned at them.

Tom hugged her back and when they broke off, he commanded the driver, "Blackwall boat yard, if you please." He turned back to Mary, excitement gleaming in his eyes. "My ship is almost ready for sail. She is being fitted out at the shipwrights. I expect she is swimming and has her masts fitted."

"What is her name?"

"The *Warley*, she is the second with the name. They sold the old one to the navy, who renamed her."

An hour later they were at the gate to the Blackwall dockyard, the traffic having been atrocious. The gateman approached the carriage. Obviously a former soldier, he carried an iron shod staff which he made look like a weapon.

"Your business, sir?"

"Captain Batrick of the *Warley*. I'm here to see my ship."

"Can I see your papers?"

A guard who can read? No expense spared! Tom handed over his commission. The guard read the papers, folded them neatly and passed them back.

"If you go down to the third dock, which is Perry's, she is moored up alongside."

"Thank you."

The carriage rattled forward over the cobbles, and Tom immediately picked out her masts. Tall enough to take royals, they soared above the docks.

"That's her masts."

"Oh my! They are so much taller than the *Rover*'s."

The carriage came to a stop beside the ship. Unladen, she loomed above the stone dock.

"She is enormous!" Mary breathed in awe.

"You had better get used to that, as she will be our home for the foreseeable future. They have given me an allowance for fitting out our living quarters."

"*What?*"

"Yes, this will be our home—you are coming with me! Come on, let's get aboard."

Mary was stunned. She had not expected to accompany her husband, but he assured her it was common practice for married captains of Company ships to take their wives along.

They walked up the gangplank and were immediately confronted by a man dressed in sailor's slops.

"Can I help you?" he said, in a Kentish accent.

"I am Captain Batrick. This is my ship."

"Oh, my apologies, sir. Graham Ferguson, first mate. They didn't warn me you were coming." They shook hands.

"They didn't have a chance—I came straight from East India House. How long have you been aboard?"

"A week. Been making sure they rig her correctly. Can I show you around?"

"Please." He felt a nudge in his ribs and stilled his impatience. "This is my wife, Mary," he said as she stepped forward, holding up her hand.

"Delighted to meet you." Graham bowed. "The masts were stepped a week ago and since then they have completed the standing rigging and the running is about half done." He led them aft, cautioning Mary not to trip over the obstacles strewn across the deck. The ship smelled of fresh tar, paint and wood shavings.

Stairs led down from a door below the raised poop deck to where their cabin would be. There were ports for two guns.

"Any provision for stern chasers?"

"No, none at all, but we could fit ringbolts so the after guns could be repositioned."

Tom nodded. Smaller ships and even frigates liked to get behind a target and rake them. A pair of guns firing through the transom would be a deterrent.

Mary asked to be shown where the partition walls would be put up, so she could envisage their living quarters. Graham obliged by taking a lump of chalk from a pocket and marking the walls on the deck. Mary took a paper from her purse and a silver pencil from her chatelain and started making notes.

"You two go ahead and see the rest of the ship, I will be busy here for a while."

* * *

The men left her to it and wandered off down the main deck. Tom glanced back through the open door and saw Mary pacing off the dimensions of the sleeping cabin. He smiled; she would be happy making their new home comfortable.

"The ports are painted the same colour as the hull?" Tom asked.

"Yes, brown. There are thirty eighteens on this deck, the other four are on the foredeck. The poop deck has twelve sixes—though what use they will be I don't know; nothing but bloody pop guns." He frowned as he thought of something more. "I still don't understand why they want a brown stripe all the way down the hull and over the ports."

"The stripe makes it harder to distinguish how many guns we are carrying. Maybe we could change the sixes for those new carronades," Tom said.

"Not if the directors have to pay for them. They are having nightmares about the cost of building ships that are heavily armed. It's all new to them," Graham huffed.

It was true. The current fleet of East Indiamen were lightly armed at best, with maybe sixteen nine-pounders. That was good for seeing off a lightly armed pirate, but not a French warship bigger than a corvette. On top of that, the guns were usually old and ill maintained.

The *Warley*'s eighteens would be coming straight from the foundry. Brand new and with the latest carriages they weighed over two tons each and cost £120 a gun. The six-pounders would probably be navy cast-offs, as they were changing most of their small deck guns for the new, large-calibre carronades.

They moved down a deck, to where the passenger cabins were located. Being closer to the waterline, they suffered less from the ship's roll. There would be cabins for high-ranking Company officers or aristocratic passengers below the forecastle, and a state room at the stern below the captain's cabin. Those were the only ones with ports or windows.

Tom and Graham made their way forward to the figurehead, which was a representation of Zeus holding a lightning bolt by his side. The figure was dressed in a white robe.

"Why Zeus?" Tom asked, puzzled.

"I don't know. It probably has some obscure meaning to someone on the board of directors," Graham said, looking at the figure with his head on one side, as if trying to divine its meaning. In Tom's opinion, whatever it meant didn't really matter—as long as it showed the way home and brought the ship luck.

In fact, Francis Baring was a scholar and understood that not only was Zeus the king of the gods, but also the patron of the marketplace, punisher of dishonest traders, and the freedom-giver. The figurehead symbolised everything Baring wanted from the ship.

Tom and Graham finished their tour and went to find Mary, who had planned out every inch of their cabin including chintz curtains for the transom windows. Tom waited until they were back at the Grapes to tell her they would be sharing the room with a pair of eighteen-pound iron cannons.

She was silent for a minute or so then went to the dresser and took up a piece of paper. She referred to her notes and sketched out a scale drawing of their living quarters. She called Tom over and handed him a pencil.

"Draw in the guns."

"What is the scale?"

"One inch to one yard."

He drew a square where the gun port lay. "That's the floor area it uses. Three yards long by about five feet wide"

"They are huge!"

"Medium-sized guns really, nowadays. The liners have guns double the size on the lower decks."

"But not in the captain's cabin! I don't like the idea of sleeping with one of these in my bedroom ..."

For the first time in his life, Tom had to open a bank account—so he went to Barings Bank and talked with the manager. The Company would deposit his salary in the account every month, and he arranged for a sum to be sent monthly to a local bank, for his mother. As they were to live aboard, most of his salary would be unspent and the manager advised Tom to invest that in government four per cent bonds.

The next day, they moved from the Grapes to the George in Blackwall, to be nearer the dock. It was where Graham was also staying, and he had recommended it as being clean, with good food. Once they had settled in, Tom went to the ship and Mary went shopping. At the docks, ballast was being delivered and placed in the bilges. Arriving by barge, it was waste rubble from the stone quarries on the Isle of Purbeck, where they mined Purbeck marble—the lowest-quality stone that had to be removed to get to the good stuff. The ballast was lifted in large buckets, raised by A frames fitted to the barges, which was a delicate job as a dropped rock could damage the hull. It also had to be packed properly, so it trimmed the ship correctly and didn't shift.

The *Warley* sat lower now, and was stable. Now they could raise the top masts. The masts were in three sections: the mast, or lower, stepped on the keel; then came the topmast; and the topgallant mast.

That gave her the capability to carry four sails per mast: main, topsail, topgallant and royal. In between the masts, triangular sails called staysails could be raised. The *Warley* carried two jibs and a staysail on the bowsprit and a gaff rigged spanker on the mizzen. The sailmaker would send the sails to arrive in a week's time.

Internally—once the ballast was loaded—carpenters started to build the cabins, which lay on two decks. East Indiamen were as much passenger ships as they were cargo carriers, with passengers paying a high price for state rooms. Company employees were also carried, and there was a high demand for the captains to carry private, high-value goods back and forth. Many a *nabob* shipped his fortune privately with the Company captains.

The *Warley* also had a larger-than-usual magazine—situated below the orlop deck and below the waterline—which could be flooded in case of emergency. They would carry up to twenty tons of powder and sixty tons of shot. This gave her a relatively low cargo capacity of just over a thousand tons, in exchange for carrying enough ammunition to fight anything up to a heavy frigate.

Almost a year later, things were progressing nicely and Tom began looking for crew. He already had his first mate, carpenter and boatswain, so he placed advertisements in the newspapers and had handbills pinned up in pubs up and down the river. He was looking for experienced seamen with gunnery experience, and was in direct competition with the Royal Navy.

Men started to trickle into the George, where he set up a desk. Some were obviously using false names and he assumed they were runners from the navy. *All's fair in love and war*, he thought, as he signed the second John Smith of the morning.

A navy midshipman appeared looking around the bar confidently. He spotted Tom and walked over.

"Captain Thomas Batrick? I hear you are recruiting for an East Indiaman."

"Yes, I am. Are you interested?"

"No, I'm here to make sure no deserters get signed up."

"Really?" Tom looked around himself and to the door, where two large bosun's mates with cudgels swinging from their belts were checking anyone who came in. "You are hardly likely to catch them with those two standing there."

"It matters not. My orders are to stop any being signed aboard a ship with immunity."

That was true; East Indiamen were immune to being boarded and having their crews pressed—much to the annoyance of short-handed navy captains.

That evening, Tom quietly set up a second, more discreet, recruiting station in a pub two streets away, and had the word put out. Getting a crew was more important than offending the navy's sensibilities.

What he really needed was a good master gunner—someone who understood the workings of the guns and could manage the magazine. He was beginning to wonder if he would ever find one, when Silas Finch walked in. He was dressed in an old navy uniform and had a peg leg shod with leather. He was not old—probably in his thirties—broad-shouldered and weathered.

The bosun's mates at the door talked to him and then, laughing, let him through. The midshipman, who lacked the courtesy to either greet the veteran or introduce himself, sneered as he stomped past.

"You Cap'in Tom?"

"Aye, I am, and you are …?"

"Silas Finch, master gunner, formerly of the *Ajax*." He plonked himself down in a chair.

"That where you lost your leg?"

"Shot off below the knee by a French nine at Cape St Vincent in '80. Navy has no use for me now." That was impressive, the battle of Cape St Vincent was a memorable victory over the Spanish. *Ajax* was a seventy-four-gun third rate. Her gunner would be among the best.

"Your ship is the *Warley*?"

"It is, have you seen her?"

"I watched them step the masts. She is going to carry a lot of guns for an Indiaman."

"Forty-six in total, mainly eighteens."

"The men you've got so far, are they trained?"

"Some, but the gun crews still need to be trained as a team. I think we will have a lot of landsmen."

Silas nodded.

"What shot you having loaded?"

"We haven't got that far yet; the guns don't arrive for another week."

"Good, I can sort that out."

"You talk like you have already signed."

"I'm the best you will get and don't worry about *this*—" he tapped the wooden leg—"I can move around a ship in any weather with this peg." He lifted the peg leg up, so that Tom could see it was shod with leather that was covered in a layer of shagreen. "That's buffalo hide covered in sharkskin, it doesn't slip."

Tom made a note in his book and turned it towards Silas.

"Put your mark there." He handed him a quill.

Silas signed, his signature flowing and elegant. Tom looked at it appraisingly: clearly, there was more to Silas than met the eye.

* * *

Another key person to recruit was a doctor. A regular ship's sawbones would not do, because of the passengers. Another advert was placed; this time for a sober, experienced medical man.

The first that applied was neither sober nor suitable. The second was a young man who was newly qualified. Barnes Redford, the third to apply, was smart, sober, confident … and seeking his fortune. He had studied at Edinburgh and gained a practical knowledge of pharmacy, botany and anatomy. He had a licence to practise and was perfect.

Meanwhile, Mary had also been busy. She had shopped frugally and bought good quality, mostly second-hand, furniture. She did not skimp on the fabrics, bedding or tableware. Aware of her husband's status, she kept the decorations tastefully functional. There was a galley attached to their quarters where their food and that of the passengers would be prepared, and it suddenly occurred to her that they needed a chef. She mentioned this to Tom.

"Damn, I was so tied up recruiting sailors I forgot about a chef. I only got a cook for the crew."

"Never mind, dear. Let me deal with that," Mary said, and smiled.

She had handbills posted in Westminster advertising that they sought a chef for a new East Indiaman, and needed somebody able to cater to the rich and noble people she would carry. Thus, the bills emphasised the quality of passenger they would be catering for.

Several men applied. The first was old, fat and not suitable. The second was experienced in cooking for a pub kitchen and while she admired his ambition, he didn't have experience of preparing high-end cuisine. The third was a newly qualified chef.

"Hello, what is your name?"

"Peter Graves, ma'am."

"Where did you train?"

"At Brooks's, ma'am. Been there seven years."

Brooks's was one of the big three gentlemen's clubs in St James Street. Their restaurant was famous, as was their gambling book. The Prince Regent was a member of Brooks's and it was the habitat of choice for gentlemen.

"You do not want to stay there?"

"They only have positions for junior chefs, ma'am. I want more freedom to create my own dishes."

Mary instantly liked the young man, who was self-effacing yet confident.

"Would you cook me a demonstration meal?"

"Certainly, ma'am."

She took him aboard the *Warley* and showed him the galley. On the way she let him choose and purchase ingredients. She sent a message to Tom that they would eat on the ship that evening.

Tom arrived at dinner time and found the large dining table, where they and the firstclass passengers would eat, laid up for an intimate meal for two. Glasses shone and silverware glinted.

"You *have* been busy," he said.

"Go and change, you smell like a pub," she said with a smile.

While he changed, she served him a glass of dry sherry. The wine was white, dry and delicious. He raised his eyebrows at it in surprise.

"Come, dinner is ready," she said.

They sat at the table and Peter brought out the first course: white soup made with almonds, meat stock and cream. Peter had spent the day making the stock from roasted beef and ham bones. The second course was Dover sole, gently fried in butter with a beurre blanc sauce and salad. The third was haricot mutton, a delicate mutton stew with carrots and potatoes. The meat fell apart and was served with asparagus. Finally, the dessert: a cheesecake. The name referred to the texture rather than the use of cheese and this one was flavoured with orange flower water and a little cardamom spice. A selection of wines was served, each chosen to match the relevant course.

"You must be our new chef!" Tom said at the end when Peter presented himself. "That cheesecake was sublime!"

"Thank you, sir." Peter beamed.

"You can start tomorrow. We move in on the morrow," Tom announced—catching Mary completely by surprise.

Shakedown

Crewed, provisioned and ready for sea, they set off down the Thames from the powder dock, where they loaded a full twenty tons of powder. While Tom was not familiar with the Thames, his first mate was—so he left it to him and the pilot to get them out to the English Channel. The *Warley* handled well under spanker, gallants, royals, jibs and staysails on the river and as soon as they were out of the estuary and the pilot had left, they turned south.

"We will take it slowly to start with, let the crew bed in," Tom said. "Set mains."

The crew leapt to it and the big sails dropped as the topmen let loose the gaskets. Well used to standing on a rope and leaning into the yard, these were the elites who worked up in the rigging to set, reef and take in the sails. Having to handle salt-stiffened canvas in all weathers meant that not one had a full set of nails on their fingers. On deck, the landsmen hauled on the sheets to trim them to catch the wind, then tied them off.

Tom watched with a critical eye. The teamwork was off, but that would come with practice.

"Set the topsails."

When she was pulling on all sails to his satisfaction he went to the wheel and steered her for twenty minutes, by which time they were out of the Channel. The sea increased. Going with the wind she sailed well, but then he turned her, so she closed with the wind.

"She's griping. We need to trim her further aft." He handed the wheel to Graham, who agreed. They could feel it through the wheel and their feet.

"We will pull into the Solent and anchor," Tom decided, after considering whether it was the press of sail contributing to the problem or just the trim. "Let's see what happens when we set the staysails and studding sails."

That didn't make any difference, so he tried sailing closer to the wind. The gripe got worse the closer to the wind they sailed, it was definitely the trim. They anchored behind the Isle of Wight, off Lee on Solent, and the crew shifted ballast aft raising the bow a few inches and giving the rudder more bite.

The following morning, they sailed on the morning tide.

"That's better, now let's really test her."

He headed west beyond Land's End, then south into the Atlantic where the winds were higher and the waves bigger.

"She sails like a witch!" Tom rejoiced as she crashed through the waves.

"Aye, we must enjoy it while we can. With passengers and cargo aboard, we will have to treat her more gently," Graham said with a grin.

"That's true, but we can have some fun now!"

Tom had the crew perform sail evolutions more suited to a frigate than a merchantman: changing sails on the fly; raising and lowering the top masts until they could do it in their sleep. They pulled into Lulworth Cove, where he had the crew kedge the ship out, back in again and anchor. They repeated the exercise several times—to the amusement of local fishermen—until Tom was happy.

He addressed the crew.

"You seem to have the measure of the ship in terms of sailing her, and what a joy she is to sail!" The crew shouted their agreement. "Now it is time to train on the guns. We exist to teach both pirates and the French that Company ships have teeth. Now we need to sharpen them and fight as well as the ships in His Majesty's navy."

He let that sink in.

"Clear for action!"

Feet pounded as the men ran to their stations. Bosun's mates yelled orders and a team went into his quarters to clear it so the guns could be used.

Then Tom had a sudden realisation; he had forgotten to tell Mary they would be doing this.

"Oh bugger," he said, as Mary came out of the door on to the main deck and looked up at him. She had her hands on her hips and a look that said "Explain!" He rushed down the steps.

"Sorry love, I forgot to warn you. We are practising going to quarters," he said as he ran down the steps.

She held up a hand, stopping him in mid-step. "They had better not break anything," she said—through gritted teeth—and turned away. She stopped and looked back over her shoulder. "Is this likely to happen often?"

"Until the crews are bedded in, yes."

"Then we will leave what we don't use in the hold."

Graham stepped up to him and said, "Cleared, skipper."

Tom looked at his watch. "Fifteen minutes, that's too slow. We will repeat the exercise after we have run the guns in and out in dumb show."

It was a shambles. The experienced men yelled at the inexperienced men who stood in the wrong place or picked up the wrong rope or got in the way. Silas Finch looked on. Then …

"*Stop*!" Finch bellowed.

The men froze.

"Get those guns back in their sailing positions and tied down."

More shouting and hauling until the guns were stowed.

"Everyone, gather around the number three gun. That's the third from the front for those who do not know."

The men did as Silas Finch told them. He pushed his way through them until he stood behind the gun.

"Now crew, take your positions."

"What do you do?" he asked a man who stood to one side.

"I worm and ram, sir."

"Do not call me 'sir', I ain't an officer. You can call me 'Guns'. You should be holding the ram."

He pulled the ram from the stowage.

"Do you like your toes?" Guns asked him.

"Aye, I do," the man said, confused.

"Then don't stand there or you will lose them." He grabbed his arms and moved him. "The rammer stands *here*! Who is the loader?"

"Me, Guns," another said, and raised his hand.

"Have you got a charge yet?"

"There ain't none up here."

Guns rolled his eyes. "It's fucking practice! *Pretend!*"

He went around the eight-man crew and pushed them into the correct positions, sometimes kicking their backsides with his peg leg. "Now everyone, look at these men and fix in your mind where you should be stood at your gun." He left them standing for a full two minutes then said, "Load your gun and run it out."

The crew, being in the right places, pulled the gun back without incident and went through the motions of loading and hauling it forward.

"*Stop*! You, why are you standing there?" He addressed a man standing behind the gun.

"Guns?" the man said.

"Are you the gun captain?"

"No, Guns, I pull on the rope."

"If you stand there when the gun is fired, the recoil will kick it back and squash your soft, flaccid body." Guns pushed him and two of the others into their firing positions. Then he turned to the other gunners. "Remember where you should be standing."

Tom watched on as Silas went through the steps, and had the gun crews chant them as the number three crew walked through them. When he was happy with that, he had them go to their guns. The word "stop" punctuated the first couple of run-throughs, but thereafter it was used less and less. Silas walked to the foot of the steps to the poop deck.

"I think we can go for a live fire now, skipper," he called up.

"By all means, please do, Guns," Tom said with a grin, then looked up to the lookout. "Lookout, please let us know if it is safe to fire a broadside out to sea. I don't want to sink any fishing boats today."

Given the all-clear, they went through the steps for real. The chant echoed, "Worm, sponge, charge, wad, ball, ram, prime, runout." There was a pause as Guns checked their positions, correcting some. Satisfied, he looked up at Tom and nodded.

"Lookout?"

"Clear!"

"*Fire*!"

The gun captains touched off their guns, which belched smoke and fire while slamming back on their tackles. No one was hurt, but Guns had set up a surprise. He had placed pig trotters behind the wheels of one of the guns. Before he allowed them to reload, he held up the mangled remains.

"If this is what those wheels can do to a trotter, imagine what they can do to your toes!"

He walked down the guns so they could all get a close look. When he had finished, he looked up at Tom and nodded.

"Excellent," Tom said. "Now do that two more times."

The rate of fire was, as expected, slow, but that would improve with practice.

"Take us to sea, Graham. Let us see how they get on with the ship rolling."

The guns were stowed, and the tampons replaced. The *Warley* was kedged out of the bay and set sail heading due south. The small crowd of locals from Lulworth village, that had come to see what the big ship was doing in their bay, waved. Tom raised his hat to them.

The Atlantic had long slow rollers travelling from the south-west with a following wind. Sailing due south made the ship corkscrew, which Tom thought was too much of a step up for his novice gunners.

"Head north-east and put the sea on our stern," he ordered, to reduce the roll component.

"Guns, two broadsides from the port battery, then two from the starboard," he ordered once they were in clear water.

He took out his watch as the procedure began. Graham stood beside him. "Will Guns always command the battery, skipper?"

"No, you will. He will be busy down below in the magazine if we get into a fight."

"Then I should run the next practice?"

"Indeed, you will my friend, indeed you will."

Graham took over command of the guns from then on and proved to be a natural with them. Soon after, Tom sat with Mary, Silas, Barnes and Graham over dinner.

"We have one more month of shakedown before we have to return to India Dock," he announced.

"We will be at sea for Christmas?" Mary said.

"No, I plan to put into Poole on the twenty-third and spend Christmas with Mum."

Mary beamed; she had been afraid that the old lady would have to spend Christmas alone. Tom wasn't finished. "The men that want to go ashore can in watches, but Christmas Day will be spent aboard. Peter will prepare the officers a Christmas feast and help the cook to prepare one for the men. Mum will be aboard with us. Peter has made a list of what will be needed and will go ashore as soon as we anchor, with a party, to procure it."

"We need two replacements, can I recruit?" Graham said. They had lost one to injury and the other was being put ashore as he was a waste of space.

"Poole is as good a place as any and better than most," Tom replied. "Only let me know who any prospective candidates are, as this is my home town, and I will probably know of them."

"Will do, skipper."

* * *

The twenty-third saw them anchor in Poole Harbour. The water, as usual, was flat calm as it was sheltered by Sandbanks Spit. Fishing boats drifted across as men fished for plaice. A boat took Tom and Mary ashore, followed by Peter and his team. The men would start their shore leave by watch—once the ship had been cleaned to Graham's exacting standards.

Tom opened the door to the house and called, "Mum, it's Tom and Mary!"

"What be you doin' 'ere?" she exclaimed in surprise, her Dorset accent sounding strong to his ears after their time away.

"We've come for Christmas," Mary laughed.

"But I ain't got nothing in!"

"Don't worry, we will be having Christmas Day on my ship," Tom said as he hugged her.

"Your ship?"

"Yes, she's anchored in the harbour."

Anne wanted nothing but to go down to the dock and see his ship then and there.

"My Lord! She's a big 'un!"

"She is a fair size," Tom said modestly.

They stood looking for a while and Tom answered his mother's questions. Then, a voice hailed them.

"Is that Tom Batrick?"

"Hello Aaron," Tom said and shook his old friend's hand.

"Is that why you didn't take my offer?" Aaron said, nodding to the *Warley*.

"She is."

"Tom is captain," his mum said.

Aaron laughed. "I know, Anne. I don't think there is a soul in Poole who doesn't. You know, as soon as she got your letter, she was telling everyone she met."

Anne looked embarrassed and Tom put his arm around her shoulders and hugged her. "Never you mind, Mum, he is only teasing."

"But it's true!" she said, looking at him with a tear in her eye. "I am so proud of you. I wanted everyone to know."

They walked back up to the house, Aaron tagging along to catch up with Tom.

"It's what you always wanted," he said.

"Aye, and she is a fine ship. The crew has come together well."

"You will be taking her on her first run, then?"

"Aye, we will return to London before the new year and take on our first cargo and passengers. We will go to India and China, then back."

"That will take … what, a year at least?"

"Yes. Will you look after mum? The Company is sending part of my salary home to her every month."

"A salary! You will be saying you're middle class next!" Aaron teased him.

"*Pfft*, as if that matters. Will you?"

"Of course; my Sarah visits her every day or so anyway."

Mary nudged Tom and whispered in his ear. He nodded.

"And would you and Sarah like to join us on the *Warley* for Christmas Day?" Tom asked.

Aaron beamed. "Why, we would be honoured."

Peter returned to the ship with two sides of beef, a five-rib of beef, a goose, sausages, a ham, pork knuckles, beef bones and bacon, kale, parsnips, Swedish turnip, carrots, onions, potatoes, leeks and Brussels sprouts. A basket of thyme, sage and parsley topped off the savouries. He had bottled peaches and pears in sugar syrup, several gallons of cream, suet, flour, dried fruit, preserved lemons, cheeses and nuts. Another boat followed with casks of best Dorset beer, cases of wine, sherry, port and brandy. He had spent the entire budget.

From then on, the ship was enveloped in the smells of cooking. First, he had the ship's cook roast the beef bones and pork knuckles then put them in kettles of water with beer, carrots, onions, leeks, herbs, pepper and cloves to make a meat stock.

A blacksmith delivered a large iron double trough with spits mounted above on frames, along with ten sacks of charcoal. The troughs were placed on a double layer of sheet iron that was fixed to the foredeck cargo hatch cover, well clear of any rigging.

Stuffing of several types was made with forcemeat; one of breadcrumbs, suet, onion and sage, another with parsley and thyme instead of sage. A third was made of sausage meat, rehydrated dried mushrooms, herbs and chopped bacon. All were liberally seasoned with salt and pepper.

The goose was pulled and plucked; the giblets went to make more stock while the feathers were gathered for stuffing a pillow at a later time. The bird would be stuffed later.

They made dough for fresh bread and soon the smell of yeast drifted on the breeze. Special biscuits were made; some sweet, some savoury. Plum puddings and preserved lemon and sugar syrup puddings were all set to steaming.

Mid-morning on Christmas Eve, the fire troughs were filled with kindling and charcoal and set alight. The sides of beef were threaded onto the spits and wires used to hold them in place. When the coals were well alight and an even white colour, the spits were mounted on the frames. The crew took it in turns to rotate them and the cook regularly basted them with dripping. They would cook for a whole twenty-four hours.

Now, the smells were maddening.

Peter was up at four in the morning on Christmas Day, and baked fresh bread for breakfast. He and the cook made enough for the entire ship to have with bacon and eggs at eight bells.

The goose had been stuffed and was roasting when a boat pulled alongside with three buckets of sprats—small silver fish that were a speciality in Poole. At that point, the skipper left to fetch his guests.

Tom was pulled across the short reach of water to the dock where Aaron, Sarah—who was about six months pregnant—and his mother were already waiting. He hugged the women and shook hands with Aaron before getting them aboard. The group was largely silent as they rowed towards the big ship.

"My goodness, how am I to get up there?" Sarah asked as she looked up at the curve of the tumblehome.

"On that," Tom said as a bosun's chair was lowered. "You as well, Mum."

The crew were extra careful with their precious cargo as the women were lifted aboard. Aaron and Tom took the battens to the main deck.

The ship's stewards, of which there were a dozen, were laying out vast trestle tables for the feast. Anne demanded a tour, but Sarah just wanted to see Mary and sit down, so Tom took them all down to the cabin first.

"My word, it's bigger than my house!" Anne gasped as she took in the extent of the captain's quarters.

Aaron also raised an eyebrow, for compared to the little cabin in his coaster, this was palatial. They looked in on the dining table that was laid with the silver tea service. Aaron whistled; even if it was plate, it was beyond his reach.

"Come on, Mum, let me show you around the ship," Tom said—as he wanted that out of the way before the midday service that would be held on deck. A local priest had agreed to come and take it.

"She's armed like a warship. Are you sure she is an East Indiaman?" Aaron said softly, while Graham was explaining to Anne how the capstan worked.

"We have to be able to defend ourselves against pirates and French privateers," Tom replied.

"Your men know how to use them?"

Tom nodded.

"Then God help any who try and take this ship on!"

Anne was amazed by the cabins and astonished at the price someone would have to pay for one. She had never seen that much money in her life.

The ship's bell rang: *ding ding, ding ding, ding ding, ding ding*. It was noon, and the crew assembled on the main deck. It was chilly, but mild for the time of year.

The priest stood on the poop deck so he could look over his flock. Tom, Mary and their guests stood with the crew. Seamen were not overly religious in the main, but did enjoy a good service on special occasions—and Christmas was one of those.

The priest had been instructed to keep the service down to forty-five minutes and to include lots of carols. A fiddler and a crewman with a penny whistle were on standby. The Reverend

Postlethwaite—a Protestant, of course—was a rotund, jolly man with a red face that told all he enjoyed the odd tipple. He reminded Tom of Friar Tuck in the ballad, "Robin Hood and the Curtal Friar", that children sang in May.

The Reverend Postlethwaite kicked off the service with "Christians Awake", a popular carol. He then led prayers, finishing with the Lord's Prayer, then quoted St Bernard of Claivaux.

Let your goodness, Lord, appear to us, that we, made in your image, may conform ourselves to it.
In our own strength we cannot imitate your majesty, power, and wonder nor is it fitting for us to try.
But your mercy reaches us from the heavens through the clouds to the earth below.
You have come to us as a small child, but you have brought us the greatest of all gifts, the gift of eternal love.
Caress us with your tiny hands, embrace us with your tiny arms and pierce our hearts with your soft, sweet cries.

That was followed by "Hark the Herald Angels Sing" and "Silent Night". The blessing followed:

May you be filled with the wonder of Mary, the obedience of Joseph, the joy of the angels, the eagerness of the shepherds, the determination of the magi, and the peace of the Christ child. Almighty God, Father, Son and Holy Spirit bless you now and forever.

The finale was a roaring rendition of "Oh Come All ye Faithful". Drinks were served, and the Reverend Postlethwaite stayed for

Christmas dinner with the men. Tom had a feeling he would have to shoot him from a cannon to get him to leave.

As soon as the service was over, Peter and the cook grilled the sprats over the fire troughs—now empty, as the beef was down below outside the galley, on scrubbed wooden boards resting before being carved. The fish were served as a sort of canapé which everyone could eat with their first drinks. Large platters of them sat on the tables in the berth deck, along with fresh bread to mop up the juices.

Tom, Mary and their guests retired to the cabin, where they had the sprats and potted shrimps on thin toasts and were served sweet sherry. Then the stewards told them that dinner was ready, and they went through to the dining room.

The table fairly groaned under the weight of food: roast beef—rare in the middle; a baked ham studded with cloves; roast goose; crispy roast potatoes and parsnips cooked in goose fat; mashed, buttered swede; whole boiled turnips; sausages wrapped in bacon. There was also gravy, rich with port and thick with the root vegetables from the drip pan that the meat had been roasted over. As the stewards served wine, Tom took up the large carving knife and fork laid in front of his place and carved for everyone.

Down on the berth deck the men were getting stuck into their beef and vegetables. A feast like this was uncommon and did more to earn Tom their respect and loyalty than anything else. The Reverend Postlethwaite joined the men, and they swore he drank two tankards of beer for every one they did. The main course was followed by plum pudding and boiled cream.

* * *

In the captain's cabin, dessert was a choice of plum pudding or steamed lemon pudding with a choice of boiled cream or thick fresh cream. A sweet madeira was served with the dessert. Anne was getting quite tipsy—in fact they all were—and laughter echoed around the dining room to match that of the crew below.

Later that afternoon, they all sat around with full bellies and played games: Questions and Commands, Nip Nose and Fly, Feather, Fly! among others. The guests returned to shore the next morning having slept in the guest cabins, feeling happy and *very* hungover.

The First Voyage,
1797–1798

India Dock

They sailed from Poole on the twenty-seventh on the early tide and made their way up towards the Thames estuary in the teeth of a storm. It was so bad that they could not contemplate entering the river, and so anchored in the Downs, where they sat for two days waiting for conditions to improve. Eventually, as all storms do, it passed; the winds dropped and settled to come from west of north. The sea grew quieter, and they could get a pilot.

"It's a fair muzzler of a wind," Graham said, looking at the flag.

"Jibs, staysails and spanker," Tom ordered. The triangular sails would allow them to sail closer to the wind.

"Bring her up to her anchor!" Graham bellowed through a trumpet.

The capstan clinked as the men marched around bringing in the anchor cable. The nippers ran back and forth, busily attaching the anchor cable to the messenger.

"Up and down!"

"Belay hauling."

"Set the jibs and spanker. Ready the staysails."

As the sails filled: "Haul away."

As the anchor broke from the holding ground: "Anchor away!"

"Helm catch her! Steer north-east."

"Steerage!"

"Bring her up to the wind, set staysails."

The sails shuddered as they got as close to the wind as they could. There was nary an ounce of gripe. They passed Ramsgate and Broadstairs—Tom wanted as much sea room as he could get, so maintained that course until they were another eleven miles north.

"Wear ship to starboard, bring her around to due west."

The *Warley* swung around in a 270-degree turn that ended with her heading right into the centre of the Thames estuary.

"Set the gallants."

Their speed increased a little to five knots, which was sedate by an Indiaman's standards.

"Pilot, you have the deck."

The pilot took command while Tom watched and learned. They passed the Isle of Sheppey to port and Sheerness, then, as the estuary narrowed, Canvey Island to starboard. A ninety-degree turn to almost due south, and they passed East Tilbury. Now they were in the river, with an incoming tide pushing them along.

They got to Blackwall and hove-to; the entrance to the docks was through a lock. A boat took across messenger lines so they could pull across cables that would be looped on to bollards. Then it was through main strength at the capstan that pulled them into the lock. Once through the second gate, they were in the outer basin and had to repeat the process through a second lock to enter the dock proper.

A man on shore shouted that they should moor at the number four dock. He came aboard as soon as they were tied up and the gangplank was lowered.

"Captain Batrick?"

"Aye," Tom replied.

"Wilberforce Grange, dock manager."

"Pleased to meet you, Mr Grange."

"I have been asked to tell you that you should report to East India House at your earliest convenience."

"No time like the present," Tom said and turned to Graham. "Make her ship shape. I will let you know what is happening later."

"Oh, you are not going anywhere soon," Grange said, looking at a sheaf of papers. "Your cargo will be coming in over the next couple of months and you are scheduled to sail on the eighteenth of March with a full set of passengers."

Tom reconsidered.

"Take down the top masts and set a harbour watch. The rest of the men can have shore leave," he told Graham.

Tom went to his cabin and changed. Mary had heard the conversation through the skylight.

"Will we get time ashore?"

"I expect so, but wait until I get back before packing."

He took a Hackney carriage to East India House and announced himself to the clerk in the entry hall. He was asked to sit and wait while a messenger was sent. An hour later, he was summoned.

"Captain Batrick. What have you to tell us?" Francis Baring spoke as soon as Tom walked through the door to the boardroom.

"Good afternoon, gentlemen. I can report that the *Warley* is in all respects ready for sea," said Tom, with gravitas.

"As a fighting ship?" Mr Lushington asked.

"As a fighting ship *and* as an Indiaman."

"You are satisfied with her sailing qualities? She is a new design, and we want to have more built," Baring said.

"She sails very well in all weathers. She needed to be trimmed a little to the stern to give the rudder more bite and to prevent griping, but other than that she is weatherly, stable and fast."

"Excellent, excellent. Well, you can leave her in the hands of the dock for the next month or so. You will sail on March eighteenth for India and China." Baring checked a paper. "You are due a commissioning bonus of one hundred pounds. It will be paid to your bank."

That was enough for a gentleman to live in London for six months! Tom decided he would treat Mary to some more new clothes and invest the rest.

Tom and Mary took rooms near Goodman's Fields in Heydon Square. It was far enough from the river to avoid the stench, and close to the countryside while having the centre of London within easy reach. They visited the theatre and playhouses and even got a taste for Shakespeare having seen a version of *The Taming of the Shrew* at the Theatre Royal in Haymarket.

Living the life of a middle-class gentleman was alien to Tom, but he was philosophical about it—and Mary took to middle-class life as if she had been born to it.

"We are warm, well fed and comfortable. I can give my mother a much better living than she ever had with Dad. It's a good life," Tom told Arnie Champion, another sailing friend who came to visit on his stopover in London. Arnie had been the bosun on the *Rover* when Tom was first mate. The two had exchanged letters ever since. Arnie had moved back to England and was now sailing out of Hull on a merchantman that traded in the Mediterranean.

"Do you need a bosun?" Arnie asked.

"Not right now, we have one, but if he leaves, I will contact you."

"He's all right then?"

"He was transferred from another Company ship."

"Aah, I see—a known man."

"The Company trusts its own. Once you are in, and are a Company man, you are set for life."

"So, I've heard. I'm staying in London for a week or so; I will keep me eyes peeled for adverts."

"I will write you a letter of introduction and a reference. That will help."

Arnie was very grateful, and a week later Tom got a note to tell him he had signed on to the *Hindustan* as a bosun's mate.

"Won't be long before he is made bosun," Tom said to Mary once he had read it.

Two months flew by, and Tom wasn't surprised to see Graham at his door in mid-February.

"They will start loading her next week," Graham announced, knocking the rain from his hat.

"We had better get back aboard then," Tom said—as he had no intention of letting anyone else organise the cargo. "Do you know what the cargo is?"

"Manufactured goods for India, wool cloth, that sort of stuff."

"We will probably pick up more in India for China and tea, pottery and silk for the run home."

So, Tom and Mary upped sticks and moved back to the *Warley*. The harbour crew had kept her in top condition and their cabin was just as they had left it—including the chintz coverings over the cannons.

The crew came back aboard and the loading began. They had to be careful that the cargo should not fill the holds; room had to be left for the passengers' baggage.

"Looks like we have a full ship," Tom said as he looked down the passenger list. "We have a supercargo coming aboard in India who will supervise the buying and selling in China."

"Supercargo? What's that?" Mary asked.

"It's a man. A senior Company official, who will be the most senior man on the ship and will direct me. Apparently, that's normal for trade in China."

The passengers started coming aboard on the sixteenth of March. Some had large amounts of baggage as they were moving to India to work and live. The Company paid their passage and recovered the costs from their salaries over time. If one was canny, one could become rich by sending high-value goods back to England with trusted captains. Likewise, canny captains brought home their own private cargoes and made their fortunes that way.

Tom had every intention of retiring rich.

The cabins filled, from the smallest up. Clerks joined early to avoid paying for another night in a hotel. The wealthy sauntered up in their carriages on the seventeenth with their cartloads of baggage. It all had to be loaded and sorted into what was to be stowed in the hold and what would go to their cabins. People who were moving out for the long-term also brought household goods and even furniture. Tom thought that was crazy, as it would be cheaper to buy new, once you were out there.

Some passengers—mainly the military types—were very low-maintenance. Some of the toffs, on the other hand, were showing signs of being a pain in the arse. One woman in particular was on her way to India to marry a senior Company man. She behaved as though she owned the ship and demanded almost constant attention from the stewards. Tom rolled his eyes as he heard her asking for—no, *demanding*—a fresh pot of tea to be brought to her on the main deck.

During this event, the pilot was aboard, and they needed to be moving. Tom walked over to where the demanding lady had a steward set up a canvas chair.

"Good morning, Miss Alvis," he said politely.

"Who are you?" she asked rudely.

"I am the captain."

She looked him up and down and managed to look down her nose at him, even while seated.

"Really?"

Tom reined in his temper. "Yes, and I have to ask you to remove the chair and table as we are setting sail in an hour, and you will be in the way."

"I am sure I'm not." She looked away, out across the basin of the dock.

Tom took a deep breath.

"Miss Alvis, as the captain of this ship I can have you clapped in irons if I wish. There is no higher authority than me—and God. Now *move*, or I will *have you moved*."

"You would not dare! My husband …"

"… is not your husband yet and is not here. And even if he was, the request would be the same. You will be in the way and in danger of being injured. You can stand over there to watch, if you wish."

Tom signalled to a steward, who came over. "Take Miss Alvis's chair and table below. Now."

Tom held out his hand to help her to her feet. "Miss?"

She huffed, took his hand and stood. The chair was removed as soon as her weight left it.

"Thank you. If you watch, you will understand."

He led her to the area that was out of the crew's way, where other passengers were gathering. Cables were run from the ship to bollards positioned to aid departure. The men manned the capstan, the nippers went to their positions.

"Cast off forrad," Tom called. He watched what the ship did. There was an offshore breeze.

The wind in the rigging gently started to push them away from the dock. "Cast off aft." He waited until they were twenty feet out, then called, "Haul away." The men stamped and heaved and the pawls on the capstan clinked. The cable came in and was coiled where Miss Alvis had been seated. The ship moved to the lock and slid in between the walls; the lock keeper closed the gates behind them and opened the sluices to let water in and raise the level. It was high tide.

The gate opened and Tom had the fore topsail set to push them out. That single sail made just enough headway to give them steerage way as they sailed through the second lock, which was open at both ends. They were in the river.

"Set jibs, topsails, gallants and spanker."

Men rushed to set the sails, hauling on halyards, clew lines and sheets. The *Warley* got underway.

Miss Alvis looked at the place she had been sitting as a rope whipped through it as it was tensioned.

"Oh my," she said.

The Crossing

They joined a convoy of four ships at the Downs. Another Indiaman, the *Amiston*—which was also on her first voyage but only armed with twenty-six nine- and twelve-pounders—and two independent traders attached to the EIC.

As the *Amiston* was obviously armed, she took the lead, her ports forming a black and brown checkerboard. She set a sedate pace of ten knots: her captain, Willoughby, had ten years of service with the EIC and knew that speed was not of the essence, the comfort of the passengers was. The first leg was west, to give them the sea room to pass the Bay of Biscay at a comfortable distance.

Tom knew that he was giving the passengers a chance to get their sea legs, and smiled as he saw the entitled Miss Alvis rush to the side and cast her accounts to the sea.

"The sea is a wonderful leveller, Graham," Tom said, piously.

"Aye, skipper. That she is." Graham chuckled.

They sailed until sunset, then the *Amiston* signalled that they should reduce sail for the night. Tom dressed for dinner and admired Mary, who wore one of her new dresses.

"You look lovely!"

"I will be plain compared to the ladies, I fear."

"Never in my eyes. Come, it is time."

The passengers weren't ready to be visiting the other ships yet, so they would have a full table. Tom greeted the passengers as they entered.

"Lord Armstrong, milady," he said, greeting the first to enter. Armstrong was a major shareholder in the Company and was visiting India for both business and recreation.

"Captain Batrick, your ship is a credit to the Company."

"Thank you, milord. She is indeed a fine ship."

"Do you expect trouble?"

"Not until we pass Madagascar. Pirates operate from there, and the French from Reunion."

The lord nodded wisely and made way for the next passenger, who was a bewhiskered lieutenant colonel from the Indian Army.

"Colonel Burton."

"Captain."

The colonel didn't chat, and moved on to get a drink from a steward. The rest of the passengers filed in.

"No Miss Alvis?" Tom asked the steward.

"She is in her cabin; I fear she is unwell, sir."

"That is a shame," Tom said disingenuously.

The passengers sat at the places which bore their names, which were set according to rank and status. Tom sat at the head of the table, with Mary opposite him at the other end. Lord and Lady Armstrong sat to his right, with The Honourable Quinten Stokes to his left and an empty seat next to him.

"Miss Alvis is not taking dinner?" Stokes asked, sounding disappointed.

"I am afraid she is suffering from seasickness," Tom said.

Mary smiled from the other end of the table, proud of her husband's restraint.

Stokes was travelling to Bombay to take the position of senior writer. He was single. Tom noticed his disappointment and made a mental note to watch for any potential trouble.

"If she's sick now, what will she be like when we get moving?" Armstrong said.

"I knew a man who died of seasickness," Rafe Simpson-Thomas said from the other side of the empty chair. "Turned himself inside out!" He guffawed at his own joke.

The conversation continued over dinner as the passengers got to know each other, and continued on deck as the hardier types took the air. Tom and Mary retired to their cabin after taking a couple of turns around the deck.

"That went well," Mary said.

"Yes, it did," Tom said as he shed his coat and neck cloth. "What did you learn about the passengers at your end?"

"Reinhold Mueller is a mercenary and travelling across India to eventually join the army of the Maharaja of Manipur."

"That's odd, why didn't he take the *Amiston*? She is going to Madras."

"Couldn't afford it. He could only afford passage to Bombay and plans to cross India on horseback."

Tom shrugged.

"Mr Bowling is travelling to Bombay to become the head shipwright at the Company docks and construction yard. He and his wife Susan are a nice couple. She's half Portuguese and has been a clerk to an accountant in the past."

"A shipwright, that could be useful. I will make his acquaintance."

"Did you talk to the colonel?"

"Eventually; he's not a very sociable man. He is returning to India after visiting England to settle his father's estate. He is a staff officer in Bombay, and a widower."

They chatted as they prepared for bed. Tom had the watch in the morning and would rise early.

The next day, they picked up the pace and raced westwards past the Scilly Isles before turning south-east for the run down to the Cape Verde. Miss Alvis stayed in her cabin; her maid was the only person who saw her. Mary went to visit and recommended she saw the physician. Barnes prescribed two drops of laudanum in brandy once a day in the morning. "It's not a cure but should relax her," he said.

The weather was typical for late winter: rain, shifting winds, moderate to high seas. They got past Biscay without incident and ran down the coast of Africa. The weather improved and Miss Alvis reappeared. The seasickness had not changed her attitude of entitlement, and she continued to make the stewards' lives miserable.

Indeed, that entitlement became so bad that by the Canaries, Lord Armstrong took action when the steward bringing tea to him and his wife was intercepted by the demanding miss and bullied into fetching her a fruit punch. Tom was not privy to what was said, but a thoroughly chastened young lady emerged from Armstrong's cabin, her ears burning.

Along with the lieutenant colonel there were four other junior officers who had not paid for dining and ate from their own supplies in their rooms. They started exercising on the main deck in the mornings, much to the interest of the ladies. One of the officers approached Tom.

"Captain, may I have a word?" He called up to the poop deck from the bottom of the steps.

"Certainly … Lieutenant Beaumont, isn't it?"

"I am, sir," he replied as he climbed the steps.

"Well, what can I do for you?"

"My fellow officers and I would like to practise our swordplay. I would like your permission."

"You have it. Set up a training area aft of the main mast." Then Tom had an idea. "Lieutenant, would you be prepared to train my crew?"

"I'm sure my colleagues and I would be delighted to."

"Then I will designate two times a day for weapons training. We have muskets as well, and twenty soldiers."

Beaumont smiled broadly; this would make the trip far less tedious.

That evening, Tom had food sent down to the officers' cabins. They were earning their way.

They did not stop at the Canaries or Cape Verde. Their course would take them south-west to Rio de Janeiro, making use of the trade winds. The army boys, as Tom thought of them, started training the men in close combat with sword and knife. The men were enthusiastic and carved their own practice swords, many of which were perfect replicas of the issued cutlasses. The lieutenant colonel looked on in a somewhat fatherly way.

They approached the Equator and the men started to prepare for the crossing of the line. Knowing how out of hand these occasions could get, Tom cautioned the men to keep it more or less civilised, and to leave the ladies alone. A large trough appeared on deck and a platform was constructed with a section that tipped up. The ocean was dredged for seaweed, which was used to decorate that area of the ship, and men busily sewed costumes in the off hours.

Tom warned the first-time passengers of what was to come. The colonel woke up and recounted his first crossing in lurid detail, making the ladies *ooh* and *aah*. Armstrong joined in with his own tale; the men who were likely victims looked uncomfortable and some even nervous.

The evening before the crossing, Neptune appeared on deck in all his glory, complete with seaweed beard and trident. He hailed the ship from the bow. The unwary went forward to see what he was about—only to find themselves soaked with buckets of water and the deck pump. There were no exceptions and Miss Alvis seemed to attract more than her fair share. This was the start.

Tom expected at least some complaints, but nobody came forward, not even the saturated miss. The mood was jolly and excited if anything. The next morning the passengers breakfasted amid an air of anticipation and had barely finished when, at nine o'clock, the door to the dining room burst open and men dressed as Neptune's constables rushed in and grabbed the novices—who were easily identifiable as they had dressed accordingly.

The victims were blindfolded and taken out onto the main deck, where they joined any of the crew that had been captured. Water was being thrown around liberally. Tom and the rest of the passengers stood safely on the poop deck to watch the fun.

The novices were led forward by a pair of constables to the platform, where they were presented to Neptune. He blessed them; their heads were painted with molasses and feathers applied. Then they were forced to lie down on the platform which, to a great cheer, was tipped so they slid into the bath, which was full of water and much unpleasant material. Afterwards, Tom had the stewards serve the victims a shot of rum or brandy. He reflected that it had gone well. No one had been injured or died.

* * *

They made the westward crossing without being becalmed or battered by storms. That is not to say it all went smoothly. South of the Equator they encountered rough weather and rain that put a stop to perambulations on the main deck. However, it did allow them to channel fresh water into the water barrels by setting up canvas water catchers that funnelled the rain through canvas pipes to the hold. This was particularly welcomed by the ladies, as Tom was able to provide clean water for them to wash in and even have a stand-up bath.

The turn to the south-east was made a day earlier than planned, as they had made good time on the crossing. That enabled them to pass slowly by the Cape Peninsula to get a good view of Tabletop Mountain and the Cape of Good Hope. That evening, the ships hove-to in the shelter of a bay, to allow the passengers to cross between ships and socialise with each other.

"Set double lookouts," Tom ordered as they passed the southern tip of Madagascar. The prevailing winds prevented a run north through the Channel, but pirates roamed all around the island trying to find ships.

The passengers, in the main, were blissfully ignorant of the potential peril. Only the soldiers and the regular travellers had any idea, and they did not tempt fate by talking about it. Guns quietly checked over their main armament and made sure that nets of grapeshot were hung next to each gun and clean balls were readily available. Down in the magazine, cartridges were prepared.

Tom cleaned and oiled his personal pistols and, at Mary's request, ran her through the loading procedure. Being Canadian, she had fired pistols and muskets in the past, but wanted a refresher to make sure she got it right.

One of the crew was an experienced armourer. He brought a sharpening wheel up on deck and began to put a keen edge on their stock of weapons. Several servants approached him and asked for kitchen and carving knives to be sharpened, which he did—to cover the fact he was preparing for battle.

Tom wasn't surprised when his lookouts spotted a sail shadowing them off to starboard late that afternoon.

"Keep an eye on it and have flares brought up to the fore deck," he said to Graham.

The flares served two purposes; one to signal to the other ships at night, the other to illuminate the sea around them. Red, green and blue for signalling and white, slow burning, for illumination. A blue flare was the alert that something had been spotted.

As the sun sank to the west and the eastern horizon was thrown into shadow, the lookout spotted something disturbing. The single sail had been joined by at least three others.

Graham sent night glasses up to the lookouts with instructions to watch the strange sails, especially as the commodore had ordered them to reduce sail for the night.

"Are we not stopping this evening?" Miss Alvis asked.

"Not here, miss," Graham answered.

"Why not?"

"The current be too strong, miss," he lied.

She looked confused but accepted it at face value and went to dinner. They were on the main course when the door opened, and Graham came in and spoke to Tom. Tom raised his eyebrows and asked, "How long?"

"Less than an hour."

Tom beckoned to a steward and told him quietly, "We will skip dessert and coffee. Please inform Peter."

When they finished their main course, he rapped on his glass with a knife. "Ladies and gentlemen, we have been watching some strange sails and they are approaching. I am taking the ship to action stations, and you are to return to your cabins immediately for your own safety."

There was a flurry of questions; Tom held his hands up. "The ships could be innocent, or they could be pirates. We will take no chances with your safety. Now, please, return to your cabins."

The colonel and other army officers stayed, as did Armstrong. "We can help defend the ship," Burton said.

"Thank you. Please collect your weapons and gather on the poop deck."

The ship was cleared for action in less than ten minutes.

"Where are they?" Tom asked as he came on deck.

"Approaching from the starboard quarter. They might have picked us out as unarmed," Graham said.

Tom silently agreed with him. All the other ships were obviously armed, and they were the bait. A blue rocket shot up astern of them. One of the independents had spotted the danger. Red and green rockets flew up from the lead ship.

"Now he wants us to make more sail!" Graham laughed sarcastically.

"Load the starboard guns with grape over ball," Tom said, ignoring him. He was watching the ships from the rail with a night glass. The image was upside down and back to front and it took practice to keep the object in the viewfinder. What he could see were four dhow-sized ships full of men, coming up on them. It was clear they would bypass the ship behind them and try and take the *Warley*.

"Turn the aft guns to the stern and tell them to be ready for one to try and hook on behind us."

The soldiers and Armstrong arrived. "I want you to concentrate on the stern. I expect them to try and board us from there while the other ships come up on the beam."

Tom wished he had enough men to man both sets of guns.

One of the ships separated and approached the *Warley*'s stern, one held back as the other two headed for the starboard side. There was more than enough room for both to hook on and board.

"Ready white flares."

Tom waited until the two ships were abeam and closing.

"Graham, they are a cable away," Tom called, and Graham had the gunners depress the barrels accordingly.

"Fire flares!"

Whoosh, pop. The flares shone like small suns as they floated down illuminating the sea all around them.

"*Fire*!"

The cannon roared and a wall of eighteen-pound balls and grape howled across the sea. The lead dhow was hit hard, the following one wounded.

"Reload, hit them again. Keep the flares firing."

At the stern rail the soldiers were firing their muskets in volleys under command of the colonel.

The ship's soldiers stood ready, breastplates gleaming in the light of the flares, long pikes ready to skewer anyone who came up the side.

Tom lost track of the fourth ship, his attention fully on the three that were engaged. It nearly cost him.

There was a scream and a shot. His head whipped towards the

sound, and he saw Mary frantically loading her pistol as a man climbed over the port rail.

"Soldiers, port side!" he yelled as he ran to her side leaping down to the main deck in a single bound pistols in hand. He shot the man in the side of the head from four feet as he got there, reversed the pistol to hold it by the barrel and discharged his second pistol into the face of another howling black figure that vaulted the side. He dropped the right and drew his sword.

A row of razor-sharp pikes appeared either side of him, skewering anybody that showed themselves above the rail. The guns roared again, and the smoke drifted back across the deck hampering their vision. Some pirates made it on to the deck, and the fighting became hand-to-hand. More crewmen arrived, the sail handlers had taken up arms and rushed to help. It seemed like an age as a fourth broadside roared out. Tom cut and slashed, clubbed and pistol-whipped, killing any pirate who came within range of his blade or pistol butt.

Then it was quiet. The pirates retreated, leaving their dead behind. Tom stood panting, blood dripping off his sword. He looked around for Mary. He couldn't see her, and frantically searched the deck.

"Tom, I'm up here," he heard her call.

She was on the poop deck, pistol still in hand. He just stood and looked at her for a long moment. Then he shook himself; this would never do.

"Set the main sails, let's get away from here." He looked around at the dead and wounded pirates. "Throw that offal over the side."

Live and dead pirates were picked up and thrown over the side. If the living were lucky, a blade ended their lives before they were thrown over, for the blood in the water was attracting sharks.

* * *

By morning, the ship was scrubbed and the only stains that remained on the deck would have to be holy-stoned out. Their own wounded, of whom there were only three, were being treated by Barnes in his surgery. Tom visited them.

"How are you?"

"I will be back on deck soon," John Smith the third said. His hand was bandaged. "I lost a finger when one of those heathens attacked the transom."

The doctor confirmed this. "Cauterised it. He should be climbing the rigging again in a week or two."

"You can have light duties until you get the all-clear," Tom said.

"Now these two are a bit more serious," Barnes said. "Young Zackery here got a nasty bang on the head. He is concussed and I suspect there may be a fracture in his skull. He will need to be hospitalised once we get to Bombay." The boy was unconscious.

He stepped to the third man, who just stared into space.

"Nothing physically wrong with Martin here. I believe he is having a hysterical reaction to the fighting."

"Will he recover?"

"He may, but I don't think he will be any good as a sailor on a ship like this."

Barnes looked at him sadly then looked at Tom. "I need a nurse; the female passengers need a woman to talk to about woman things and I need someone to help care for the sick ..." He finished in a rush.

Tom could have sworn he blushed. "We will look for one in Bombay. They have a hospital, so there must be trained nurses there," he said.

India

They arrived in Bombay on the fourth of July, and tied up at the Company dock. The passengers departed and each shook Tom's hand as they left. Armstrong was the last to depart.

"I will report on the voyage and the encounter with the pirates, and I will recommend you are given more men. The way those pirates attacked on three sides was unexpected."

"Thank you, milord."

"Think nothing of it, your leadership was exemplary." He shook Tom's hand and walked down the gangplank.

"That was nice of him," Mary said.

"You heard?"

"Yes. How long are we staying here?"

"Until the first of October."

"We should take a house, then."

Bombay was a largely unpopulated island. It had Bombay Fort/town at the south end, complete with castle, fortified wall and gates, a garrison, and docks. This is where they had docked. Around the island were other strategically-placed fortifications, including four more forts and a couple of batteries. There were salt pans to the north of Bombay Fort and several villages, where the locals lived.

Surrounding the fort's walls was an esplanade, on the far side of which were houses and barracks for the sepoys. Tom and Mary found a house to rent on a three-month lease, which was nicely furnished and more comfortable than their cabin. Tom enjoyed his time ashore, and his days were mostly spent with factors and agents taking on cargo for China.

In mid-September, a tall, well-dressed and tanned man came to the house and handed Tom a letter of introduction. It was from the Chairman of the East India Company Committee.

"Mr Daalderop, what can I do for you?" Tom said.

"I am your supercargo. I have arranged the special cargo."

"Special?" Tom said, momentarily confused, then remembered. "Oh, the *special* cargo."

"Fifty crates of prime resin. It must be loaded last, so we can get to it quickly."

Tom nodded. To him, opium was just another product. He knew it was a drug and that doctors used it as a painkiller and a diaphoretic. They even gave it to babies if they had a cough. The East India Company had a monopoly on the growth of opium in Bengal, and used it to fund the exports from China that could be sold for large profits in Europe.

"The last goods for trade in China will be loaded by the twentieth."

"Then it will be delivered the evening of the twenty-ninth and must be loaded immediately. You have soldiers?"

"Yes, twenty."

"Have them guard the crates round the clock."

"Just out of interest … what are the crates worth?"

"Fifty crates are worth more than this ship."

Tom blew out his cheeks. He would move back to the ship the day the crates arrived. One more surprise was that Daalderop gave him permission to increase his crew. In fact, what he said was: "You need to be able to fight your ship efficiently. How many more men do you need? I assume the commissioners pegged you to the minimum?"

Tom told Daalderop that he needed another sixty. A recruitment campaign found a few European men, but he had to resort to taking on lascars for the rest. Lascars were sailors from anywhere east of the Cape of Good Hope and could be Indians, or from any of the south-east Asian countries. They were good sailors, but Tom wasn't sure how well they would do in a fight.

The twenty-ninth dawned. A convoy of crates escorted by mounted soldiers arrived at the dock late in the afternoon. Tom had cargo nets waiting and they were lifted into the centre hold, where they were stacked and secured. They were halfway through when Daalderop arrived in a coach. He travelled light, with only a single trunk. Tom sent a man ashore to bring it aboard and put it in the main state cabin.

Tom was curious when another coach arrived, with a military escort. A tall figure—dressed in a hooded, full length, leather cloak—stepped out, looked around and spotted Daalderop on the deck. They exchanged nods.

The person reached into the coach and pulled out a blunderbuss. A pair of soldiers climbed out, carrying a strongbox—which was obviously heavy—and carried it towards the gangplank.

"Warn your men to stay back and not to try and take the box," Daalderop said.

Tom passed the word and watched as the soldiers struggled up the gangplank, followed by the cloaked figure.

"Take it to the state cabin," Daalderop said.

The mysterious figure nodded and led the way. Just then, Tom caught a glimpse of its face. *A woman*! He also glimpsed what she wore under the long leather coat. Knee-length boots over leather trousers, and a sword. *What the hell? That's unheard of!* He was shocked, it was totally inappropriate for a woman to be dressed in such a way.

The soldiers returned and left the ship without looking back or saying a word. There was no sign of the woman. More passengers arrived. Not a full load and no further dignitaries. Some were paying a low price for a ticket to go back to England: these brought their own stores aboard and would buy extras from the purser on the ship. The *Warley* was going via China, the long way round, and the cost of a ticket to England was less than on those ships going back directly.

The doctor found himself a nurse; a young Indian woman who had worked in the hospital in Bombay. Her name was Shyla and she spoke perfect English in a surprisingly deep voice, which Tom found very attractive. She was petite, barely five feet tall, a widow at thirty years old, cheerful with a wicked sense of fun, and pretty. Mary took to her immediately and the two could be seen chatting when time and duties allowed.

Once all the paperwork had been completed and they had customs clearance, the *Warley* sailed on the tide in the dawn light of the first of October. They would hop from one harbour to another down the west coast of India. Their first stop was Tellicherry in Kerala where they would pick up a load of pepper, which at the time was almost the most expensive spice they carried. Tom had every intention of taking his own private cargo of black gold back to England, where it fetched a high price. He planned to invest what was left of his commissioning bonus and some of his savings.

* * *

They docked in Tellicherry on the ninth. Two passengers left and four joined. One, a woman travelling alone back to England, was called Margret Fitch. She had taken the smallest cabin and brought hardly any baggage or stores aboard at all. Mary was concerned for her well-being, so she and Shyla cornered her and engaged her in conversation.

"She is a widow, her husband died of the fever, leaving her only a little money. She has been the subject of the relentless but unwanted attentions of a merchant in the town, who wanted to make her his mistress, and bought passage to escape him." Mary told Tom this over dinner in their cabin.

"Did she say who this merchant was?" Tom said angrily. He firmly believed that a man should act charitably and not take advantage of the weak.

"Some man called Johan Van de Peel."

Tom looked up from his plate.

"I know him! He is a pepper trader. Dutch, originally, now almost native."

The more Tom thought about the poor woman, the angrier he got. He lay in bed and thought about it and then he had an idea. He slipped out of bed and out of the sleeping cabin, carefully closing the curtain behind him.

Tom lit a candle and by its light looked through the ship's crew register. There, William Handy, topman. Just the man!

William was an excellent topman, but had a shadowy past. Tom knew it involved leaving his home town of Bury St Edmunds in a hurry when he was seventeen years old. Handy had joined a merchant ship and excelled in the rigging, having a natural ability for climbing. Tom sought him out.

"I want to ask you a blunt question and want an honest answer—but first, I assure you that whatever you answer will not affect your position on this ship."

Will looked at him curiously and nodded.

"Were you ever a roof man or cat burglar?"

"You are right, that *is* a direct question. Why do you ask?"

"To help a damsel in distress."

"That pretty lady who just came aboard? I heard about her circumstances."

Tom nodded.

"Yes, I was, and a good one too, but I robbed the wrong man."

"Would you like to help her?"

"I think I would. She didn't deserve what that fellow tried to make her do."

Tom smiled. The tale had obviously been exaggerated as it went around the ship. Now, Van de Peel was the arch villain from a half-penny novel with a heart as black as hell.

Tom knew where Van de Peel lived. He was married to a shrew of a woman whose face was as sour as her soul. Tom understood why he wanted a mistress. However, there were ways and means of getting one without forcing yourself on a woman.

The two of them made their way to the house after midnight. Tom kept watch, while Will scaled the wall and entered via an upstairs window. Tom was nervous—he was no stranger to rubbing up against the law from his privateering days, but he had never taken part in a house robbery.

The minutes dragged by. Tom stayed in the shadows, keeping watch, waiting, getting more nervous. A sound made him jump. It was a rat, scavenging in some rubbish on the road. He took a deep breath and let it out slowly. A hand came down on his shoulder.

"Jesus Christ!" he hissed. "You scared the shit out of me."

Will's teeth shone on the moonlight.

"Come on, skipper. Let's get back."

The next morning, Tom had a meeting with Van de Peel to purchase a half ton of pepper. The man looked haggard.

"Something wrong?"

"My wife is angry at me and is making my life miserable."

"Did you do something bad?"

"Something stupid, but I don't know how."

"Sounds odd."

Van de Peel sighed. "Somehow, a letter from a mistress was left where she could find it."

"Oh, that's never good," Tom said, apparently sympathetically.

"No—and now I have to get rid of the mistress and live with my wife's nagging without relief."

"I would love to spend time sympathising with you, but I need to get the cargo on my ship before we sail this afternoon."

They bargained—and Tom bargained harder than he had ever done, grinding down the merchant to the lowest possible price. The deal done, the casks of pepper were taken directly from the warehouse to the ship.

They kedged out of the harbour with the tide and Tom walked the main deck. He spotted Margret and stepped up to wish her good day. She looked relaxed and was the prettier for it.

"Captain, I have a question," she said.

"Please, ask anything you want."

"If a passenger finds something of value in their cabin, should they hand it over to you?"

"What would I do with it? If the previous occupier of the cabin left something behind, it could be years before we revisited where they left if we revisited it at all. No, if you find something, treat it as good fortune and keep it."

"In that case, can I move to a bigger cabin?"

Above them on the ratlines, Will had paused to listen in on the conversation. He smiled.

The next stop was Cochin, on the eighteenth of October. This time, Daalderop left the ship—and when he returned, he brought two carts loaded with crates with him. More opium, Tom guessed.

The mysterious woman made an appearance as well, this time without the long leather cloak. She was dressed in leather armour, her long dark hair braided. Long swords of unusual design were sheathed on a harness on her back, the hilts sticking up over each of her shoulders, a main gauche on her hip. An air of controlled violence hung around her like an aura.

She turned her gaze on Tom. He must have been staring. Her eyes were flint grey and just as hard. Tom shuddered and looked away, she was not someone he wanted to cross.

Daalderop came back on board. "Please store those crates with the others."

Tom got the crew moving and more passengers arrived. One caught his eye—a Chinese man, on his own, who made himself as inconspicuous as possible. He mentioned it to Graham.

"I saw him as well; he waited on shore until Daalderop and his woman went below. According to the list, he is to leave us at Whampoa."

"Did he?" Tom replied, thoughtfully.

The last stop in India was at Anjengo, on the twenty-third of October. Tom got the passenger list from the agent. There in the middle was the name of another Chinese man. When this one arrived, he was dressed in colourful silks and had his wife with him. She scuttled along behind him, head bowed. There was something odd about the way she walked.

"They keep their women servile," Daalderop said from behind Tom, making him start. "Do you see her feet? They bind them, from an early age, to make them as small as that." He was right—the woman had tiny feet, in strange shoes with hardly any length.

"This one's more flamboyant than the other one," Tom said, seeing if that caused a reaction.

"Other one?"

"Came aboard in Cochin. Quiet fellow."

Daalderop looked thoughtful. Tom decided to ask about the woman.

"Your companion is rather ... aah ... striking."

Daalderop gave a cold smile.

"Freyja is a Nordic warrior from a sect that consider themselves daughters of the valkyrie. She is my bodyguard—and quite deadly."

"Is she? Well, dressed like that she will get the attention of the crew."

"I would advise you to caution them against making any advance. She is sworn to celibacy and can react, let's say, *firmly*." Daalderop changed the subject. "Once we leave here, I will instruct you on our next destination."

"An extra stop before Whampoa?" Tom guessed, looking up at the rigging.

Daalderop didn't reply, and when Tom looked around, he was gone.

They set sail. There was no cargo to load at Anjengo, so the stop was short, and they warped out as soon as the passengers were aboard, destination Whampoa.

Daalderop had asked Tom to meet him in his cabin, where Freyja sat to one side and watched. She had removed her sword harness, but her swords were close by and to hand if she needed them.

"You have never sailed to China before, have you?" Daalderop asked. Tom had to admit that he hadn't.

"Then you need to know that the Chinese made opium illegal in 1729. However, there is a growing demand for it, and it pays extremely well. It is, in fact, what pays for the luxury goods we get from China."

Tom knew about the second part, but the ban was new to him.

"If it's banned, how do we import it?"

"Through third parties, smugglers. We will sell our cargo of opium to them at Hainan Island. Freyja?"

Freyja unfolded herself from her chair and fetched a rolled chart from the dresser. Tom noticed that she moved with the grace of a dancer, which the leather trousers and tight, padded bodice did little to hide. She placed the chart on the table and unrolled it. Daalderop used an inkwell and a dagger to hold it open.

"This is Hainan Island. It is where the Chinese send their political prisoners and exiles, and it is a den of thieves and smugglers. Now, we would normally send our opium on affiliate ships—but as yours is so well protected, we saw an opportunity to cut out the middle man."

The use of smugglers made sense; the Company would want to be able to deny any direct involvement with the trade to preserve the export trade with China.

"When do you want us to arrive there?" Tom said, assuming that the smugglers would have a set time when they would be at the island.

"The fourth or fifth of January would be ideal."

Tom measured off the trip with his fingers.

"Unless we get becalmed, we should be able to do that easily enough."

"One more thing: we will be passing through the Malacca Strait. Expect pirates there. The Javans, Burmese and Chinese all have pirate fleets roaming that area."

"Then we will have to thin them out a bit," Tom said, a hard look on his face.

Freyja actually smiled. She was extraordinarily pretty when she did.

The Strait of Malacca

They crossed the Bay of Bengal and entered the Anderman Sea with the crew on high alert. As a ship on its own, the *Warley* would make an attractive target for pirates both going to and returning from China. It flew the Company flag, and the pirates knew that Company ships carried valuable cargoes. As a merchant, no one would expect it to be heavily armed or manned with trained fighters. Tom had taken the time to train the new men while crossing the bay and they were now moderately efficient.

To even things out, he spread the inexperienced around the guns, making sure that every gun had an experienced gun captain. Guns then re-trained all of them, bedding in the new men and getting the old hands used to their new shipmates. They were as ready as they could be.

The south Anderman Sea was quiet, in that they only saw one other ship, but as they got closer to the strait, more appeared. Junks predominated, with the occasional European ship. Tom hailed one of the Europeans as they passed.

"Any trouble in the strait?"

"No, nothing, it is unusually quiet," the ship's Norwegian captain shouted back.

"Skipper," a hand shouted from the deck.

Tom beckoned him up to the poop deck.

"What's up, Tim?"

"I just been checking the rudder cables, and someone has cut one almost halfway through."

"What? Show me."

They went below and crawled into the space where the cables ran through. Sure enough, the starboard cable had been sawn almost in half.

"Sabotage?" Daalderop said.

"Most certainly. We will have to repair it, so it doesn't give under heavy manoeuvring," Tom replied.

Daalderop frowned, and he took a deep breath before asking, "How long will that take?"

"Half a day at sea, or we can anchor in George Town to effect the repairs, which should be done in less than half a day."

Daalderop paced up and down.

"Freyja, be a dear and fetch the Chinese man." She grinned and stalked out.

"You think it was him?"

"If it was, they know we are coming and what we carry."

The door burst open, and the Chinese man landed at their feet. Freyja followed.

"Sit him on that chair."

She picked him up bodily and plonked him on the wooden chair.

Daalderop started talking to the man in Chinese. The man shook his head. Freyja stepped up and backhanded him across the face. It was a hard blow, and he ended up on the floor. She picked him up and put him back on the chair. Blood ran from one of his nostrils.

Daalderop asked again—and again Freyja clobbered him, this time with a clenched fist holding a knuckle-duster. Tom was no stranger to beating information out of someone, and watched with professional interest.

Eventually, the man had enough; he started to talk, and when the flood gates opened, he told them *everything*.

"In summary, there is bad news and worse news," Daalderop said. "They know we are coming and what we carry. His job was to sabotage the ship so that we would be disabled and become an easy target."

"That's the bad news?" Tom said.

"Yes—the worse news is that he works for the Chinese Red Flag fleet which is extremely large and run by Zheng Yi Sao. I heard she has something like eighty ships."

The ship rolled gently, anchored in George Town. Men swarmed the rigging looking for any more sabotage, more as a precaution than anything else, as the Chinese man had apparently told Daalderop that he had only cut the rudder cable.

"Skipper," Graham said as he climbed the steps.

"Find anything?"

"One of the fore mast stays had been cut and tar rubbed over it. There were also signs that the tackles on two of the guns had been attacked. We are changing all of them."

"Check the priming holes. If I wanted to sabotage a fighting ship, I would spike them."

On inspection, it was found that several guns had bamboo plugs rammed into the touch holes, which they had to drill out.

"Looks like chopsticks," Daalderop said.

"What are they?" Tom asked.

"They are what the Chinese use to eat, instead of knives and forks. He would have several pairs."

The crew was called together, and the Chinese man was brought before Tom. He was badly bruised and his face was swollen. Daalderop translated Tom's words for him.

"You are guilty of sabotaging my ship. An act of piracy. As captain, it is my duty to pass sentence on you." Tom looked around the men; they were hard-faced and unforgiving. "I sentence you to hang."

The man spat a gobbet of blood at Tom's feet. Tom shrugged and said, "String him up."

Two men dragged the condemned man to the rail below the main yard. A rope was thrown over the rail; it had a loop in one end, formed by a wooden grommet spliced on to the end of the rope, and the other end was passed through to form a noose. A second leather collar prevented the wooden collar sliding too far up the rope. The noose was placed around the condemned man's neck and tightened so the grommet sat at the back, and a hood was placed over his head.

Freyja stood close by, watching.

"Tell her to step back, he will shit and piss himself when we haul him up," Tom said. Daalderop called down to Freyja and she hurriedly stepped out of range.

"Haul away!"

Four men quickly hauled the man up until he dangled ten feet from the deck. He strangled to death over twenty minutes.

"A heavier man would have died quicker," Tom said dispassionately once the man had stopped twitching. The passengers, he noted, had watched with interest. Some even laughed and made bets on how long it would take for the man to die.

* * *

They started down the strait. It was almost a full moon, and the skies were clear except for a few scudding clouds. They sailed south, then south-west with the wind on their beam. The crew, like all sailors, could sleep at a moment's notice and wake up just as fast. Many lay by their guns, fast asleep … but, like cats, if you kicked one, they would all rise spitting and scratching.

Tom stayed up all night, and in the wee hours, Freyja came up on deck. Her hair was unbraided and tied in a simple ponytail.

"When do you think they will attack?" Her voice was husky and accented.

"I would go for an hour before dawn, in the hope that the crew was at the end of their watch and not attentive. The moon will have gone down by then and the east will be dark."

"When is dawn?"

The moon was on the horizon.

"In about an hour."

She laughed. "You have a strange sense of humour."

Tom didn't get to answer.

"Deck, there is something to the east blocking out the stars low down."

"Action stations!" Tom roared.

Men jumped to their feet. There was no need to clear as they had done that at George Town. Mary was down in one of the empty passenger cabins. Tom wasn't about to let her be on deck during the fight again.

Daalderop came up on to the poop deck. Tom was looking for'ard with a night glass.

"How many?"

"A lot."

Graham appeared. Tom issued his orders. "We will maintain our speed, so only clew up the mains and do not take them in. I want everything else set. Load the guns with grape over ball and aim low. We will kill as many as we can before they have a chance to close. I want extra preventer stays fitted on the aft side of all masts, and nets strung to catch any rigging that falls."

"What if they try to get under your bow?" Daalderop asked.

"Then we run them down. Our hull is triple planked, and the bow is reinforced with bracings as well as being an extension of the keel," Tom returned.

"We are making twelve knots and a fathom," Graham called from forward.

"Good, they will have to run to keep up." Tom smiled.

Graham looked forward and could see the line of ships ahead of him. The moon had disappeared below the horizon. Only the stars shone bright across the sky, but that starlight was enough. The pirates started to form into an arc, like the horns of a buffalo, trying to envelop the *Warley*.

Tom waited and watched. Then he bellowed, "*Fire*!"

The guns fired in a ripple from fore to aft, both sides belching fire and smoke illuminating the sea.

"Fire rockets."

A pair of ship's boys were tasked with firing a rocket every twenty seconds and white rockets shot into the air and burst, illuminating the sea around them. Anybody near them could hear them count, "One little monkey, two little monkeys, three little monkeys ..."

"They are trying to envelop us, thinking we will slow."

The guns fired again. "Under two minutes, that's good!" Tom said to no one in particular.

The forward lookout yelled, "There's one crossing our bow!"

"*Hold on*!" Tom shouted at the top of his voice.

The ship lurched and hesitated for a split second before carrying on. A crunching noise came from the bow, along with screams, and they could see a square sail pulled downwards as they ran over the junk. Tom walked to the side and calmly looked over. The front half of a junk floated by with a few pirates clinging to it. The guns fired again.

A crewman shouted, "Skipper astern!"

Tom went to the stern rail. A pair of junks were being rowed furiously up behind them. Men in the bows were twirling ropes with grapnels attached. He watched, fascinated, then smiled. The stern guns had been turned to face aft and blasted forth a load of grape, over balls that could smash a thin-hulled junk to matchwood.

Freyja appeared beside him just as the right-hand junk's bow was hit. The man with the grapnel was picked up and thrown back onto the ship's deck as a grape shot hit him in the chest. The left-hand junk was missed; the gun had fired too high, so the grapnel flew and caught on the rail. Freyja turned to cut it but a half dozen more came up and they were well and truly attached. The junk's crew hauled her up behind the *Warley* and men started climbing the ropes.

Tom drew his sword and a dagger. "Repel boarders!" he cried.

To his astonishment, Freyja screamed a war cry and leapt over the stern, swords in both hands. He had no chance to see what she was doing as a head and shoulders appeared at the rail. He drove the point of his sword through the man's throat, and his victim fell back. He could hear screams coming up from below. Tom slashed the rope with his dagger but only succeeded in cutting it halfway through before he had to stop a man on another rope getting aboard.

Suddenly, the ropes went slack. He killed another pirate and looked over the side. The junk was falling behind them. "Freyja!" he cried. *She must be still on it!*

Freyja landed on the deck amid a surprised mass of men. She didn't give them time to react. Her swords wove a sphere of steel around her as she dispatched man after man. She was invincible, the song of death ringing in her ears. She could feel the valkyrie within her.

The forecastle was clear of the living. Men on the main deck were reluctant to advance and hesitated. That gave her all the time she needed. Sheathing one of her swords, she started to slash through the ropes holding the junk to the *Warley*. Now men started to come forward, driven by the captain. There were two ropes left. She grabbed one with her left hand and with a mighty slash severed them both. The junk fell away, leaving her hanging over the sea. She sheathed her sword and started to climb.

Tom couldn't see anything in the dark behind them, the junk had disappeared. What the hell was he going to tell Daalderop? He stood, looking aft, trying to pick out the junk. It was nowhere to be seen. He sighed and started to turn away when a hand appeared on the rail, he raised his sword, but something made him hesitate. There was a grunt and a head appeared, wreathed in blonde hair.

"That was a nice little fight," Freyja said as she pulled herself aboard.

Tom stood, open-mouthed, not knowing what to say.

By the time the sun came up they were clear of the pirates, and with the mains fully set were making thirteen knots. The crew set about repairing the transom windows that had been smashed when the pirates tried to board.

Tom hadn't noticed that during the fight the ship had taken several hits from stone, twenty-four-pound balls. The triple-thickness hull had not been breached but showed signs of damage where the wood had been dented and paint scarred. The rigging had been damaged in places as well.

The crew had come out of it relatively unscathed, with a few minor wounds and injuries, the worst of which was a gunner who lost some toes when the gun rolled over them. They were busy making repairs and cheerfully exchanging experiences. Freyja sat on the deck polishing a nick out of her sword with a stone, looking for all the world as if nothing extraordinary had happened. She didn't have a scratch on her, but her leathers were bloodied and the men looked at her in awe as the story of her role in the fight circulated.

"What shall we do with the dead pirates?" Graham asked.

"Throw them overboard. All of them."

"Wounded as well?"

"All of them. We don't want them cluttering the ship up and the Company will hang them anyway."

Graham looked grim and pulled his dagger; he would finish any that were alive before feeding them to the sharks.

Daalderop was happy.

"You did very well, Captain," he said.

Tom just nodded.

"Freyja is happy, she is one step closer to becoming a shield maiden."

Tom looked at her, then turned to Daalderop.

"A *what*?"

"She is, what you might call, a journeyman. She is on a journey to gain experience so that she can be made a shield maiden. It's akin to how a man became a knight in the olden days."

Tom shook his head; warrior cults were all queer. There was rumoured to be one in England that modelled itself on the Knights of the Round Table.

They came up on Hainan Island and Daalderop directed them around to Haikou Bay on the north side, where there were several junks anchored. He had Tom raise a blue pennant and get the opium crates up on deck. After they had anchored, several boats came across with their captains.

"We will run an action. Mr Woo will preside," Daalderop announced.

Mr Woo was the well-dressed Chinese man who was aboard with his wife.

Why am I the only one not knowing what is going on, on my own ship? Tom silently fumed.

Mr Woo had a crate selected at random by one of the captains and opened it to reveal the spheres of opium inside. The captains inspected it and some even took a piece and tasted it.

The auction was done in lots of ten crates, and proceeded at a furious pace. Tom watched with interest. Mrs Woo sat behind her husband at a portable folding desk with a sheet of parchment, brush and ink. Her job was to record who bought and for what price. Tom noted that the bidding got fiercer as the number of available lots decreased.

Then, as quickly as it had started, it was over. Piles of silver were placed in front of Mrs Woo, who weighed them with a set of balance scales and made notes on her parchment. Freyja stood behind her, quietly watching.

"A good auction," Daalderop said, looking at the neat heaps of silver. "We made more than I expected."

Canton and Home

The *Warley* entered the Pearl River estuary on the eighth of January 1798 and took on a pilot who guided her through the maze of islands. They entered Blenheim Reach and crossed the first bar noting the battery on the north side, passed behind Dane Island and anchored on the southern side of Whampoa Island by the town. Tom could see a tall pagoda in the distance and noted it as a landmark. *Gaijin* (foreigners) were only allowed to land on the island and the Thirteen Factories area outside Canton, on the mainland. They were forbidden to travel anywhere in China without permits, which were almost impossible to obtain without huge bribes.

Daalderop asked to be taken ashore and he, Freyja and Mr Woo were boated across. Tom stayed with his ship; she needed maintenance, and he got the crew to work mending and replacing rigging and generally cleaning the ship. Daalderop returned with the others later in the day.

"We need to move the ship up to the anchorage by the factory," Daalderop said.

The pilot returned in the morning, and they took Fiddler's Reach upriver to the city, anchoring close to the bank. The city itself was separated from the Thirteen Factories area by a high, fortified wall. A Chinese customs inspector came aboard and checked their cargo against the manifests. Tom saw Daalderop pass him a purse. Apparently, corruption was the norm.

Once they received their clearance, boats came alongside to take the cargo and any passengers ashore, along with men who would monitor the unloading. Tom was told, "Let the Chinese do the unloading and instruct your men not to interfere."

Daalderop pointed to a cocky-looking fellow holding a baton. "See him? He is the boss of the stevedores. He has a contract with the Company. If you interfere, he will lose face and we will be in all sorts of trouble."

Tom had heard that the Chinese were prickly about losing face and quickly had the word spread to the crew to stay back and not do anything, whatever they saw. He was sure there would be a fair amount of petty pilfering going on. So, he relaxed. The Company had its own warehouses ashore and its own security arrangements. The cargo was no longer his problem.

What *was* his problem was the state of the ship. The voyage had taken its toll and he wanted to get her bottom cleaned and timbers checked. "Are we allowed to careen here?" he asked Daalderop.

"I can book us in for a place on the beach. There are warehouses for rent where you can store the guns and other things."

"Are they secure?"

Daalderop barked a laugh. "As secure as anything around here."

Which meant not secure at all.

Tom took a boat to the careening beach. He blew out his cheeks as he looked at it. It was deep enough for a fair-sized junk but nowhere near able to take the *Warley*. He returned and looked for Daalderop who, he was told, had gone ashore. Mr Woo was there though, and he asked him.

"Mr Woo, is the careening beach on Whampoa Island bigger than the one here?"

"Yes, twice as long."

"I am thinking more of how deep it is. Is it big enough for us to get the *Warley* out of the water?"

"I think so, you should go look."

"Do I need any permissions to do that?"

"No, as long as you stay in your boat until Whampoa Island, you OK."

That was all he needed to hear, and he took the gig down to the island. A Chinese patrol boat shadowed him. The island's beach was better suited to the *Warley*, and a ship of similar size was having her bottom cleaned.

Tom was hailed as they passed another Company ship called the *Exeter*: a three-decker, carrying twenty-six twelve- and nine-pound guns.

"Ahoy there, what ship?" a distinctly north-eastern accent called.

"The *Warley*," Tom shouted back.

"Wey aye man, come aboard and have a cuppa an' a natter."

Tom laughed at the man's insistence and ordered his men to pull alongside. The boat was tied off and they all went up.

"Tom Batrick," he said, introducing himself to the bluff, blond, ruddy-faced skipper of the *Exeter*.

"Lestock Wilson. The *Warley* … was that the big, black-hulled ship that arrived a couple of days ago?"

"That's her, she's being unloaded at the Thirteen Warehouses."

"Aye well, she'll be back here come the morrow. The Chinese don't like us 'anging around down there." He pronounced down as *doon*.

Wilson had a Chinese servant, who made them tea. It was highly scented.

"Jasmine tea, ever tried it?" Wilson asked.

"No, this is my first trip."

"Aah, wey man. Then you will be thinking about goin' ashore."

"I'm thinking about cleaning my ship's bottom."

"Are you rich? Because you need t' be if you wanna do that here! You can't use yer own crew, like."

Tom sighed. "Don't tell me, the Chinese have the monopoly?"

Wilson grinned. "You are catching on! You're better doing that in India or at home."

Tom sipped his tea; he found the experience grew on him and decided it was something Mary might like.

"Where can I get some of this?"

"Any tea shop will sell you a pound or two, but I can give you a quarter to be gettin' on with."

"That's very kind. Will you join my wife and me for dinner when the *Warley* comes back here?"

"I would be delighted."

Tom went back to his ship and had the boat row him around her. *Her bottom will have to wait,* he thought, convincing himself it wasn't that bad.

Wilson was right: as soon as they were unloaded, they were told to return to the island anchorage and stay there. They had to be towed—the wind was contrary, light and constantly shifting.

Tom took Mary ashore to explore the island. It wasn't very big, at under six square miles, but had a very tall pagoda on the south side and another in the town on the north-east corner. In any case, it was good to stretch their legs. The southernmost of the two pagodas was built on top of a large, truncated pyramid which served as a temple. They bought a painting of it from a street vendor for practically no money.

Having exhausted the sights on the south coast, they walked up to the village, where there was an active market. Tom kept his purse close to his skin—the locals looked a shifty lot. Mary attracted attention: not many European women were seen there. A youth shouted something, and an old lady, sitting on a mat outside her house, cackled gleefully at whatever it was. After a few purchases, they decided that it would be prudent to return to the ship.

Wilson came over for dinner and explained a little more about the Chinese way of doing things.

"You will need to employ a comprador to get provisioned for your journey home. I can introduce you to one that is halfway honest."

Tom rolled his eyes at Mary; he had told her about the bribes and the way the Chinese controlled everything. Wilson continued.

"When your crew goes ashore, they need to be on good behaviour. The local Mandarin imposes heavy fines on any that get arrested, and they are very intolerant of bad behaviour. There are bars and a couple of brothels to keep the boys amused."

Mary blushed. She knew all about what went on, but to hear it so blatantly spoken of. Well …

Wilson didn't notice and carried on.

"All of it is run by Chinese gangs called Triads. Nasty bunch that are not averse to murder if you cross them. The upside is that the island isn't big enough to hide opium dens."

"We saw soldiers patrolling," Mary said.

"Corrupt as everyone else," Wilson snorted.

"Is it really that bad?" Tom said.

"Look, every official is on the make, the soldiers are in the pay of the Triads. The locals that work for themselves pay the Triads for protection. The stevedores work for their bosses who pay graft to the Triads and the officials. It's a way of life—and don't expect to be able to barter. Bartering is a sport here, they love it. I've seen two Chinese men go a whole day bartering over a few pennies."

Wilson stopped for a gulp of wine.

"I wouldn't give the Chinese the time of day, but they have tea, silk and porcelain …"

Mr Woo and his wife had joined Daalderop in the Thirteen Warehouses, where he had taken rooms and an office. Tom was obliged to travel back and forth between the ship and the office.

"I need you to send me the soldiers," Daalderop said on one such visit.

"Why?" Tom asked.

"Because we will be receiving a shipment of porcelain which will be stored here until the rest of the cargo arrives."

Tom understood: pilfering was rife.

"I will have them boated down. How long will we be here?"

"Probably to the middle of March."

"Good, we will miss the monsoon. The winds should be in our favour," Tom said.

The soldiers were dispatched, and the comprador employed. Peter was frustrated that he could only buy small amounts of goods for the kitchen and made up a list of what he wanted for the return journey. The comprador didn't understand half of it and just bought what he could get.

Reloading the ship was very different to unloading it. No gang of stevedores appeared when the boats came out, and Tom had the crew load the *Warley*. He found out from Wilson that this was a common practice, as the skippers wanted their ships trimmed precisely and only their crews could do that.

Wilson sailed before them, and they were towed out of the harbour and over the second bar on the twenty-fifth of March.

"Do we need to go through the strait again?" Daalderop asked.

"Not necessarily," Tom replied, and showed him a chart of the area. "This is the Pearl River estuary, and this time of year winds are from the north-west, so, we could sail south and pass through the strait between Java and Sumatra then pick up the south-east trades."

"Is it much further?"

"It is, but not by much—as long as we're not calling in at India."

"We aren't. Take that route. I do not want to risk our cargo going back."

He's brought something aboard that's worth a lot then, Tom thought later, when he was alone, and smiled to himself. But then, so had he: in his cabin was a chest of silks and another of jasmine tea. In his strongbox sat a bag of sapphires that he was carrying for a Company man in Calcutta.

They had a hard time rounding the Cape of Good Hope. Contrary winds and big seas slowed them down to a crawl. By the time they were in the Atlantic proper, they were running short of water.

We will have to call in at St Helena, Tom decided. The rock was used as a watering stop by the navy, thanks to its convenient location in the Atlantic.

* * *

James Town was on the north coast of St Helena, and had a deep-water harbour where a ship could tie up at the dock. They arrived there on the fifth of August, rewatered, stocked up on fresh food and left within a day.

The crossing west saw them chased by storms coming off the coast of Africa. These were the seeds of tropical storms and even hurricanes that would beset the Caribbean. They had very few opportunities to reduce sail overnight.

One particularly large storm came up behind them. "Deck there, dark clouds coming up astern," the lookout called down.

Tom climbed into the ratlines to get a view. *Bloody hell, that's going to be a big one.*

"Take in the mains and topsails, put a single reef in the gallants and royals," Tom ordered.

The men went to work, the topmen fisting the stiff canvas into folds against the yards. Their speed dropped and there was a strange sort of calm before the front edge of the storm hit. Being an anticyclone, the winds rotated around the storm counterclockwise, and Tom watched the pennant and tell tails swing as the wind changed from an easterly to a northerly, driving them south. Then came the rain, a deluge of warm fresh water so hard they couldn't see a quarter mile in any direction.

It was two days before it passed, and the trade wind returned. Then the skies cleared and they could get a fix.

Tom put down his sextant and made the calculation. "Two hundred miles further south than we want to be. Helm steer north-west." That would make the trip a little more uncomfortable, as they would cross the swell at a slight angle. The passengers would notice, of course, and some would get seasick again.

They reached the coast of Brazil and continued north-west to the Caribbean, where they picked up the Caribbean current. Passing between Granada and the Grenadines, they entered the Caribbean Sea. A ship-to-ship shouted chat told them that a hurricane had passed through a fortnight before.

They stayed away from the Windward Islands, where most of the hurricanes formed, and sailed west past the Lesser Antilles then west by north-west into the Gulf of Mexico. There, the winds and current took them around the gulf and out between the Florida Keys and Cuba. Then it was up to North Carolina to pick up the westerly trades—and home.

They arrived at the Downs—after suffering several summer storms—on the eighteenth of October. A message from the Company told them to proceed to Portsmouth and dock, having first unloaded their powder at the Upper Harbour powder dock.

The Second Voyage, 1799–1800

Portsmouth and Poole

Tom and Mary had time at home once the *Warley* had been unloaded at Portsmouth. She wouldn't sail again until June. The Company would look after her until then, and Tom and his crew were given leave to stay ashore.

Christmas was held at the house in Poole, and was all the finer for Tom having made a very nice profit selling the silks to Ede & Ravenscroft, the king's costumier, in London. The jewels had been delivered and Tom received a healthy bonus from that, as well. The tea had been sold to Twinings on the Strand. He had got it at a very good price and, again, made a very healthy profit. Even better, the Company paid gun money for the actions taken against the pirates which, as captain, Tom received a quarter of.

So his bank balance was good, and he started looking for a grander house when Mary announced, "Tom, I have something to tell you."

"Yes, love, what's that?" Tom said without looking up from the paper.

She frowned at him. "It's important."

He put his paper down, looked at her and said, "I am all ears. What is it?"

"I'm pregnant. You are going to be a father."

His joy was unbounded, and he picked her up and swung her around—before realising what he was doing and putting her down gently. Anne was far more pragmatic.

"When's it due?" she asked.

"May, I think."

"You *think*?"

"Well, we …" She blushed.

"Long voyage home?" Anne said, and laughed.

The need to buy a new house thus became immediate, and Tom went to the local banks to see if they knew of any for sale. A couple came up. One was available because the owner had died with no issue and the relatives wanted to sell it so they could split the money. The other was for sale due to a bankruptcy; the bank had foreclosed on it. It was just outside Poole, in Branksome Park, and had been built in the first part of the century.

Tom took a horse and went to have a look. The grounds covered 250 acres of parkland, laid out as pine and beech woods. The house was large, well-built and rather handsome. But it was too big, with too much land.

The next day he went to the second house, which lay on the edge of the village of Bourne. It had been built in the time of Elizabeth I, with oak beams showing through the whitewashed walls and a thatched roof. It sat in an acre of garden. He went inside and looked around. The ceilings were low and the living room had a large inglenook fireplace. There was a separate kitchen that had a fire with built-in ovens. Upstairs were four bedrooms off a central hallway. Outside were sheds, a walled garden for vegetables and the thunderbox. The vendors wanted £450 for it, which included the freehold of the land.

He went back to the bank. "Will they consider an offer?" he asked the manager.

"I am sure they will," the manager replied.

"It needs new thatch."

"But it comes with all the furniture," the manager reminded him.

"Old and mostly worthless. I will offer four hundred pounds."

"No more?"

"Not a penny."

"I will ask the sellers. Will it be a cash purchase?"

"Yes."

He had no intention of selling the house in Poole. Most people rented their houses and there was high demand—he could make twelve pounds a year from it.

Tom had to wait a week for the bank to return with the sellers' decision. The relatives all had to agree. Some had wanted more while others took a "bird in the hand" attitude to the transaction. In the end the chance of some easy cash overcame their greed, and they agreed to sell. Tom had a banker's draft sent down from Barings and employed a local solicitor for the conveyancing.

A few weeks later, it was done. The house was theirs and they could move in. The village wasn't far from Poole and Tom bought a pony and dogcart that Mary and Anne could use to get there to see their friends. The pony, a mild-mannered New Forest type of thirteen hands, was called Jasper and was three years old. Hardy, strong and trained to the saddle as well as the harness, he would do them for years to come.

Tom and Mary were settling in when they received a visitor. The man was well dressed and obviously of some means. He introduced himself as Gerald Goldsmith.

"To what do I owe this pleasure?" Tom asked.

"I am a jeweller, as my name suggests, and I understand you brought back a selection of sapphires from India for a Mr Clairmont."

"And what business is that of yours?" Tom asked.

"Oh, I mean no offence, I bought those stones. What I want to know is, will you bring more back from your next trip?"

"That depends on two things. Whether my ship stops in India and whether anybody asks me to carry some home for them."

Goldsmith leaned forward eagerly.

"I have a third way."

Tom looked at him and waited.

"If you buy them yourself, I will guarantee to take whatever you bring back. Which takes the risk out of the transaction."

Tom smiled. "At a discounted price, no doubt."

"Naturally, I want to pay a reasonable price. Shall we say twenty per cent under market value?"

"Mr Goldsmith," Tom stood and held out his hand, "good day to you."

The dismissal was ignored, Goldsmith remained sitting.

"A hard man you are, Captain. Fifteen per cent."

"Ten and you have a deal."

"Meet me in the middle, my boy, twelve and a half per cent."

Tom looked at him and pursed his lips thoughtfully. He had looked into precious stones while he was in India but didn't have sufficient capital at the time. Emeralds. sapphires, diamonds and rubies were all available, one just had to be careful about the quality—and that was knowledge he lacked.

"I'll tell you what. I will go with twelve and a half per cent off the market value at the time of the sale, and in return you will teach me how to assess stones for quality."

Goldsmith looked surprised.

"That is good to hear: I think we have an accord."

It was spring and the banks along the roads and tracks of Dorset were yellow with primroses, and the woods blue with bluebells. Every morning the birds set up a symphony of song loud enough to wake the dead. On the chalk hills, skylarks flew and sang their hearts out, too. Mary was in her final trimester.

A courier delivered Tom's next set of orders on the twelfth of May, and he was pleased to see he would have a short revictualling stop in Penang on his way to China. There would be no opium on this trip as there were no stops in India and he would be carrying a mixed cargo of wool cloth and iron goods on the outward journey.

He would be able to acquire some stones in Penang: rubies, sapphires, topaz, amethyst and garnets were all found locally. Goldsmith had given him a jeweller's loupe and an extensive education in stone appraisal. It was a fascinating subject and he turned out to have a good eye.

Mary was due any day, her stomach gravid, and the baby was impatient, kicking her hard. But Tom had to go to Portsmouth. Anne took charge, and had him stop in Poole to get a midwife she knew to come to the house.

He found his ship partly crewed, with Graham on board and the rest of the crew arriving in dribs and drabs depending on how far they had to come. He was surprised to see Freyja.

He asked Graham, "Is Daalderop aboard?"

"No, she just arrived and hasn't said anything."

Tom raised his eyebrows, he would question her later, but for now he had other things on his mind. "Have we a passenger list yet?"

"Yes, it's in your cabin with the initial manifest. Oh, and by the way—they cleaned her bottom."

Tom walked over to where Freyja was standing. "Come with me." He led her to his cabin. He found the passenger list and there was no supercargo. "No Daalderop. So, what are you doing here?"

"Hello, Tom," she said, in spite of his rudeness. "I am here to sign on."

He looked at her incredulously.

"Sign on?"

"Yes, as your captain of soldiers."

"Why?"

"Because your ship gets into fights."

"And following Daalderop around doesn't offer as many opportunities?"

"Exactly."

"I thought you and him were …"

She burst out laughing. "If he had tried, I would have cut his balls off."

"You are celibate?"

"Only by choice." Her tone left no doubt that the subject was now closed. "By the way, has your wife given birth yet?"

He knew when to let things go, and entered her onto the ship's books as a working passenger.

Tom got the chance to return home for a couple of days before the ship sailed. He knew as soon as he got out of the carriage that something was different. All the windows of the house were open and bed linen was strung out on the washing line. Carpets were being enthusiastically beaten by a pair of village boys. His home was being spring cleaned. He opened the door and called, "Mary! Mum!"

A young girl appeared holding a duster and asked, "Be you Master Tom?"

He nodded, somewhat confused.

"Mistress Mary is upstairs with the baby."

"*What*?" he cried and took the stairs two at a time. He burst into their bedroom to find Mary sitting up in bed, suckling a child at her breast.

"He arrived just after you left," she said.

"He? It's a boy?"

Mary smiled, radiant and beautiful. Tom stepped up slowly, sat beside her and gently stroked the baby's head. He kissed Mary.

"He was impatient to get out. It was lucky the midwife was already here, or she would have missed him."

Anne stuck her head through the door. "Abigail said you had arrived."

"Abigail? Is that the girl who I met downstairs?"

"Yes, your maid of all works. She started yesterday."

Tom looked at Mary. "That's a good idea."

"Mum's idea. It's a big house."

"You should get a cook, as well."

Mary and Anne exchanged a smile.

"We have one already."

Tom knew when he was beaten, and laughed, but then sobered and said, "What will we call him?"

"I thought Thomas Henry,"

"Henry after your father?"

"And grandfather … and Thomas after you and your father."

The baby was christened before Tom returned to his ship. Most of the village was at the church and he got to know his neighbours. He found they looked up to him and called him Captain Batrick. That was a long way from his upbringing in Poole where, out of school, he had been a street urchin. For his next voyage, Mary would stay at home with their son, and he was happy that they were going to be well looked after. The cook was a bustling middle-aged widow who cooked good country food. Abigail was a village girl, the third daughter of the local baker who was blessed with six of them—and happy just to reduce the number of women in his house!

The ship was fully loaded and the passengers were starting to arrive when Tom got back to Portsmouth. Freyja had taken charge of the soldiers. Graham told him that some had objected to being commanded by a woman, and so she had demonstrated her superior skills by dumping them on their backsides. They were being made to exercise and the sight of ten burly and slightly overweight men puffing and straining as she put them through the routine made him smile.

"Baby arrived?" Graham asked.

"Thomas Henry is well, always hungry and has a pair of lungs to give a bosun competition."

Graham laughed and slapped Tom on the back in congratulations. The word got around the crew in no time, and soon men approached with gifts of toys they had carved from bone or wood. Tom was amazed that they knew. Graham told him that he was probably the only one who *didn't*, at the end of the last voyage. Tom spliced the mainbrace in celebration.

The passengers arrived and, as usual, the poorest were first. Two clerks—one for the Company's office in the Thirteen Warehouses and the other for Penang—who were sharing a cabin. A Chinese couple returning home. A single man who looked like an adventurer and was destined for Penang. Then an army captain, which was odd as they were not stopping in India. And finally, a wealthy couple who were starting some kind of grand tour.

It was the eighteenth of June and time to sail. The wind was fair from the north-west, and they warped away from the dock before setting the jibs and spanker to take them out to the island which served as the powder dock. They confined the passengers to their cabins and enforced a strict policy of no naked flames or smoking.

"Was that *entirely* necessary?" the army captain, Sedgwick Farrington, asked over lunch.

"In your case, probably not, but the civilians are not experienced in being around more powder than they can carry in a powder flask. We took on twenty tons."

"That would make a big hole in the water if it went up!" Farrington laughed.

Mrs Scarborough whinnied a nervous laugh. "That seems an awful lot of powder for a merchant ship, Captain."

"We are a new breed of ship, Mrs Scarborough. The Company is successful and that attracts the highwaymen of the sea. The *Warley* is designed to be able to protect herself from anything."

"Including the French?" Farrington asked.

"We should be able to take on anything up to their smaller two-deckers and certainly any of their privateers," Tom said modestly.

The door to the dining room opened and Graham poked his head through.

"Skipper, there is a pilot cutter approaching, signalling that they have someone aboard for us."

Tom put down his knife and fork and excused himself. Once he was on deck he said, "Mount the handlines and reduce speed so they can come alongside. If we heave-to, the rolling in this sea will have everyone's food in their laps."

The cutter expertly came alongside, matching their speed. A ladder was lowered, and a man jumped to the battens, grabbed the handlines and climbed up. A rope was sent over and a sea chest was brought aboard as well.

"That was exciting. Permission to come aboard," a man of about thirty said, and grinned.

"Granted, now who the hell are you?" Tom barked.

"Lieutenant Edward Westcliff, Company Marine."

The man held out a packet of papers and Tom opened it. He looked around to see a lot of men standing and watching. "Make sail, get us back to eight knots."

Graham grinned and shouted the orders.

Tom read the papers. In summary, Westcliff was being granted passage so that he could take command of a new sloop in Penang. He would join the *Warley* for the trip to China and back to Penang.

"Are you going to be escorting Indiamen through the strait?"

"Yes, sir. The *Aurora* is a new ship, built in Bombay and armed with ten thirty-two-pound carronades."

"Why didn't you join in Portsmouth?"

"I come from Falmouth, and I didn't get my orders until the day before you sailed—so my friend, who sails that cutter, offered to intercept you. We had another friend who works in one of the semaphore towers between Portsmouth and Falmouth, watch for you."

"Have you eaten?"

"Not today, sir."

"Come with me."

Tom took Westcliff down to his cabin, where he had him shed his tarpaulin coat. Underneath it, he wore Company Marine uniform.

"That'll do. As an officer of the Marine, you will eat at the captain's table, although you disturbed my lunch."

The steward made a place for Westcliff while Tom introduced him to the other guests.

"Ladies, gentlemen, I would like to introduce Lieutenant Edward Westcliff of the Company Marine, who is travelling to Penang to take command of a new sloop of war.

"Is that what the French call a corvette?" Farrington asked.

There he goes again, referencing the French, Tom noted. His nose twitched as if he smelled something off.

"Yes, it is. Sloops are effectively small frigates," Edward Westcliff said.

"Will you fight the French?" Farrington asked.

"If they decide to send ships to try and disrupt trade, yes. But our main task is to patrol the Malacca Strait between Penang and Whampoa, looking for pirates."

Penang and the Strait

Tom watched Farrington, who went ashore as soon as they docked. Something was off about the man, but Tom was damned if he could put his finger on it. He half considered having him followed, but told himself that he was overreacting. Then the Company agent came aboard, and he had no more time to dwell on him.

"I have cargo for China and to go back to England," Dewi Pritchard told Tom in a broad South Wales accent, as he handed over the loading manifests.

"We need to rearrange the holds. What is the cargo for England?"

"Pepper and rare woods."

Tom considered the situation, thinking of weight distribution and trim. He made some notes on the manifest and then called Graham over.

"The pepper for England goes in the forward hold, the woods in the centre. Anything for China goes in the aft hold."

"Aye, aye, skipper."

"Where can I buy gems?" Tom asked Dewi.

"You want to get them direct from the miners if you can. Uncut gems make the most profit. I am looking at some this afternoon, if you want to tag along."

"Do you need them taken back to England and sold? I have an arrangement with a jeweller there."

"Good prices?"

"Twelve and half per cent below the day's market price for high quality stones."

"That is good, I usually get twenty per cent below."

The deal was struck. Tom would get a shipping fee for his trouble, of five per cent of the gems' value. Dewi would still be up on his usual deal and was quite happy. That afternoon, the two men wandered through the town to a … well, Tom didn't quite know what to call it. It was like a market but without stalls: men sat on mats or just on the dirt and showed the products of their labours. Traders wandered among them, picking what they wanted and bargaining for the best price.

"This starts every afternoon at around two o'clock, with the miners coming in and taking their pitches. The traders know who generally produces the best stones, but you never know, until you look, what you might find."

Tom agreed and simply went from man to man examining their wares. Dewi watched him.

"You seem to know what you are doing."

"I was shown how to assess stones by my friendly local jeweller." He held a ruby up and used his loupe to examine it, turning it in the light. "This is a nice stone. It has good colour and clarity and a single inclusion which can be lost when it is cut. I think something around two and a half carats would be the end result."

He asked the price through Dewi. The miner asked for a silly amount, so Tom offered an equally silly amount in reply. The miner got the message. Tom haggled and bought the stone for a good price. Not finding anything else with that man, they moved on to the next who was selling amethysts from the northern part of Malaya. He had travelled a long way and had a variety of stones. Tom picked out half a dozen that were an even reddish-purple in colour.

The next few pitches had nothing of interest. Dewi bought some garnets and beat Tom to a couple of sapphires. A friendly competition developed.

Tom noticed a man arrive and sit quietly on the edge area. He wandered over, as he now recognised from the man's dress that he came from the central part of Malaysia.

"What do you have?" he asked in bad Malay, which he had picked up from Dewi.

"Sapphires."

"Can I see?"

The man opened a bag and tipped it out onto a cloth. A dozen or so lumps of blue rock were scattered, varying in size from a thumbnail to a heart-shaped lump of about two inches across. Tom picked up some of the smaller stones and examined them. They were nice, with some being better than others. He put the best to one side. Then he picked up the heart-shaped stone. It had inclusions—most sapphires did—but it was generally clear and of an excellent colour. It was the find of the day.

Tom haggled, but the miner knew the stones' worth and was prepared to haggle all day if he had to. In the end, it took all of Tom's available cash to get the stones he wanted.

"I'm done," he told Dewi when he found him.

"Me too, let's go and get some food."

Dewi led him through the streets to what looked like a tavern. It was moderately busy and had a mix of local and European customers sitting at the tables.

"Best food in Penang, I come here all the time."

A girl came out and bowed. "Mr Dewi, what can we get you?"

"Hello Nazra, is your father cooking?"

"He is; we have mutton rendang or laksa."

Dewi ordered when Tom shrugged, not knowing what they were. "Two rendangs please, and beers."

What arrived amazed Tom, as it was unlike any of the dishes he had eaten in India. Slow-cooked mutton—probably goat—in spices and coconut. The meat simply fell apart, and was delicious.

He was just about to praise the dish when he heard a familiar voice from behind him. He turned his head, as if looking for the waitress, and confirmed his suspicion—it was Farrington. Tom listened harder and for a moment was confused as he couldn't understand what was being said—then realised the man was speaking French.

Tom leaned closer to Dewi and said softly, "Dewi, there is a man at a table behind me in a dark brown coat. Can you have a sneaky look and see who he is talking to?"

Dewi looked surprised, but leaned back as if stretching his back.

"I know him. He is a French-Canadian trader, a really nosy type—always watching what everyone is doing. Oh, and *that* is interesting."

"What is?"

"Another man has joined them, who purports to be French-Canadian but I believe is actually French."

Tom had to restrain himself from turning around then realised he could use his knife as a sort of mirror.

"Did I just see him being given a purse?"

"You did. The French man passed it over. Look out, they are leaving."

They both made a show of concentrating on their meals until the three men had departed.

"Well, that's a rum do," Tom said.

"How's that?"

"He is supposed to be an army captain en route to China."

"Then what is he doing talking to French-Canadians?

"Are they?" Tom asked, looking concerned.

"What, French-Canadians? I don't know for sure but as I said, I have doubts about one of them."

Tom returned to the ship, his troubled mind popping up questions that he couldn't answer. Farrington was back on board and acting as though he didn't have a care in the world. Freyja noticed Tom's troubled frown and came to speak with him.

"Is something bothering you?"

Tom felt the need to talk things through with someone. "Let's go to my cabin and I will tell you."

Ten minutes later, he sighed and said, "So you see, I have my suspicions about Farrington and about who the two men he met were. But have no idea what to do about it."

"Well, I do not like Farrington, he is what you call a paper soldier."

"Paper?"

"You know, not a real soldier, one that children play with."

"Oh, a *toy* soldier!" Tom did not laugh.

"Yes, a toy soldier. He has the uniform but knows nothing about soldiering."

"Is that a fact? I wish I knew more about those other two."

"I can help you there," Freyja said and stood up. "I will return before the ship leaves."

And that was it, she left.

Oh Lord, what have I unleashed?

* * *

As it was, they had another day in Penang because the wind was in the wrong direction to leave, so Freyja took as much time as she could.

"The trader is a French-Canadian and very unhappy about the British holding Canada. However, the other man is not from Canada. He is French."

"And how do you know this?"

"The French man has servants, and one has gone missing. Before he died, he told me that his master was Monsieur Bescond from Paris and that he worked for the Ministry of Foreign Affairs."

"Before he died?"

"Yes, he drowned."

Tom swallowed hard. *She drowned him? Oh, my Lord.* Tom coughed, "Did he tell you anything else?"

"Yes, that Bescond and the trader, who is called Michel Roi, are collecting intelligence to feed to French ships that will be coming to this area soon."

Tom did not know what to do with that information. He had no time before they sailed to talk to anybody in authority in Penang, and as the thought crossed his mind, he heard Graham shouting the orders to get them underway. He wrote down everything that Freyja had said and put the paper in his strongbox along with his and Dewi's jewels. Freyja was a useful person to have around, but now he knew that he would have to put constraints on her in the future—otherwise, she would leave a trail of dead bodies behind her.

Lieutenant Edward Westcliff read himself in as master and commander of the HEIC sloop, *Aurora.* She was a beauty, built in Bombay of teak, launched in 1790 and bought by the EIC in 1798. He was her first proper commander, the outgoing one having merely been responsible for ferrying her to Penang.

Her carronades gave *Aurora* a punch that was well above her weight, and she had two long nines mounted as bow chasers. Her crew of sixty men could easily fight on both sides and sail her.

Westcliff would accompany the *Warley* through the straights to Canton. He wondered at that order, as the *Warley* was a big, well-armed ship even if she looked like an unarmed merchant.

She looks like an unarmed merchant!

The realisation hit Westcliff like a brick. She was manned and armed as a fighting ship but dressed like a merchantman. Furthermore, a merchantman being escorted by a Marine ship must be carrying something valuable. They were bait! They were inviting the bloody pirates to take them on!

His midshipman interrupted his train of thought.

"The *Warley* is warping out, sir."

Damn. Any questions would have to wait for later.

Westcliff called the orders to get them to sea. He would make sure his gunners were up to scratch.

Tom had reached the same conclusion. It fell into the general orders he had to engage and destroy pirates and any enemies of the British Empire. It seemed the Company was intent on making it happen.

"She looks pretty," Graham said, looking astern.

Tom looked at the *Aurora*. "She certainly is. Let's see what she can do. Make all sail."

Graham shouted the orders, and the men ran to their tasks. Sails blossomed up the masts and their speed increased. On the *Aurora*, the same orders were given. There was no way on this earth that Edward would let a bloody merchantman, armed or not, outpace him.

The passengers generally enjoyed the speed, knowing that it would make their journeys shorter, but one of them looked over the side and was troubled. Farrington had reported to his contact in Penang that the *Warley* was a well-armed ship—now she was proving to be a fast one, as well. She hadn't shown her full speed all the way across the Atlantic but had cruised at the most comfortable speed for the conditions. Now, on a flattish sea with a fair wind on her quarter and going with the current, she was racing along.

Leaning on the mainmast, cleaning her nails with a dagger, Freyja watched Farrington. She didn't like him, and if he *was* a spy, he was putting her and her friends in danger.

She knew that he liked to spend time on deck at the beginning of every day, so she left him there and went below. The door to his cabin was unlocked, as a steward was cleaning it. Freyja stepped inside and looked around the small sitting room. Nothing looked suspicious, so she went into the sleeping cabin.

The steward looked up from making the bed. She put her finger to her lips. "*Shhhh.*" He was a little wide-eyed, but pointedly concentrated on his task. There was a small folding writing table which Farrington had brought on board. She checked it over; he used the new steel-nibbed pens. She admired these, knowing they could also be used as a weapon.

The writing table had a drawer which wouldn't open, so she ran her hands around it to see if there was a release. Then a hand appeared, as the steward reached under the drawer and released it.

"The skipper asked me to have a look," he whispered.

She nodded her thanks and the two went through the contents.

They entered the strait at speed, the *Aurora* keeping up and then moving ahead to windward. Tom grinned; Edward knew how to do his job. Tom didn't expect trouble yet, he had too much sea room for manoeuvring for the Javanese and Sumatran pirates who infested these waters to take them on. No, he expected them to make a play when they got to the bottom of the strait and got among the islands approaching Singapore Island.

He saw the steward whom he had tasked with searching Farrington's cabin come on deck, followed by Freyja.

"Graham, you have the deck. I am going below. Inform me if anything happens."

He went down from the poop deck to his cabin and was joined by Archie, the steward, and Freyja who came in via the steward's pantry.

"Well? What did you two find?"

They both started talking at once and Tom held up his hand. "Archie?" He gave Freyja a look that told her he was in no mood for arguments.

"We searched his desk and found a drawer with a hidden lock. It were no problem as I seen them before. Oh, by the by the desk is French made. In it were a number of papers addressed to a Pascal Crémant and written in French."

"Anything else?"

"Yeah, he has a bag of Napoleons hidden in a compartment in his trunk, along with another letter to Crémant with a seal on it. The trunk also has a false back and there are weapons hidden there that a gentleman officer would never carry."

Freyja looked surprised at the revelations and Archie looked smug.

"Thank you, Archie." Tom flipped him a coin.

Archie left and Tom turned to Freyja.

"Archie was a cabinet maker before he got caught robbing the house of a man who had failed to pay him. He figured that going to sea was better than going to gaol. I asked him to search Farrington's cabin while he cleaned it. Have you anything to add?"

Freyja noticed he didn't reprimand her.

"Only that one of the letters was an introduction to people in China and Penang from someone called Serge Dallaire. The others were from a woman in Paris."

"You read French?"

"I speak it as well, along with Spanish and Italian."

"A woman of hidden depths," Tom said, looking at her appraisingly.

She gave him a smirk.

He looked at her seriously. "I do not want to suddenly find Farrington missing or turning up dead. We know who and what he is now, and I am sure the Company will have its own way of dealing with him. Am I making myself clear?"

"Yes, skipper."

"Good, now leave me in peace. I have letters to write."

"Skipper, we are coming up on the islands," Graham called down through the skylight.

Tom went up on deck. The *Aurora* was three cables ahead and to windward.

"Is she too far ahead?" Graham asked.

"No, she is fine where she is," Tom replied. In fact, she was just where Tom wanted her—as he wanted the pirates to think they could separate the two ships.

The Carimon Islands were coming up on the starboard side and he knew they were approaching the line where the tides met between the strait and the South China Sea. According to his almanac, the South China Sea would be approaching high tide in the next couple of hours. That meant they would be seeing an increase in the current as they got among the islands—which would favour the pirates.

"Good weather for a fight," Tom muttered to himself.

"Skipper?" Graham said.

"Get the passengers below and clear the ship for action. Tell them it is precautionary."

The crew, well-practised now, ran to their stations and the ship quickly became silent and expectant. Tom focused his telescope on the *Aurora* and saw that she was prepared as well.

Now, we wait.

Ahead of them, a flotilla of Sumatran pirates waited behind Tree Island, with another behind Sultan Island to the north. The channel that British ships took passed right between them and the vessels slowed because of the current.

The war junks were manned with banks of twenty oars, each manned by two men, and were two-masted with the typical sails of the region. Because of the oars they relied on large cannon in the bow, sacrificing fire power for manoeuvrability. The decks were full of men, ready to overwhelm the merchant ships by boarding.

The word had come down from Penang that there was a British ship being escorted by an East India Company sloop. It must be carrying important people or valuable cargo. Either way, it would make a lot of money.

The commander waited until the ship was two miles away, then fired the rocket that gave the signal. They started to close the trap. This was close enough that their prey could only come on, knowing that to try and turn and run would just make things worse.

Edward saw the rocket and gave a grim smile. "Load the guns with small ball over chain and be ready to wear ship fast. I want to pass through those ships coming from the north and serve them royally."

Between his main guns he had swivels mounted which, if they got close enough, would fire canister into the junks to kill as many men as possible.

On the *Warley*, there was an air of expectation. The guns were loaded with chain over ball. The soldiers were in place, with Freyja commanding.

"Clew up the mains," Tom ordered.

The corners of the mainsails were raised to get them away from the gun's flash.

"Stand by!"

Edward judged the time as right.

"Wear ship."

The *Aurora* spun on her heel as only a well-handled sloop could, and charged directly at the northern group of junks. Puffs of smoke from the junk's bows showed they had panicked and fired early. The shot splashed harmlessly in the sea, not getting close enough to wet the hull.

"Bow chasers, as you bear!"

The nines roared and the centre junk shuddered as she was hit by at least one of the balls. The *Aurora* gunners rushed to reload.

"Steady, lads," midshipman Jamie Martin said, an eye on the skipper.

The sloop jinked to pass between the middle and next junk to the right.

"Fire as you bear," Edward shouted.

Jamie had instructed the gunners to fire as they passed the foremast, and that is exactly what they did. *Boom*! *Chuff*!—the carronades blasted their loads. Jamie didn't look to see the effect; he was exhorting his men to reload as fast as they could.

Edward *did* see the effect. Wood shattered, throwing splinters across the crowded deck. Men were pulped by the small ball which passed through the hull, them, and out the other side.

"Wear to starboard! Pass behind them."

The second broadside was just from the port guns at a cable's range, right along the deck of the junk. That one was out of action until they could clear the dead out of the way of the rowers.

Tom saw the carnage wrought by the *Aurora* on two of the junks and knew that now she was behind them, Edward would continue to rake the targets as they presented themselves. His problem was the six junks heading up from the south. *What's good for the goose is good for the gander.*

"Steer directly for them."

That had two effects, the junks were suddenly presented with a much smaller target, and it was approaching at speed. Suddenly ports flew up and guns—a *lot* of guns—ran out. The junks fired, a hole appeared in the fore mainsail and some rigging was cut. Another ball ricocheted off the figurehead and passed down the port side.

"Fire as you bear, hit them between wind and water," Tom bellowed.

The gun captains bent, looking along the barrels, linstocks in hand. The bow of the junk appeared in the port, and the gun captain stepped to the side, dabbing the slow match into the priming hole.

Fzzzz . . . Boom! The gun sent its load outwards and recoiled back.

On the junk, chain howled across the deck low enough to decapitate or smash heads. The ball crashed through the side just above the oar ports sending splinters careening through the rowers—it had a slightly downward trajectory and took out two benches of rowers on the other side.

Like the *Aurora*, the *Warley* turned back to the east. To give the pirates their due they recovered quickly, and turned to try and get alongside at a point where they could board. More fell to the big guns before they managed that.

"Swivels," Tom ordered. The guns would keep firing without him telling them to. He took a blunderbuss from a rack by the wheel and pulled back the hammer to full cock. He saw Freyja and she waved; he nodded back.

The first junk came alongside, and hooks arced over to pull the ships together. There were too many to cut, so the men concentrated on thinning out the pirates before they got aboard. The main guns, depressed to the limit, could send grape down into any junk that tied up next to the first junk. The swivels and blunderbusses fired down into the ship immediately alongside. Of course, the pirates tried to suppress the gunners by firing muskets and arrows at them. The gunners responded by lobing grenades over the rail into the tightly-packed men.

Four pirates swarmed over the rail on the leeward side of the poop deck. Tom levelled his piece and pulled the trigger. At twenty feet the shot and scrap metal spread wide enough to take three of them down. The fourth staggered as he was hit by a solitary piece of scrap, but kept coming. Tom threw the blunderbuss at him, pulled a pistol from his belt, and shot him dead centre in the chest.

Now was the time for the hack and slash of swordplay.

On the *Aurora*, Edward was sailing his ship to cross the stern of as many junks as he could while keeping out of their clutches, for to be boarded would mean defeat. His carronades, being only three and a half feet long and mounted on slider carriages, were much faster to load than the *Warley*'s eighteens and could easily get off a round a minute or less.

He ordered another wear, and the starboard guns came into play, raking a junk as they turned past her. Their standard load of small ball and chain shredded the hull and rigging and pulverised the crew. Edward had a momentary thought, as he looked on, that they must have killed tens of men today.

The target he had in mind came into view off his port bow and he ordered the helm to steer to cross her bow. The junk was trying to get behind the *Warley* and was firing her twenty-four pounder. If he timed it right, he could cross her while the *Warley*'s stern chasers were reloading.

He soon realised that plan wouldn't work. So, he went to plan B.

"Run us alongside her at fifty yards. Aim for her oars!"

He figured that without oars the junk had no chance of catching up the *Warley* so just by taking them out they would render the pirate ineffective. They swung to approach the junk head on and the closing speed was high.

"Fire as soon as you see her bow cross your gun," he shouted to his gunners.

The foremost carronade fired, followed rapidly by the rest in a rippled broadside. He looked back. The starboard side of the junk was a mass of holes, and the majority of the oars were, well … gone.

Tom fought alongside his men, slashing and hacking with his cutlass, which dealt horrible damage to its victims. He killed the man ahead of him and found himself without a target. A high-pitched war cry from his right attracted his attention and he looked to see Freyja, who was a tornado of flashing steel. Fighting with a sword in each hand, she was decimating any pirates who stepped into range. Bodies were strewn at her feet and were soon joined by another as she kicked the man in the gut then almost beheaded him.

Her soldiers were using their halberds with intense ferocity, thrusting, twisting and withdrawing as a group. Forcing the pirates back to the rail. The pirates had lost momentum. A horn blew and all of a sudden, the deck was empty of standing pirates, as they withdrew.

Whampoa

The sixteenth of January in the year of our Lord 1800 saw the *Warley* anchor off Whampoa Island. The pilot had informed them that they would be unloaded there. Tom immediately sent the letter he had written about Farrington to the chairman of the Company Committee, who was based in the Thirteen Warehouses.

To give the Company a chance to reply with instructions, Tom did not allow the passengers to debark, giving the excuse that the customs inspection had not been completed. Which was true, as he hadn't requested one yet. This delaying tactic should buy him some time.

He was therefore surprised when a boat came alongside and a European came aboard.

"Captain Batrick?" the man asked as soon as he set foot on the deck.

"Yes," Tom said.

"Can we talk in private?"

"Of course, follow me," Tom said and led him to his cabin. He signalled to Freyja to stand guard.

Once inside, the man held out his hand. "Westfield Trafford, East India Company, head of security in China. You can call me Bill. Middle name is William."

"Pleased to meet you Bill, I'm Tom."

"I was passed your letter by the commissioner. It made for interesting reading. You think this fellow is a rum one?"

"Yes, I thought him a bit off as soon as I met him. Why would a captain of infantry be heading to China?"

"Quite. We only have a small garrison here and that's run by lieutenants. You saw him meet with the French in Penang?"

"I did, he was several tables away in the restaurant but the agent knew both men he met, and I saw the pouch change hands."

"You searched his cabin?"

"I had a steward and the captain of my soldiers search it."

"Can I speak to one of them?"

Tom opened the door and asked Freyja to step inside.

Bill's eyes widened as he looked the woman up and down, appreciating the curves inside the leather armour. Her hand went to her dagger.

"Freyja," Tom said quickly, "please tell Mr Trafford what you found inside Farrington's cabin."

Freyja described the search and what she had found in clear and succinct terms. Bill asked questions and finally thanked her. Tom asked her to wait outside, largely to avoid any reaction to Bill's obvious attraction to her.

"I should warn you that she has taken a vow of celibacy and is very good with that dagger. She threatened to cut off Daalderop's balls if he tried anything when they were sharing a cabin."

"God, the man must have been in agony. She is fabulous."

"You should see her fight. She killed at least a dozen pirates in the strait."

Bill shook his head at the thought, but then got his mind back on track.

"I want him followed. We have suspected that the French have placed a spy here for a while now. This might give us the chance to find out who it is."

"He has a big heavy trunk. What if I detail a couple of men to carry it to his lodgings for him?"

"That is a good idea, then you can set up a watch on him."

"Me?"

"You found him; you can help uncover what he is up to."

Tom called for a customs inspection and quickly received permission to debark his passengers. He spotted Farrington coming up on deck.

"Thank you for sailing with us, Captain Farrington. Can we be of any further assistance?"

"Yes, can you get a couple of coolies to take my trunk to my lodgings?"

"I can do better; my men will carry it for you. Those coolies will steal anything."

Farrington couldn't prevent a flicker of surprise, but obviously couldn't think of a way to refuse the offer.

"Thank you."

Tom detailed two of his more intelligent landsmen to carry the trunk and whispered a command for them to make a note of the address and for one to hang around and watch the address until relieved.

The men didn't bat an eyelid; obviously the crew had heard about their captain's suspicions. News of anything going on aboard ship was transmitted almost instantaneously.

Tom waited. His patience was rewarded when one of the men returned with the address. Bill was still aboard, hidden in his cabin.

"He is lodged in the Pearl," Tom announced as he closed the door behind him. "I have a man watching the place."

"Excellent, can you leave the ship?" Bill said.

"Me? Why, yes I can, my first mate is capable of managing the unloading."

"I want you and that valkyrie of yours to take a room in the same establishment. Like lovers would."

Tom was outraged at the thought but also a little thrilled, if he was honest with himself.

"I am a happily married man and father!"

Bill patted his shoulder. "I'm not asking you to shag her. Just pretend." Tom was clearly uncomfortable. "Look, this way you can legitimately be there and watch what he does and who he meets."

Tom tried to think of a way to get out of this and failed dismally. His only hope was that Freyja would refuse. He was to be disappointed: she agreed immediately.

The owner of the Pearl was a former sailor and leered at Freyja when Tom asked for a room. She ignored him. Freyja had foregone her leather armour and put on a dress. The dress was low waisted and had a tight bodice which emphasised her curves. Her blonde hair was loose and cascaded over her shoulders.

The room was on the second floor and looked down on to the street from above the entrance. It was perfect. According to the crewman on watch, Farrington had not left the building. Tom had him relieved by another, who was carefully briefed by Bill. Bill himself was keeping out of sight, as he was worried he would be known to the contact.

Having settled in their room, Tom and Freyja went downstairs for their evening meal. They chose a table in a corner, from where they could watch the entire room. Farrington came down, dressed in civilian clothes. He ate alone, then bade the waitress goodnight and went back upstairs.

Freyja and Tom took it in turns to watch the entrance from their room's window all night. Nobody left. The next morning, after breakfast, Farrington went for a walk. They followed at a discreet distance as he seemingly wandered around the town at random. Eventually, he found his way to a temple and entered. They watched him from the door.

Farrington took an envelope and placed it in the offering bowl.

"What is he doing, placing an offering in a Buddhist temple?" Tom asked when they got back to their room.

"I don't know, but it is highly unusual," Freyja replied.

"I need to talk to Bill. Keep watch while I am gone," Tom said.

"Before you go, unlace me." She turned her back on him.

The bodice of her dress was laced up and tied at the back. He released the bow and left before she could drop the dress to the floor. The Nordics had a much looser sense of decency than the British.

Bill was still on the ship and listened carefully to what Tom said.

"It must be a dead drop," he said.

"A dead drop? What's that?"

"A mechanism to exchange messages without physically meeting your contact. You leave the message on a paper at a pre-agreed place. At a crossroads under a rock, behind a loose brick in a wall, that sort of thing or, in this case, in an offerings bowl."

"You are saying a monk is the contact?"

"That's possible, but unlikely. No, the bowls are only emptied at the end of the day so the contact would just have to go to the temple and retrieve the envelope when no one was looking."

"We should put a watch on the temple, then," Tom said.

"See, you *are* catching on." Bill grinned.

Patronising arse.

"You have lots of men, I will leave it to you."

"Don't you have any men?" Tom asked, slightly exasperated by the whole thing.

"I do, but they are all tied up in an operation in Canton."

Tom sighed, and gave in. "All right, I will get a team set up."

He wasn't short of volunteers. The two men who had taken the trunk had told their mates about it and that had excited the crew, who were intrigued by the whole affair. Tom created two teams: one to follow Farrington if he left the inn and the second to watch the temple. Bill gave them tips on how to remain unseen and how to work in pairs.

"Now remember, you are just to watch and follow, not to intercept or try and grab them. Keep you distance and behave naturally," Bill said.

Fat chance of that, Tom thought as he looked at the grinning faces of the men.

When he returned to the inn, Tom saw Farrington in the common room and despite an attempt to avoid him, was spotted.

"Hello Captain, what are you doing here?"

Tom decided to bluff it out.

"Hello Captain Farrington, I am staying here with Freyja," Tom said conspiratorially.

"You are? You old dog!" Farrington chuckled, giving him a nudge in the ribs. "A girl in every port, eh?"

"Not quite, but we are at sea for a long time!" Tom smirked.

"Well, I won't keep you, I'm sure you have plenty to do." Farrington chortled, giving him a wink.

Tom took his leave and almost ran up the stairs to the sound of Farrington chuckling.

He entered the room. "Farrington saw me."

"Oh?" Freyja said.

"He thinks we are at it up here." Tom was embarrassed.

"*At it*? What is *at it*?" She asked with wide-eyed innocence.

"You know, having sex."

"That was the idea, wasn't it?"

"What?"

"To make people think we are having sex, what your sailors call 'the blanket hornpipe'."

"You are learning all the wrong things," he said grumpily, hoping to change the subject.

Freyja couldn't resist teasing him a little, he was so … British.

"You don't want to have sex?"

"No!"

"Good, because I do not either."

Tom shook his head. How had the conversation ended up going that way?

Freyja went back to the window. Tom slumped in a chair muttering to himself.

"*Hallå*," she said. "He is leaving."

Tom went to the window and watched as Farrington strolled down the road. One of the team came out of an alley and followed him. A second man would be trying to get ahead via a parallel street.

Once they were out of sight, Tom went to the door.

"Come on, we should search his room."

"It is on the first floor, at the back."

Tom paused.

"How do you know that?"

"I already searched it."

"And?"

"He is definitely Pascal Crémant. There was a letter written by him to Serge Dallaire at the Ministry of Foreign Affairs."

"What did it say?"

"I do not know; it was written in some strange language."

Tom frowned.

"Hmm, code probably."

She passed him a piece of blank paper.

"What's this?"

"The top sheet of a sheaf of paper he had on his desk."

Tom shook his head. "Why did you take it?"

"If you look at it, there are indentations where he used a pencil to write something on the sheet on top of it."

Tom raised his eyebrows in understanding and held the paper to the light.

"Yes, I can see them." He put the paper on the table and searched his satchel. "Aha!" He pulled out a short piece of charcoal that he used to sketch things of interest. He gently rubbed the charcoal over the surface then blew away any loose dust,

"*Mercredi, onze heures, marché*, signed *PC*," Tom read.

"Wednesday, eleven o'clock, market," Freyja translated. "'P' and 'C' are his initials."

* * *

Tom reported their findings to Bill, who immediately took him to the Thirteen Warehouses and the Company offices, where they talked to the chairman.

"So, the man's a spy. What do you want to do about him?" Lionel Darrell, the acting chairman, said.

Bill sat forward. "Watch him for now and see who his contacts are, then see what he does next. We should try and turn him or feed him misinformation. He is not much of a threat. We know who he is and what he is up to."

Darrell nodded. "Proceed along those lines, then." He turned to Tom. "You have done the Company a great service, thank you."

"It was not just me, sir. My crew as well," Tom replied modestly.

Darrell smiled knowingly.

"I understand that Daalderop's pet valkyrie has been involved as well."

Tom bristled. "Sir, I can assure you our relationship is purely professional."

Darrell chuckled. "Do not worry. We all know that Miss Freyja is not into men. Many have tried … and nursed bruises and even cuts for their troubles."

Tom realised he had been teased.

"Anyway, she would happily dispose of him for us if needs be," Darrell continued.

Bill stepped in to stop that train of thought. "We will continue to collect evidence with which we can blackmail Crémant or justify his arrest."

"I don't think arrest is an option," Darrell said. "I would much prefer to know who is watching us and if they will not cooperate, then eliminate them."

Tom shuddered at the cold-blooded way in which those words were spoken.

Bill managed to free up some of his men and took over the observation of Crémant. Tom and Freja returned to the ship. A package arrived from Mr Darrell with a note.

My dear Captain Batrick

In recognition of your service to the Company in uncovering the infiltration of French spies, I am pleased and honoured to award you the enclosed service as a reward.

I would much appreciate you passing our thanks to the men who were involved in the operation and there are ten guineas for each of them. Not forgetting Miss Freyja's contribution—there is a reward of fifty guineas for her.

My kindest regards and thanks.

Inside was a tea service. A solid silver tea pot, water jug, cream jug, sugar bowl, sugar tongs, tea strainer and teaspoons along with a set of eight fine Chinese porcelain teacups and saucers packed in straw. A pouch contained the reward for the men and Freyja.

He called the men to his cabin.

"Men, the Company has seen fit to reward you for your sneaking and watching. They have been generous, and you each get ten guineas."

The men grinned or blew out their cheeks in amazement. Tom continued. "That is a large amount of money, so I give you the choice to leave it with me until we reach London, or to take part or all of it now. I will add that I do not want this flaunted in front of the other men unless you wish to collectively share your good fortune with them."

One man spoke up after a brief whispered consultation with the others. "Skipper, if we might be so bold, we would like to throw a party, we all missed Christmas at sea and would like to make up for that."

Tom thought that was a grand idea.

"If you each donate two guineas to a party fund, I will add six more. Thirty guineas will pay for a sumptuous meal and drink."

Once they were gone, he summoned Freyja. She looked at the golden guineas in amazement.

"What am I to do with this?"

"I don't know, buy yourself a dress or three. You do look good in one."

She looked at him in surprise and then her eyes went soft. "Do you think so?"

"Freyja, you are a frighteningly good warrior, but you are also a woman and a very pretty one at that. You should show that side of you more often."

"If anyone other than you said that, I would gut them."

"And for that, I am eternally thankful."

She gave him a look that he didn't quite understand, picked up her coins and left. She saw him on deck later and passed him five coins. "For the party," she said.

Did her hand linger just a moment too long?

The party was held on board, but the food was cooked ashore where there was less of a fire hazard. Ducks by the dozen, a pig and a bullock were roasted. Large woks, manned by Chinese cooks, were used to prepare vast quantities of fresh vegetables. Noodles and rice replaced potatoes. Rice wine by the crate and local beer washed it all down.

The men sat at tables that ran the length of the deck on both sides, with a table across in front of the poop deck for the officers and senior ranks. Tom looked on indulgently from his place at the head of the tables. Chinese servants, hired for the day, ran back and forth with plates of meat and bowls of steaming vegetables, rice and noodles.

The men laughed and sang carols. Then Freyja stood and called for silence. She nodded to one of the crew, a Swede, who pulled out a pipe and started to play a tune. She started to sing, her voice full and strong. It was a Swedish song celebrating Christmas. A third Swede stood and joined in with a strong baritone:

Jul, jul, strålande jul, glans över vita skogar,
himmelens kronor med ljus.
glimmande bågar i alla Guds hus,
psalm, som är sjungen från tid till tid,
eviga längtan till ljus och frid!
Jul, jul, strålande jul: glans över vita skogar!
Kom, kom, signade jul! Sänk dina vita vingar
över stridernas blod och larm,
över all suckan ur människobarm,
över de släkten som gå till ro,
över de ungas dagande bo!
Kom, kom, signade jul, sänk dina vita vingar

The men listened in silence and when they finished there was a long pause before they started to cheer and bang the tables. They didn't need to know what it meant, their voices and emotion were clear to see. She smiled and sat down.

Tom leaned across the table and just said, "Thank you."

Bill turned up, and updated Tom on the Farrington affair.

"We spotted the person who picked up the letter at the temple and followed her. She is Vietnamese and is the servant of a man who goes by the name of Smith, not very original I know, who is posing as a tea trader. We watched them meet at the market and a packet was exchanged. Later, Farrington turned up at Company headquarters with a letter of introduction looking for a post as a shipping clerk."

"Did he get one?" Tom asked.

"Oh yes, and he is blissfully unaware that we know what he is up to."

"So, he will be allowed to pass information?"

"Practically encouraged to."

"Which you will control?"

"Absolutely."

Tom sipped his jasmine tea and felt the satisfaction of a job well done.

London and Home

They raised anchor at slack tide on the twenty-ninth of March, and were towed out of the estuary and across the second bar as the tide turned.

"Make all plain sail," Tom ordered. They only had a couple of passengers; a Company clerk who was returning home and a member of the Marine who was returning home as he had inherited his father's estate. The clerk was a proper little *nabob*, having made a small fortune while he was in China. He had taken a good cabin and showed off his wealth conspicuously. Tom had the misfortune to have him at the dinner table every day.

The clerk was well into his cups when he said, for the ... what was it, third time, "I made a fortune from silks, you know."

"Really?" Tom said, knowing what was coming next. He usually tuned out when the man, Clifford Arbuthnot, started waffling on about how he had made his fortune. But suddenly he said something that caught Tom's attention.

"Sorry, what did you say?"

"Hmm? About what?"

"You said the name of your supplier."

"Philip Smith."

"The tea merchant?"

"You know him?"

"I have had dealings with him, but didn't know he dealt in silks."

"He sold them to me at a very good price," Arbuthnot hiccupped.

"Did he ever ask for anything from you?" Tom asked.

"Not really, he was always chatty though."

Tom poured him another glass of wine and had the steward bring in the brandy.

"What about a letter of recommendation?"

"Yesh, he did *actuaaally.*" Clifford Arbuthnot burped, then hiccupped. Tom stopped refilling his glass, worried the man might pass out on him.

"Did you write one?"

"*Yesh*, well, no … but I did tell him what the correct form was." He was slurring his words even more, now.

"Did you tell him about cargoes?"

"Only chatted …" Arbuthnot slurred—and then he was snoring.

"Take him to his cabin," Tom told the steward, who got one of his mates to help him carry the unconscious clerk away. Tom immediately wrote down his findings in a letter to Bill and asked the next Canton-bound ship they passed to take it.

Freyja was bored. They had passed through the strait without even seeing a pirate. She wandered about the deck, looking for something to do.

"Hello," an unfamiliar voice said. She turned, and saw it was a passenger.

"Good morning," she said politely.

"My name is Clifford, what's yours?"

"Freyja."

"I must say, you are a very pretty girl. Why do you wear leather?"

A crewman sniggered as he heard the question, and stopped what he was doing to watch.

"I beg your pardon?" She spoke in a tone the crew knew meant danger.

"I mean no offence, but your garb is somewhat unusual."

The crewman signalled to the others nearby and they all stopped what they were doing to see what happened next.

"It is armour."

"Yes, I can see that, but why are you wearing it? Women do not fight."

Several men grimaced as they heard that; a couple laughed and started making bets.

"I see. Do you fence?" Freyja said in a flat voice.

Clifford struck a pose and said, "I have had lessons."

"Then get your sword and show me what you can do."

He looked surprised, but scuttled off to do as she bade him, convinced he would impress her.

The word spread around the ship like wildfire. A steward burst into Tom's cabin. "Miss Freyja is going to fight a duel!"

Tom got to Freyja as Clifford emerged with his small sword in hand.

"Do *not* kill him," he said in her ear.

"I will only teach him a lesson," she replied, and put her hand on his arm reassuringly.

Tom walked away, muttering.

The crew marked out a fighting circle on the deck with a rope. Freyja stood in the centre, waiting. Clifford joined her and swung his sword around to loosen his wrist.

"Are you ready?" he asked, and swished it back and forth a couple of times.

"Absolutely," Freyja said in a little-girl voice.

Clifford didn't notice but stepped forward and assumed the classic ready position. Freyja stood square on; her sword was still sheathed. She looked him over and shrugged.

"On guard," she said and pulled her main gauche, a foot-long basket-hilted dagger, with her left hand.

"Don't you have a proper fencing sword?" Clifford said, and stepped back.

"I don't fence. On guard!"

He resumed his stance, looking a little confused.

"Fence!" called Tom when Freyja nodded to him.

Clifford tried a standard, fencing lesson two attack, which Freyja parried easily. He recovered and tried something a little more complex. She stood still and parried; her reactions lightning fast. He stepped up his attacks and she stood like a rock, unmoving, her dagger a blur. The crew cheered.

Clifford stepped back; he was breathing heavily. He wiped the sweat from his brow. Freyja was not breathing heavily and hadn't even broken a sweat.

He circled to her right. She didn't move. He flicked his point at her. It hit empty air. She slapped him on the backside.

"I'm here!" He felt her breath on his ear. She was behind him, the dagger pricking his throat as he turned to find her less than a foot away.

"You are dead."

"How?"

"You will never know, you are dead."

She stepped out of the circle and walked away, putting the dagger back in its sheath behind her back.

The crew laughed and went back to work. Tom heaved a sigh of relief.

They reached St Helena and rewatered on the fifteenth of July, which put them in the eastern Caribbean at the beginning of August. This was not good timing, as it was coming up to the height of the hurricane season. They suffered successive tropical storms as they made their way towards Bermuda—and narrowly missed a hurricane that passed south of them—through the Leeward Islands, into the Caribbean Sea and on into Louisiana.

The *Warley* took the route that passed the Lesser Antilles, and they reached a point fifty miles off the Bahamas on the twenty-sixth of August. The sky to the south-east that evening was dark and angry. The waves were growing larger by the minute and the wind was increasing.

"That, my friend, is a hurricane," Tom said to Graham who had joined him on deck.

"Will it hit us?"

"Not directly. I have been watching it and I think it is heading for the Bahamas."

Lightning etched the forward edge of the clouds. The storm was over 200 miles wide and travelling at fourteen miles an hour, though Tom had no way to know that.

"I think it will be over the islands by tomorrow morning, by which time we will be another hundred miles north of here."

A hundred miles put them in the forward edge of the storm, which had slowed to a crawl as it passed over the islands. It would batter them for two days. They managed to sail north by north-east in the howling gale, the sea on their stern. Tom hardly left the poop deck.

"Sir, we have three feet in the bilges," Frank Wilton, the carpenter, reported.

"Get the pumps started and let me know the depth in an hour."

The crew manned the chain pumps and the *clank, swoosh* as they turned them could be heard throughout the ship. The pump worked by the simple arrangement of a crank attached to a sprocket which moved an endless chain through a pipe that ran down to the bilges and back up in a continuous loop. Bell-shaped buckets fitted to the chain lifted the water and dumped it into a sluice that took it overboard.

After an hour, they had reduced the height to eighteen inches. That meant no serious leaks and Tom had the men stand down. He would pump again when the water reached three feet. As they followed the current north up the coast of America, towards North Carolina and Virginia, the wind dropped as the trade winds returned to normal and swung to blow homeward.

The crossing east was lumpy to say the least, but the waves were mainly on their stern and they were going with the Gulf Stream. It was with a sense of relief, at least among the passengers, that they reached the Downs on the twenty-third of September.

And there they sat, waiting for permission to enter the river and make their way to India Dock. It wasn't until the first of October that they got permission and a pilot. They docked on the second and Tom was summoned to attend the board of directors, who were waiting for him.

"Take care of the unloading and give the crew shore leave if I'm not back in time. We won't be leaving again until the new year," Tom told Graham; for he had decided that if he could, he would head to Poole forthwith.

Dressed in his best, he presented himself to the doorman at East India House and was told to go up to the boardroom's anteroom and wait.

There he sat and read a copy of the *Times* which a previous visitor had left behind. It was only a day old, and he was just reading an interesting account of a murder trial when the door to the boardroom opened and he was asked to step inside.

"Captain Batrick, welcome. Please take a seat," Francis Baring said from his seat at the end of the table. He was bracketed by Mr Lushington and Mr Inglis. A third man in a black suit sat to the side of the table, opposite Tom.

"Gentlemen," Tom said in greeting, nodding a bow.

Baring introduced the man in black. "This is Captain Franklin from the War Office."

"Your servant, sir," Tom said.

"We have received a report from our man Trafford which told us of your exploits in China," said Baring.

"That was quick, he must have sent it on the Hindustan. She left two weeks before us."

"He did indeed. We, in turn, told our friends at the War Office and Captain Franklin here has an interest in your tale."

Franklin leaned forward. "Tell me, what alerted you that something was off about Farrington?"

Tom pursed his lips and looked at the ornate ceiling, gathering his thoughts. "To start with, his general demeanour. He was supposed to be a military man, a captain of infantry, but he never talked about the army or what his posting was in China. Another thought I had was that captain was a surprisingly senior rank for a post that supposedly had only a handful of men."

Franklin nodded and made a note on a paper before him. "Carry on."

"Also, he referenced the French several times. Will we fight them, was the *Aurora* the equivalent of a corvette, that kind of thing."

"So that triggered your suspicions?"

"Well, yes, why would an army man compare a sloop to a corvette?"

"Indeed. You had him followed when you arrived in Penang?"

"Oh, no. I was having lunch with the Company agent Mr Pritchard and he—Farrington—was on a table the other side of the restaurant with another man. I heard his voice and got Dewi—Mr Pritchard—to look and see who he was with."

"That's when he recognised that the two men were French?"

"He said he had suspicions that *one* of them was."

"And that prompted you to have his cabin searched? A major imposition that, if discovered, could have got you into a lot of trouble."

Tom felt as if he was being cross-examined in a court. He took a breath and let it out slowly, to control his emotions.

"I felt it was justified, given the circumstances, and in any case we were proved right."

"We? Oh, Miss Freyja and you?"

"Yes."

"We know all about Miss Freyja."

"Oh?"

"Don't worry, she is on our side."

Tom was immediately suspicious. "She is one of your agents?"

"No," was all that Franklin said. Then, after he had finished making another note, he said, "Tell me what happened on Whampoa."

Tom recounted the tale, leaving nothing out. Franklin asked questions at different points, prompting Tom to fill in with more detail.

"Excellent, you did a good job," Franklin said when Tom had finished.

"Thank you," Tom replied, feeling relieved it was over.

Franklin stood and bowed to the board members. "Thank you, gentlemen. I will take my leave now. You have all been most helpful." He bowed to Tom and left.

"Well, that's a bit rum!" Inglis said.

Baring nodded then looked at Tom. "We thank you for your service. The report of the battle with the pirates in the strait made interesting reading. I understand the China office rewarded you and your men for your efforts in Whampoa, and as your report has been confirmed by the Marine you will receive gun money for the action."

"Thank you," Tom said, wondering what else was going to happen.

"Your ship will not sail again until May, so I wish you a restful time with your lady wife."

When Tom returned to the *Warley*, a stream of stevedores were unloading her, and he met Graham and the agent at the top of the gangway.

"All in order?" he asked.

"Aye skipper. The first of the crew have left already, the rest will go as soon as the cargo is unloaded, and her sails and yards are brought down."

"Has the magazine been swept?"

"Aye, Guns did it with his mates. Place is spotless."

Just then Guns—Silas Finch—came on deck, carrying his sea bag.

"Skipper, Graham. I'm all finished up. Magazine is clear, shot is stowed, armoury locked. The keys are on your desk."

"Thank you, Silas. Are you going home?" Tom asked.

"Why, yes, and here be my missus to meet me."

Tom looked at the dock, where a woman half Silas's age stood waiting. He did a double take as the one-legged gunner swept her into his arms and kissed her deeply. She was a looker as well!

"The old devil!" Graham laughed as the two walked away.

Tom waited until the ship was stripped to bare masts and sealed up for her stay in dock before leaving. He went straight to the Pool of London to find a ship heading down to Poole.

He found a Thames barge that carried stone from Purbeck to London; it was on its way back and could take him. This modest craft suited him fine, as he was carrying a fortune in gemstones and with a crew of just three men from his hometown, he felt safe. However, he kept a pistol under his blanket all the same.

He was met at the door of the house by Mary and a toddling Thomas junior. *Damn, he is growing fast.* Mary, who had regained her figure, hugged him fiercely before introducing Thomas to him.

"Thomas, this is your father," she said and picked him up.

Thomas looked at Tom with big eyes and sucked his fist.

He met Goldsmith a few days later and the jeweller was very happy with the stones Tom had brought back. Tom had checked the price of stones in London before he left and knew what to expect. The deal was done with no haggling and the money was deposited in his and Dewi's banks.

He was sitting in his study when he had a sudden thought.

Where does Freyja go between trips?

The Third Voyage, 1801–1802

Addiction

Tom discovered he was very much a hands-on father. He enjoyed playing with his son and introducing him to the toys the crew members had made for him. The boy was quick to learn and was saying "Mama" and "Dada" and had started to point to things when he wanted them. He would either crawl or, increasingly, toddle around and bring his father a toy, which he would name. He was playing this game in the nursery when Mary answered a knock at the door.

"Tom, there is someone to see you," she called.

Puzzled as to why she did not just show them in, Tom put Tom junior in his cot and went down the stairs. As he walked down, he saw a cloaked and hooded figure standing in the doorway.

"Freyja?"

"*Ja*. I need your help."

"Who is this lady?" Mary asked with a look of concern. The thought that this was his mistress was clear in her eyes. Tom spoke firmly and looked at his wife directly.

"Freyja is the captain of the soldiers on my ship. She is a Nordic warrior from a sect that consider themselves daughters of the valkyrie; she is currently a journeyman, working her way around the world until she can become a shield maiden. She is sworn to celibacy."

Mary looked him in the eyes as she took in what he was saying. Then she humphed and stood aside to let Freyja in.

Tom took her into the living room, where his mother sat knitting. They remained standing.

"What's the problem, Freyja?"

"Daalderop has gone missing," she said, dropping the hood.

"What? You mean you can't find him?"

"His servants haven't seen him at his London home for two months now and the Company is looking for him. He is not at any of the usual places he goes to. No one has seen or heard from him."

"Probably a woman," Anne muttered, loud enough to be heard. They glanced at her, then turned back to their conversation.

"Why are you down here?"

"He has business interests in Portsmouth."

"Have you checked them?"

"No, I do not know the town at all. That is why I came to you."

Mary had overheard most of the conversation and asked, "Who is this Mr Daalderop?"

"He is a senior supercargo with the Company, an important man whom Freyja was guarding before she joined the ship."

"Do you know where he stayed when he visited Portsmouth?" Mary asked.

Freyja shrugged. "We stayed at an inn."

"The Company men would use the Royal George. It is the best inn in Pompey and is conveniently close to the docks and warehouses," Tom said.

"That was it!" Freyja exclaimed.

"Well, you had best start there then," Mary said.

Tom was surprised when, during the evening, Mary and Freyja seemed to get on quite well, chatting and laughing. The tall warrior wore her leather armour but had replaced the trousers with a long leather skirt.

They would start the search tomorrow. It was winter and the roads were easier to pass early in the morning.

Tom and Freyja set out at dawn, which was at a half after seven. It was cold, crisp and slightly misty. Mary had made sure he was dressed warmly, and Freyja donned a heavy cloak trimmed with wolf fur. Even so, the cold had crept into their bodies by the time they reached the Royal George.

Tom handed the horse and the dog cart over to a groom and they went inside, where a log fire was burning in a large inglenook fireplace, making the place pleasantly warm.

"Can we talk to the landlord please?" Tom asked a serving girl.

"He's out back. He'll be here in a minute," she replied.

Tom sighed, stood, then walked over to the bar, lifted the hatch that was set into one end and walked through. He was followed by Freyja.

"Oy, you can't go back there!" the girl squawked.

Tom ignored her and took the door to the room where the beer barrels were kept. The landlord was just finishing the preparation of a barrel for drinking. He held a large mallet and had a tap positioned on the bung.

"Just a moment," he said, and brought the mallet down firmly on to the end of the tap, which went through the bung cleanly with hardly a drop spilt.

"What do you want?" he said, looking at Tom—then frowned when he saw Freyja.

"Do you know Mr Daalderop?" Tom asked.

"Yes, he works for the East India Company and stays here sometimes." The landlord was guarded and looked at them suspiciously.

"Has he been here in the last couple of months?"

"Why do you want to know?"

Freyja stepped forward. "He is missing, and we are trying to find him. You know I stayed with him here a year ago."

"Oh yes, I thought I recognised you. You are the girl in leather."

"Have you seen him?" Tom asked again.

"He stayed here, let me see ..." He looked up at the ceiling as he thought. "About five weeks ago now. Stayed for three days, then left."

"Was there anything unusual about him?"

"Now you mention it, he did seem rather melancholy."

"Melancholy? What is that?" Freyja asked when they got back into the bar.

"Sad," Tom explained.

"Why would he be sad?"

"I don't know, we need to find out."

Their next stop was the local East India Company office.

"Mr Daalderop? Haven't seen him for weeks. He popped in a month or so ago and I haven't seen him since," the clerk told them after they had explained the situation.

"Do you know what business interests he has in the town?" Tom asked.

"He has a small warehouse in the docks. It's in the secured area near the Company warehouse. I heard he also has an interest in a wool merchant. Let me see." The clerk shuffled through a drawer of filing cards. "Yes, here it is. Mayhew and Donaldson on Union Road."

"Thank you," Freyja said.

"Please, if you find him let us know. Everybody liked him here," the clerk said sincerely.

* * *

The warehouse was their first port of call. They had to pass through gates that were manned by guards armed with cudgels, and Tom was asked for identification. He showed his commissioning letter.

The door looked as if it was locked, but when Tom rattled the padlock the hasp fell open. He looked at Freyja, who drew a pistol from under her cloak. Tom pulled the door open and stepped inside, Freyja came in behind him and then stepped to one side to clear her field of fire. It was gloomy inside the warehouse and they stood still to let their eyes adjust.

Tidy stacks of crates filled one end of the building, and there was a desk with a chair in the corner. Tom went over to it and lit the lamp hanging above it. There didn't seem to be anyone around.

He ran his finger over the desktop. "Dust. This hasn't been used in weeks." He started to look through the papers lying on the desk.

Meanwhile, Freyja explored the rest of the building. She came back and put her gun away.

"Nobody here. Find anything?" She looked over his shoulder as she spoke.

"Just a few manifests, looks like he is doing quite well."

"He is a good businessman."

They left and closed the hasp on the padlock as it had been before.

"Next stop, Mayhew and Donaldson's."

The company's office was a mile away and they walked briskly to keep warm, Tom's cane tapping as they walked.

"Are you not armed?" Freyja asked in her rather appealing Nordic accent.

"I am, actually," Tom said and held up his cane.

"Sword stick?"

"Yes, twenty-four-inch blade."

"I wondered. There are no bulges in your pockets, and you are not wearing a sword."

They found the office easily, as it had a large brass plaque on the wall by the door. Tom pushed the door open, and they stepped inside.

"Can I help you?" said a man who was sitting just behind a door to the right of the entrance hall.

"We are looking for Mr Daalderop."

"Aren't we all?" the man said.

Tom explained their visit and said, "You haven't seen him?"

"A few weeks ago. He came in, withdrew some money and left. Haven't seen him since."

"Was he in good humour?"

"His usual self, he just seemed to be in a hurry."

"Are there any places he frequented?"

"You can try the Old Harry pub; he went there now and again."

The pub was only a few streets away and was a middling sort of establishment where clerks and workmen went to drink. The landlord was a taciturn sort.

"Daalderop? Don't know anybody by that name."

Tom put a half crown on the counter but kept his finger on it. "Tall man, dresses well, has a slight accent, blue eyes."

The landlord looked at the coin and licked his lips.

"You should try Mary Baker's. He went there from time to time."

Tom knew full well who and what Mary Baker's was. The house on Water Street was a well-known bordello. The owner was a local personality who wore a fancy red wig, extravagant clothes, furs and hat.

He warned Freyja, who shrugged. "Such places are common all over the world."

The brothel was in an old lodging place called Gloucester House. The name was emblazoned on the wall above the door. Tom pushed his way inside past a drunken sailor who grunted and collapsed to the floor after trying, unsuccessfully, to grope Freyja.

The bordello's madam herself met him in the reception room. She looked at the prone sailor in the doorway. "Bert! Clear that rubbish from my door," she shouted.

A large man appeared through a door at the back of the room, wiping his mouth with the back of his hand.

"I was 'avin me lunch, wun I," he muttered as he picked up the sailor and carried him away. He came back without him.

"Now, what can I do for you, me darlin'?" Mary said.

"We are looking for Henrik Daalderop," Freyja said.

"'Enry? You need to talk to Greta." She looked hard at Freyja, then shouted, "Greta! Get your arse daan 'ere."

She smirked at Tom. "Can we do anything else for you, my lover?"

"No, thank you," Tom said politely.

Greta entered from the back and Tom did a double take. Apart from being hardly dressed at all, she could have been Freyja's twin.

"Oh my," Tom said.

Greta looked at Freyja, who looked back in surprise.

"You must be Freyja," Greta said.

They sat around a table and Greta explained, "He would visit, and I would have to pretend to be you. We would do it and then he would cry. He was in love with you, I think, but you were untouchable, he said."

"When was the last time you saw him?" Tom asked.

"Nigh on two weeks ago. He was in a bad way. I think he had been smoking that opium stuff."

That was not good news.

"Do you know where he smoked it?"

"There's a den off Church Street. You have to go down Fiddler's Alley to get to it, but that's a really rough area—you will need protection."

Tom looked at Freyja, who looked upset, and said, "I have some."

Church Street was a slum, the home of the lowest of the low, and was ruled by thugs. Fiddler's Alley was notorious. Tom put his hand in his pocket and pulled out a set of brass knuckles which he slipped on to his right hand then held his cane at the ready. Freyja drew her swords and held them ready under her cloak. She grinned at the bar of brass adorning his fist.

"Nice," she said.

They entered the alley and became aware that, as soon as they were ten feet in, a pair of men closed off the entrance. The alley was narrow and ended in a small courtyard. The opium den was in a ramshackle building on the other side. Three thugs stood between them and it.

"What's yer business?" one said.

"We are looking for a friend," Tom replied.

"Well, he ain't here."

"You don't know who it is yet."

"No matter, he ain't here."

Tom sighed and twisted the top of his cane. Freyja shrugged her cloak off her shoulders, so that it hung behind her.

"Are we going to have to do this the hard way?" Tom said.

The men didn't answer, but produced knives and clubs. Tom heard a crunch as a foot trod on something behind them. Freyja reacted, spinning around, swords flashing. Tom pulled his blade and advanced, not waiting for them to come to him.

He held the cane in his left hand and sword in his right. He slashed the middle thug across the chest with a high-to-low diagonal cut then hit the thug to his left across the side of the head with the cane. The cut thug howled and the other staggered away, dazed from the blow. The third tried to get close enough to stab Tom.

Tom spun the cane, swishing it towards the man's head. The thug ducked and Tom punched him in the side of the head, the brass knuckles leaving a visible dent.

The dazed thug had recovered at least some of his wits and charged at Tom, roaring. Tom sidestepped and punched the man behind the ear as he passed.

Then Tom looked around: two unconscious, the third sitting on the ground holding his chest together. He checked Freyja. She was fine, wiping her swords on a prone man's trousers.

"Shall we?" he said, and the two walked into the den.

A wide-eyed Chinese man stood in the hallway that led back from the door. Alcoves lined it, in which recumbent addicts smoked pipes of the sweet-smelling drug. Tom and Freyja walked down the hallway, blades drawn.

Daalderop was about halfway down. He was thin, dirty and stank of his own piss and shit.

"Oh, my Lord. You silly man," Freyja said.

Tom took the pipe from him and threw it away, then grabbed Daalderop by the lapels and hauled him upright.

"Fuck it, I'm going to have to carry him."

He sheathed his blade in the cane and pushed it through his belt. He left the brass knuckles on. Then he ducked and hauled Daalderop over his shoulder. The smell was appalling.

"Lead us out."

Freyja advanced, swords at the ready.

They got him back to the Royal George after dark, and took rooms. Tom ordered hot water and a hip bath and got Daalderop cleaned up. He threw his clothes on the fire and bought some clean ones from the landlord. They were ill fitting but would keep him warm. Daalderop was largely unaware of what was going on, and passed out on the bed when Tom manhandled him onto it. Halfway through the night, he woke up screaming. Tom subdued him with a sleeper hold that cut off the blood to his brain, rendering him unconscious. He had seen a surgeon use it once and was grateful he had him demonstrate the technique.

In the morning they put Daalderop in the dog cart and took him to Tom's home, where they put him to bed. Freyja stayed with him, only leaving his side when Tom or Mary replaced her so she could sleep. They had him checked by a doctor, who only wanted to bleed him, so Tom thanked the man and sent him on his way.

Deprived of his drug, Daalderop went through purgatory. He raved, hallucinated, cried and shivered. After a month he was through the worst, but his mind was still affected. By then, it was Christmas time. In January, they took him to London by mail coach and brought him to his own house. The Company was informed—and did just as Tom expected. They washed their hands of him, pensioning him off.

Tom and Freyja discovered that he had a brother who was a lawyer in London. They had little choice but to put him into his care. His brother hired a nurse and confined Daalderop to his home. It was better than sending him to an asylum.

London

Freyja returned to Poole with Tom and stayed with the family until it was time to leave for London, to prepare the *Warley* for its next voyage. The whole Daalderop episode had deeply disturbed her, and she spent a lot of time talking to Anne, whom she seemed to treat as her mother.

"Take care of her; she is vulnerable when it comes to relationships," Mary told him as he pulled his coat on for the trip to the Big Smoke, as London was called in the countryside. "And I think she sees you as a father figure."

"That's all I need," he grumped, then smiled and hugged her. They had said goodbye in a passionate and loving way the night before.

"See you in a year. Next time you can come with me, as little Tom will be old enough."

Their goodbyes said, Tom and Freyja climbed into the carriage. The driver flicked the whip and the horses started out. It was April. The lanes were lined with blackthorn and wild cherry blossom and the banks swathed in primroses and celandine. The fields were dotted with dandelions and cowslips. Birds sang their stories of nests and challenges over territory. As the day warmed, early butterflies emerged.

Freyja decided she liked Dorset in the spring and travelling by coach gave her ample time to admire the countryside. Tom had decided to travel to Portsmouth to use a Company ship to get to London, rather than rough it on a coaster from Poole. This was only partly in consideration of Freyja, whom he watched looking out the window at God's own countryside. There was no better place to be in the spring, in his opinion.

"What is the black and white bird?" she asked.

"That's a magpie. If you see one on its own you should say 'Good morning, Mr Magpie, how is your wife today?' to ward off bad luck."

"Why are they unlucky?"

"I don't think they are, but most people believe seeing a single one is bad luck. There's a rhyme. 'One for sorrow, two for joy, three for a girl, four for a boy, five for silver, six for gold, seven for a secret never to be told'."

Freyja laughed. "People are the same about ravens at home, but we don't have a rhyme."

Portsmouth was just as it usually was: dirty and smelly after the fresh countryside air. The stench of humanity hung over the place like a cowl, along with the smell of rotting fish. The Company ship was at the dock, and they went aboard immediately upon arrival. Tom had timed everything perfectly, and they settled down for the short trip around the coast. The tide was at its height at a half after two in the afternoon, when they slipped their moorings and trotted past Portsea Island and Gosport before turning east with the wind on their stern.

They had cabins. The trip would take at least a day, depending on whether they had to hold at the Downs. Tom had talked to the captain, who said he expected to pick up a pilot as soon as they entered the estuary. They would see—Tom knew better than to rely on any planning.

* * *

The ship, EICS *Ceres*. was towed into India Dock and moored close to the *Warley*. Tom shook Captain Stevens' hand and thanked him for the passage.

The *Warley* looked sad in her harbour dress—almost abandoned. They went aboard and Tom looked her over.

"She hasn't been touched." He frowned. He had expected the Company to at least do *some* maintenance, but apparently she had been forgotten.

Some of his crew were back, and Tom put them to work cleaning the bird shit from the rigging and deck. He personally inspected the rigging and made a list of the parts that needed replacing. When the carpenter arrived, he had him inspect the hull. The Company, being interested in profit, would only refit a ship after three crossings—and that was fine if all they did was sail back and forth. However, the *Warley* had fought and fired her big guns, which added a lot of wear to the hull because the recoil flexed it.

His requests for a dry dock fell on deaf ears. He received the rigging he asked for, and a stock of timbers and caulk was delivered. The sailing date remained the nineteenth of May.

"The bilge needs pumping, but the hull looks to be sound enough," Frank Wilton reported.

Tom thought back to that solitary magpie they had seen in Dorset and shuddered just a little.

A letter was waiting for him, from Daalderop's brother, who thanked him for rescuing his sibling. He said that they had been forced to confine him, as his craving for opium was overwhelming at times and he would try and escape to find a den. Daalderop's businesses had been dissolved and there was enough money to care for him till he died. Tom wondered again about the morality of the opium trade, if it could ruin good men like that.

Inside the letter was a deed through which Freyja had been given, at Daalderop's insistence, a property in Kent to do with as she wanted.

"He gave me a house?"

"Apparently so. The deed is in your name, Freyja Gulbrandsen."

"Yes, that is my name, but why?"

"Only he knows, and it will be a long time before he is well enough and strong enough to venture outside his house."

Freyja took the deed and for a moment looked as if she would screw it up and toss it overboard. But she relented and tucked it away inside her bodice.

Their destination was China via Rio de Janeiro and Penang. Tom had the lading sheets in hand. They would deliver wool cloth at Rio and pick up silver, coffee and sugar. They would offload some coffee at Penang and pick up "general cargo". Tom frowned; that was a phrase he had never known the Company to use.

What the hell is that?

He shook his head; the Company was probably up to no good. He moved on to the passenger list. One for Rio, a Mr Borges, must be Portuguese. Two, no three for Penang, a Company clerk and a trader with his wife. Finally, four for Canton. A Chinese diplomat returning home with his wife and two children. The dinner table would be international, to say the least.

The cargo was loaded, Graham took care of that, and then the passengers arrived. Borges was a haughty man who came with servants. He had the largest suite. He was followed by the Chinese man, Mr Qiu, and his family. Richly dressed in traditional Chinese clothes and accompanied by a pair of servants and four small dogs, they came aboard in a clatter of wooden-soled shoes and barking. The trader and his wife were well dressed in smart, yet serviceable, clothes and had no servants. She, a little woman who scurried rather than walked, was bossy and obviously strong minded. The clerk, Ernest Brown, arrived last, and only just in time. He rushed up the gangplank carrying his own luggage and tripped as he came on deck. A sailor caught him as he staggered forward before he fell. Brown's bag slid across the deck and was stopped from sliding into the scuppers by one of Freyja's booted feet.

Oh yes. Tom smiled grimly to himself. *This is going to be an interesting trip.*

The tide was high at a quarter after one in the morning and reached low tide at a half after seven. They planned to start the trip at false dawn to get as far down river as possible, and hopefully out to the estuary. Tom had the *Warley* out in the river before high tide and stood looking at the moon, which was rising over the city. It was a clear, cold night; could he make the trip down river now?

The pilot was already onboard, and Tom had him brought up onto the poop deck.

"Can we sail down by moonlight?"

"We could, there will be enough water under our hull at slack tide before it starts going out," Cyrus Stemp said. "You will need a couple of good men in the chains measuring the depth."

"Prepare to raise anchor. All hands on deck," Tom bellowed.

The men came up, some rubbing their eyes, not having expected to be sailing yet. Graham appeared, looking sleepy.

"We're leaving now, skipper?" he asked.

"Aye, the tide's right and there's a good moon."

Graham took over organising the men and soon the cry came: "Anchor up and down!"

"Jibs and spanker, once we are out of the docks, we will set staysails," Tom said.

The *Warley* broke free of the land and glided forward. Tom stood at the wheel with the helmsman watching a lookout in the bow, who held a lantern with coloured glass in its windows. He guided them past other anchored ships by showing them white for straight ahead, red for turn to port and green for turn to starboard. It helped that every ship showed harbour lights and Tom could see their silhouettes against the night sky, but the lamp was his guiding light.

Then they were clear and the staysails were raised to increase their speed a little. The monotonous call of the leadsmen in the chains echoed back to the poop deck. Cyrus gave the helmsman quiet instructions. "A half point to starboard, steady as she goes." They were making only two knots over the current.

They rounded the curves past the Isle of Dogs, and the river got wider as they passed Woolwich, with more curves as they passed Crossness and Coldharbour. Dartford was followed by a sharp left, right, left—then they had to thread their way past ships moored in the river at Tilbury.

Tom heaved a sigh of relief as they entered the top of the estuary and the river opened out. Cyrus left them; he had a boat that was being towed behind and he waved as his sail filled and he started back up the river. It was dawn; their progress so far had taken them six hours of concentrated sailing. Tom smiled as they entered the Channel and turned south of west past Sheerness. They were on their way.

Rio de Janeiro

The Atlantic crossing was rough. Storms plagued them, tiring the men and working the ship's timbers. Tom was concerned and made a personal inspection of the hull, down to the bilges, with the carpenter.

"She's working out her caulking," he shouted above the thumping of the sea against the hull.

"Aye, she needs docking and refitting," Frank shouted back.

The timbers of all ships flexed, that was part of their strength, but over time—and especially in rough seas—the caulking between the timbers would work itself out.

"Get a team down and try and hammer it back in," Tom yelled as a squirt of water hit him on the neck.

On deck, the men dressed in tarpaulin coats and hats in an attempt to stay dry. None of the passengers ventured out and food was served in their cabins.

Then, twenty days into the trip, the wind dropped, the sky cleared and they were all but becalmed. The passengers came on deck to exercise and to take the air.

"Can we not go faster?" Borges demanded.

"Unfortunately, sir, we are at the mercy of the wind," Tom said, thinking what an idiotic question that was.

Borges stomped off, and Tom watched other passengers. Mr Qiu and his family, the children running around and letting off steam and the strange little dogs called Shih Tzus. He wondered who got to clean up the shit that four dogs would deposit. As if on command, one squatted and deposited a pile on his deck. It had no sooner finished than one of the family's servants rushed forward with a small straw brush and a pan and scooped it up before depositing it over the side.

Well, that answers that.

Freyja worked off her confusion and sadness over Daalderop by drilling the soldiers. The children imitated them and made a game of it. A sailor gave them cut-down boarding pike shafts so they could copy the moves made with the halberds. Tom knew that most sailors liked seeing children aboard. If they didn't, they kept it to themselves or risked losing their berths. People who could afford to take their families with them were almost exclusively rich and powerful.

The light winds did not last long. They were soon overtaken by another storm coming off the African coast. While this got their speed up again, the combination of wind and waves had all the passengers back in their cabins.

In time, Rio appeared off the bow to the lookout, who shouted, "Land Ho! Sugarloaf Mountain three points off the port bow."

Graham had the watch. "Steer three points to port. Tell the skipper that we have Rio in sight."

Tom stayed below. They were still eighty miles off and, from the sound of the ship, making less than ten knots. He could sleep for another hour or so. He had just settled down when there were a series of thuds and raised voices.

What the hell is going on?

There was a knock at the door.

"Skipper, can you come on deck?"

Resigning himself to having to get up, he dressed and went on to the main deck. Borges had his cabin luggage on deck and was demanding that the rest be brought up from the hold. Tom walked up to him.

"Mr Borges …"

"*Dom* Borges!"

Tom took a deep breath and let it out slowly. "Dom Borges, what is the problem?"

"They will not bring up my luggage!" Borges, looking ready to stamp his foot, stood quivering with outrage.

"What do you want it for? We are still a day from port," Tom said as mildly as he could.

"I heard them say they could see Sugarloaf Mountain. We must be closer than that."

A tired Tom decided to be blunt rather than diplomatic. "Please, Dom Borges, let me explain. Sugarloaf Mountain is about thirteen hundred feet high, and the lookout is one hundred feet above the sea. He can spot the mountain from around eighty miles. At ten knots it will take us around eight hours to get there and it will be dark. As pilots are not available until it gets light, we will heave-to until dawn. Then we can get a pilot and negotiate the entry to the bay and find our dock."

Borges looked as though he didn't understand a word of it but chose to keep his peace, as other passengers were nearby and he didn't want to appear a fool.

"Thank you for the explanation, I will return to my cabin," he said huffily, then walked to the stairway. His servants scurried after him with his bags.

Graham joined Tom.

"He wouldn't listen to me."

"I wonder why he is in such a hurry?"

"Maybe I can shed light on that, Captain," Cedric Ambridge, the trader, said. Tom gave him a quizzical look and Cedric clarified matters. "I overheard your conversation with the Dom, we had dinner with him several times during the passage. He is getting married. The lady is waiting for him in Rio, where her family are big plantation owners."

"An heiress, lucky man." Graham said.

"She is undoubtedly from a rich family, but the Dom is wealthy in his own right. He met her in Porto, and they fell in love, but her family went back to Brazil, taking her with them. According to him, she is the most beautiful girl in the world."

"Love does that to you. I fall in love with the most beautiful girl in every port," Graham said, and laughed.

As the sun came down, they anchored in the lee of the Ilha de Rasa with another three ships. The Portuguese ships made no attempt to communicate, so they kept their distance and Tom set an extra watchman to keep an eye on them. He wasn't needed, and they had a quiet evening, so Tom invited all the passengers to dinner.

Peter had done what he could. They had soup made from beef broth—which he had made from roasted beef bones, the last of the onions and carrots that had been packed in boxes of sand—to which he added some small dumplings. That was followed by tuna. The large predatory fish had been caught on a handline trailing a shiny piece of tin. It had taken four men on the line and two with gaffs to get it on board. Peter served steaks of it, griddled, with a wine sauce. The meat course was a goat stew that he had learned to cook in Malaysia. Tom recognised it as the one he had eaten in Penang. Dessert was nuts and what was left of the cheese they had brought on board in England. The wines, however, made up for the lack of fresh ingredients and flowed freely.

A pilot arrived at ten o'clock the next morning. Dom Borges had taken to pacing the deck impatiently and audibly huffed when the pilot announced they would be the third ship in. The pilot heard him and walked over to him. Tom watched as they exchanged a few words, at the end of which the Dom burst out in a beaming smile.

"What did you say to him?"

"I told him Dona Calista is waiting for him. She sent a message for him."

"Well then, you had better take us in."

The pilot grinned and started giving directions. Tom set a speed of five knots and they headed towards the inlet to Guanabara Bay. The pilot asked that they raise a pennant that signified they were under the command of a pilot and Tom saw why. There were a number of forts and redoubts guarding the entrance and they had to pass between one on an island called Forte Tamandaré and one on a peninsula or headland called Fortaleza de São João. They then had to sail north to the docks that were behind Ilha des Cobras.

They berthed at a stone dock and immediately the gangplank was lowered, Dom Borges left the ship—and his luggage—behind, eager to get ashore as fast as he could. Tom saw why when he followed his course from the poop deck. A carriage was waiting, from which a woman stepped down as soon as they pulled alongside. He looked at her through his telescope and whistled.

"What does she look like?" Graham asked.

"He was not exaggerating."

"What? Let me see!"

Tom grinned and handed him the glass.

"Oh my." Graham smiled.

Dona Calista was probably five feet two inches tall, curvy—well, that was the polite way to describe her—had a pretty face in a round sort of way and was bouncing up and down in excitement.

"Beautiful in her own way," the pilot said as he gathered his things to disembark.

"Absolutely!" Graham said and snapped the telescope shut.

Peter went ashore and ordered supplies to get them to Penang. He spoke no Portuguese, but he knew how to haggle. He also knew what would last and what would rot in a week. The ship's stores had plenty of dried peas, so he looked for other dried pulses, fruits and vegetables, cured meats and dried or salted fish. Beer, spirits, wine, fresh vegetables, live chickens, a pair of goats with kids and a pair of bullocks were also on the list to be delivered to the ship, along with the preserved stores. To keep everyone healthy he needed demijohns of lime juice.

Rio was not a safe place, and he was accompanied by Freyja, who carried the money. She caused outrage among the women in equal parts with admiration from the men. Any man stupid enough to attempt to touch her found himself looking down the wrong end of a pistol or pricked with a dagger. After the fourth such occurrence, a space magically opened up around them wherever they walked.

There was a stock dealer selling two-year-old bullocks at the end of the market. These were well fed and kept, but the asking price was high. Peter knew the asking price for a prime bullock was four pounds and a quick conversion told Peter that the dealer was asking for six.

Peter shook his head and offered three pounds. The dealer counter-offered at five and they settled at four pounds ten shillings. Buying goats for milk was easier. Another dealer had a pair of milkers with four four-month-old kids for sale and he took the lot for two pounds.

The rest of the provisions were easy to find. Rio was an active port, with ships coming and going every day. Merchants either set up stalls on the docks or had premises adjacent to the docks. A steady stream of carts arrived at the *Warley*.

The passengers also took the opportunity to replenish their personal stores and were soon ashore shopping. Some bought sensibly, others less so: these would end up eating or throwing away a lot of fruit and vegetables that were going rotten.

Tom looked around Rio for investments. Diamonds had been discovered nearby in 1729 and he visited a dealer. The man, who was Portuguese, spoke English and tried to palm off some sub-standard stones. Tom produced his loupe and proceeded to evaluate them in a loud voice.

"Full of inclusions, colour poor, clarity average ..."

"Sir, you are obviously expert ... let me show you our choicest stones," the dealer said, and snatched the stones back. A velvet bag was produced, and five cut stones were emptied onto a black velvet cloth.

Tom selected the biggest and evaluated it. *That's better. A small inclusion, otherwise good clarity and colour is good. About four carats.* He placed it back on the cloth and picked up the next: this was a beauty. *Flawless, colourless, well cut as a drop and about five carats.* The other three had inclusions and were smaller—ranging from two to four carats—and coloured.

"What is your price for all five?"

He was quoted a price that exceeded that charged in London. Tom declined to buy. The dealer, seeing any kind of profit walking out of the door, quickly revised his price.

"Look, diamonds are not in fashion right now and I can buy them in London for two-thirds of what you are asking," Tom said. "Do you have garnets or emeralds?"

He did, and Tom bought a few of the best specimens at a good price. He was about to leave when he had a thought.

"What price for just the five-carat diamond?" He had it in mind to have that made into a something for Mary. Diamonds would come back into fashion at some time.

When Tom returned to the ship, it was to the smell of coffee being brewed. It was enticing and he followed his nose to the captain's pantry.

"That smells wonderful," he said to Peter.

"I got some roasted beans to see what it tastes like. The shopkeeper told me to crush the beans and boil some in water. This looks like it should be ready."

Tom took a cup and tasted it. "Strewth! That is bitter."

"Maybe we should add sugar—he did say that a lot of people drink it with milk and sugar."

"Put some of both in."

Tom tasted it again. "Now *that* is nice. It still has a bitter edge, but much more pleasant."

"I think it would wake you up in the morning," said Peter.

"Yes, but I wouldn't want to drink it all day."

Peter nodded; his captain was very keen on his jasmine tea.

Penang

They arrived in Penang on the thirty-first of October. Dewi Prichard met them and oversaw the unloading of the coffee and sugar, and Tom took him aside once that was done.

"Now, Dewi. What is the *special cargo* I see on the sheets?"

Dewi chuckled. "Oh, you are going to love this."

Tom was not chuckling. "Come on, spit it out."

"Your *special cargo* is Sultan Tegku Muhammad of Kelantan and his family. He has been ousted by his brother. You are to take them to England."

"Why are they going to England?"

"The British have offered him sanctuary. His brother wants him and his issue dead."

"Bugger me, they play rough here, don't they?"

"Politics and power, my friend."

The sultan was snuck aboard in the middle of the night along with his two wives, six children and five loyal retainers. They were given the state cabin plus four more, and Tom let the sultan sort out who slept where. Freyja set up guards. One outside the state cabin, and two in the corridor that led to the other cabins. In the morning, at the sultan's request, a brick hearth was built so his cook could prepare their meals.

The newly boarded people were just one of Tom's problems. The sultan had managed to bring along a significant amount of gold and jewellery.

"We need a strongroom," he told Frank.

"Where do you want it built?"

"Aft hold. Wall off a six-foot deep section at the stern end with heavy teak timbers and install a door with the strongest lock you can find."

"I will go ashore and find the wood."

Tom handed him a purse. "That should cover it."

They had to shift some cargo to create space, but Frank had the strongroom built in a day. The walls were made of three-inch-thick teak, as was the door, which had reinforcing iron bands and four concealed hinges. To secure the door, Frank had found a smith who forged iron hasps and bars that were secured with padlocks and a sturdy plate lock. Without all three keys, the locking arrangement would stop anything but an extended attack with an axe.

Tom gave one key to Graham, one to Freyja and held one himself. That way, all three of them needed to be present to gain entry. The sultan's wealth was as secure as he could make it, and the strongroom was an ideal place to keep his own special cargo of gems and any other exceptionally valuable cargo.

In Penang, Tom visited the little gem market and added to the purchases he had made in Rio. He had more silver to trade this time and he had a substantial haul to lock away for the journey home. He had found some excellent rubies, sapphires, yellow topaz and garnets.

Away from the market, he stumbled over a Burmese trader who was selling jade. Tom had learned about jade in China. Out of interest he had asked how it was appraised, and learned that there were two forms, jadeite and nephrite; colour, transparency, texture, cut size and weight all had to be considered. He knew that the most sought-after colours were imperial green and lavender, and that jadeite was more valuable, because it was rarer.

What he was presented with was jadeite, both in its raw form and carved. The carved items were obviously for the Chinese market, as they resembled items he had seen in Whampoa. He chose a few that he thought would sell in England and bought a large lavender lump that had good transparency and nice texture, which he planned to sell in Whampoa.

On his return to the harbour, Tom decided to take a walk along the docks and see what ships were moored up. Junks of various designs predominated. He could see Chinese, Javanese and Malaysian junks, but there was another ship he didn't recognise. It was high sterned, with a ladder-like mast set well forward. It looked as though it could be powered by oars as well as the sail, unlike the junks. Behind the mast was what could only be described as a hut. He described it to Dewi.

"Sounds like a Burmese Pain Caw. Where is it?"

"Up at the end of the dock."

"What's that doing up there?"

"It was just sitting there when I saw it."

Dewi looked concerned. "I want to see it."

Just to be safe, Tom asked Freyja to accompany them and picked up a pistol from his cabin.

The ship was still where he had seen it and Dewi spoke to a fisherman who was mending a net.

"They came in yesterday and haven't unloaded anything. Our friend there doesn't like them."

"Why? Because they are Burmese?"

Dewi talked to the man some more.

"He thinks they are here to look at the ships and where they are going."

"Pirates?" Tom said.

Dewi nodded, thoughtfully. Let's have a closer look."

They walked up to the ship's gangplank. A man appeared and shouted something. A half dozen others came out of the hut carrying long knives or swords.

"I don't think they want us aboard," Freyja said.

Tom walked up the dock to the prow and then down to the stern. He returned to the others and raised his hat to the men on board.

"I've seen all I need to," he said, and walked away. The others followed.

After a hundred yards Freyja said, "One of them is following us."

"Probably wants to see what ship we are on," Tom replied, and turned down between two warehouses. He stopped and put his hand in his pocket. When it emerged, Freyja caught the glint of brass knuckles.

Their follower stepped into the passage and was met by a blow to the chin that felled him.

Dewi winced. "Ouch, that is going to hurt when he comes round."

"He will live, although he may be drinking soup for a while," Tom said as he dragged the man deeper into the passage. He quickly searched his victim and took a long knife from him.

"Leave him there." He stepped out of the passage and continued walking as if nothing had happened, tossing the knife into the sea.

Forewarned is forearmed, Tom thought as he prepared to get them underway. He had noticed several things about the Burmese craft. First, it was low in the water at the bow, and he could see a shadow below the surface sticking out. So, she probably had a ram fitted. There were no signs of cargo but many signs of provisions and water for a large crew. He assumed that they had put off all but a handling crew to visit the port. There were also signs that something, probably a gun, had recently been mounted in the bow.

He discussed it with Graham and the master gunner.

"They must have trimmed her to try and hide the ram," Tom concluded.

"Well, if we see them coming, we know what to expect," Graham said.

"We need to be able to stop them coming head on," Silas said. "And that isn't easy. Grape might do it, but I'd want something better."

"Can you suggest anything?" Tom asked.

"What are they made of?" Graham asked.

"Not teak. It looks like an oversized riverboat, so I imagine something like hardwood for the base, which looked to be carved from a single log, and softwood for the upper hull, which showed a lot of scratches and gouges," Tom replied.

"Small ball," Silas said. "That's what the *Aurora* used."

"Do we have any?" Graham asked with a frown, as he mentally went through the inventory of the shot locker.

"No. The Company only supplies grape, which is half the size. Small ball is three inches round and about three and half pounds in weight. We can fire half a dozen or more per cannon. They will smash right through their upperworks and carry on the length of the ship."

"And not only that—our gunners are capable of aiming the guns well enough to make a hit," Tom added. "There is a Company armoury on the island. See if they have any."

* * *

They set sail with piles of small ball stacked on the centre line, that would be hung beside the guns in nets of eight once they were at sea. Tom anticipated that they would fire once any pirate got to a cable and a half, so Silas made up three-quarter weight charges. There was no point in wasting powder.

The Burmese boat had disappeared the night before they sailed and, given the valuable cargo they carried, Tom in an excess of caution had doubled the lookouts posted.

The sultan came on deck, accompanied by one of his retainers.

"You fear we will be attacked?" he asked through the retainer, having seen the men bagging shot and hanging it beside the guns.

"I am told your brother wants you dead, and given the riches you brought with you, I expect there will be some who are ready and willing to take a risk to get them," Tom replied.

"My brother will have put a bounty on my head as soon as he learned of my escape. He does not want my supporters to use me as a figurehead."

"I assume he has spies in Penang?" Tom said.

"Most assuredly."

"Then we can expect company. I would appreciate it if you could take your family and servants down to the orlop deck if we are attacked. You will be safer down there. One of our stewards will take you down if I deem it necessary."

The sultan agreed. Then he saw Freyja.

"Who is that?" the sultan asked.

"That is the captain of my soldiers," Tom answered,

"But it is a woman."

Tom had noticed that the sultan's wives were veiled. He decided to turn the conversation around.

"You do not have women in your army? They can make very good fighters."

"Women should be at home having children."

"You will find that Europe is very different from Malaysia."

The sultan looked a little troubled, but held his peace.

Eventually, they spotted a ship following them. It was not the Burmese ship that was in the harbour, but a large junk. Whether it was an innocent trader or a pirate, they could not tell. Whatever it was, it was keeping up with them and they were making eleven knots.

Tom decided to go to the top of the main mast to have a look. Graham raised his eyebrows but said nothing. He had never known Tom to climb the rigging. As he got to the lower futtock shrouds, Tom regretted what seemed now to be a rash decision. His climbing days were a long way behind him and he wasn't as fit as he used to be. He gritted his teeth. *I'll be damned if I will use the lubber's hole.* He took the outer route hanging at forty-five degrees. *Easy does it.* He made it and continued to climb. The lookout was on the topgallant yard, he passed him and went up to the royal yard. Once there, he sat, caught his breath, swung his telescope around and adjusted it to his focus mark.

He swept the arc of the horizon aft of them. There was a sail to starboard just poking above the horizon—the one aft and nothing to port. He concentrated on the one aft of them. She was a large two-masted junk sailing with all sail set. He guessed she was probably sailing as close to the south-westerly wind as she could as her sails were canted well around. He checked his own sails. They were running with all their square sails, the triangular staysails and jib; the spanker was gaff rigged.

"Bring her up to the wind a point!" he bellowed down.

The *Warley* turned another eleven and a quarter degrees south. The trimmers got to work, and the log was run.

"Ten and a half knots!" the log man shouted.

Tom studied the junk. She was trying to match their course, but with the wind full on her beam she lost power and slowed. *Yes, she is definitely dropping back.*

Tom shifted position so he could face forward. There was a sail broad on the port beam, heading more west than they were. He swept around the horizon. Nothing else. He sat for half an hour and swept the horizon again. They should be passing Port Klang on the Malaysian coast now. He checked behind, the junk had dropped below the horizon.

"Bring her back a point to port."

He felt the rigging ease as the wind shifted slightly astern.

He turned and scanned forward. They would be passing Rupat Island soon, on the starboard side, which would suit any pirates hiding behind it perfectly. He waited patiently. The strait was a scant twenty-four miles wide at that point, which was only a little wider than the English Channel.

There! The distinctive shapes of Sumatran and Burmese ship sails. He watched and calculated; they were definitely closing faster than he liked. He took a stay to the deck.

"Bring us to quarters and get the sultan and his family down to the orlop deck."

For ten minutes, the ship was all of a-bustle. Then, she waited.

"Ships to starboard five miles," the lookout called.

"We will employ the same tactics as before. Maintain as much speed as we can with clewed up mains. Guns will target any ship directly approaching us and fire as they bear at no more than one and a half cables. It is my belief that the Burmese will try to ram us while the Sumatrans try and board us."

Graham knew what to do, they had discussed tactics over dinner many times. He walked down the crews.

"Aim between wind and water. They will be using oars and sails. If they have a bow cannon, duck if they fire. The stone balls will smash and shower shards."

He kept the men calm. As the ships approached, gun captains called for the guns to be trained around left or right. They had no sights to speak of, so looked along the top of the barrel. The gun crew worked with jack staves to turn the heavy pieces, sweating and grunting. When he was satisfied, the gun captain facing the nearest ship called, "*Clear*!" The men stepped aside. The linstock hovered. It dipped.

FFFFFTTTTT. BOOOM.

Smoke and flame erupted from the barrel and the carriage slammed back against the tackles. The gun beside it fired a moment later at the same target. The crew didn't dwell on whether they had scored a hit or not. They got on with swabbing and reloading the gun while the gun captain closed the touch hole with a gloved hand.

Graham waited for the smoke to clear as the other guns fired and smoke drifted aft. They had scored hits on the two closest ships and damaged them enough that they were being left behind. But more ships were coming on. The first gun had reloaded and was being run out.

"Left, left, a bit more. *Clear*!" the gun captain cried.

The gun fired again.

* * *

Tom gave orders to the helm; the pirates were coming on from broad on their starboard bow. He steered a little more west to bring the wind more on their starboard quarter.

There was a crash and the deck shuddered. They must have been hit. He went to the stern rail. There was a junk behind them. He leaned out and looked down. The stern chasers had fired and there was no visible damage to the windows of his cabin, so the ball must have hit lower on the sultan's cabin windows. As he looked, the starboard chaser emerged as it was run out and the barrel jerked right as it was trained. He ducked back just before it fired.

He looked at the ships coming at them. One, a Javanese type, had avoided getting badly damaged and was approaching on a course that would impact the starboard side back from the bow. He wished the *Aurora* was with them. He could use their support right now.

He watched as the ship approached.

"Hard to starboard."

The wheel spun.

Lord, have I timed it right?

The bow turned towards the threat.

It was just enough. The ram hit, but at such an oblique angle that it skittered down the side of the hull.

"Get us back on course."

The manoeuvre had cost them speed, and a Sumatran junk got alongside and grapnels flew. Tom grabbed a blunderbuss from the rack ahead of the wheel, cranked back the hammer and went to the side.

The ship was slightly ahead of where he stood but he had a clear view down on their stern castle. He fired, and bloody holes appeared in the back of the steersman and the man who stood beside him. Tom dropped the gun in the scuppers and grabbed another. This time, he leaned out so he could see along the side. He aimed and fired, sending the load into the mass of men climbing the side. Several fell.

Freyja saw the grapnels and shouted orders; her soldiers, who stood between the guns, levelled their halberds. She had a sword in her right hand and a pistol in her left, and positioned herself at the end of the line. A gunner grinned at her over the barrel of the gun he was training. She grinned back then shot a pirate that appeared at the rail beside him. The pistol was dropped in favour of her second sword.

The soldiers waited until heads appeared above the rail, then swung their razor-sharp blades along it. The heavy blade sliced through necks and shoulders with ease, sending sprays of blood spurting out to rain down on the men below. Corpses fell back into the ship they had come from, now just dead meat that got in the way or landed on their former shipmates.

Gunners used jack staves to batter anyone that the soldiers missed, swivels were fired down at the mass of men on the deck killing five or six men at a time.

The *Warley* ploughed on.

Freyja was like a tornado. Her twin swords spun and glittered in the light, sprays of blood arcing off them as they slashed, decapitated and amputated. Tom and any crewman not manning the guns or sails joined her in pushing the pirates back into their ship and cutting the grapnel lines. The pirates threw more to replace what they had lost. They shot at the *Warley*'s men who cut the ropes and grouped to reboard. Peter had reloaded his blunderbuss and Tom returned fire.

* * *

Then they were clear. It felt as though they had been fighting for ever, but it was just a matter of minutes. The pirates' strategy had been to slow or stop the *Warley* so they could board in numbers, but they had failed. The *Warley* sailed on, leaving wrecked ships and dead men behind her. The men cheered, but Tom was more cautious.

"Get the guns cleaned and restock the nets. We aren't safe yet."

Graham nodded grimly.

As the ship was quiet, the sultan came on deck and looked with wide eyes at the number of dead. Tom did not notice him and ordered, "Throw that offal overboard and get my deck clean!"

A soldier picked up a head and made a joke, causing the sailors around him to laugh. He tossed it over the side.

The sultan turned a funny shade of green and went to the starboard side. Tom saw him and shouted, "Not that side! The other side. The leeward side!"

A sailor grabbed the sultan and half carried, half dragged him to the port side, where the wind was on his back. The retainer was aghast. No one touched the sultan. The sultan didn't care at that moment, as he was too busy throwing up his lunch.

"That's funny, I would have thought he was used to seeing things like that," Graham said to Tom.

The lackey came over and said, "Your man must be punished for touching the sultan."

"Is that what the sultan wants?" Tom said.

"It is the law."

"Well, it is not the law on my ship. All my men know that you don't piss, spit or puke into the wind. He did the man a favour. Tell me, isn't he used to seeing this kind of thing?"

"This was the centre of contention between my lord and his brother. My lord is a scholarly, gentle man and did not approve of using force to get his way or control the people, whom he thought of as his children. His brother is a soldier."

"I see." Tom nodded. "Well, at sunset we will lose the wind until the nightly land breeze picks up. We will be passing Singapore Island then and that is the time their oared junks will have the advantage. We are normally well past there by then, but tide and circumstances have put us in this position."

Tom was right—the wind steadily decreased as the passed through the Singapore Strait and they reduced their speed to naught but a few knots. As the sun set, they could see the sharks gathering. A mixture of Chinese, Malay and Burmese craft slunk out from behind the islands. Not a sail set; they moved under oars.

"To stations!" Tom bellowed.

"Most of them already are," Graham answered grimly.

"The Company needs to form convoys," Tom grumbled.

The enemy came, spurred on by the prospect of the sultan's jewels and the bounty. The guns were run out on both sides and all the topmen gathered on the centreline with boarding pikes.

A sail flapped as the wind all but died.

"We have about thirty minutes before the land breeze starts," Tom said.

Darkness fell.

"Fire star rockets," Tom ordered, and rockets whooshed up into the air bursting with a slow burning white star that slowly drifted to the sea. "Fire as you bear!"

The guns started to roar, the gunners making sure they aimed at the closest craft that were speeding towards them. They did not need or want to waste a single shot. Tom held a musket and tried a shot at a steersman on a junk a hundred yards away. He missed, but the aft gun didn't, and a large, elongated hole appeared in the side of the junk as the eight small balls ripped through the soft wood. They had hit it at an angle to the hull so the balls tore through the interior of the ship, killing or maiming every soft body in their path.

The gun crews were loading like mad men. Tom swore later that they reloaded the aft eighteen in a minute and a half. In the interval, the poop deck six-pounders were sending their loads of canister into any ship that got close enough. Small and quick to reload, they were effective shotguns.

But there were too many of them and inevitably one got across the bow, stalling their already slow progress. Freyja and her men went to work. Grenades were dropped into the ship and swivels fired at the climbing men. Halberds were put into play with deadly effect.

They fought; men died on both sides. Tom had Peter reloading for him, and he used two blunderbusses in rotation firing down into any ship that came near. He shouted for grenades when they ran out of ammunition, and threw those instead.

A sail flapped, then boomed as the land breeze came on.

"Clear that ship out of the fucking way!" Tom yelled and ran forward to help.

Freyja heard him and climbed over the bow to cut away the grapnel lines. Tom joined her crawling along the bowsprit, slashing with a cutlass. More star rockets whooshed up. He saw Freyja drop onto the deck of the junk. *Here we go*. He grinned to himself and followed her.

Freyja was already clearing the deck of men, swords flashing in the harsh light of the stars. Tom joined in the slaughter, wincing as a blade scored across his shoulder blade. He spun and ducked as a blade whistled over his head, arm extended. His cutlass ripped the belly out of the man. Freyja had eliminated the men around her and was cutting the ropes holding the junk to the *Warley*. The junk twisted as the bigger ship pushed forward and then, like a series of gunshots, the remaining ropes snapped one after another.

Well, that was unexpected, Tom thought as the *Warley* ground down the side of the junk. A pirate charged him, and he concentrated on dispatching him. By the time he had finished, the *Warley* was past.

Freyja stood beside him, looking like the angel of death as blood dripped down her face.

"Is that blood yours?"

"No. Where is our ship?"

Tom turned and ran to the stern where there was a boat—well, more of a skiff really.

"Come on, we will take this."

Freyja looked down at it.

"Fucking hell, that's …"

"One, it's all we have and two, you have been spending too much time with the soldiers," Tom said and dropped over the stern into the little craft. Freyja joined him. "Cut the tow line."

The skiff had a single oar and no sail. Tom looked around and spotted the U-shaped wooden rowlock in the stern. He would have to scull it. Star rockets were still being fired and he headed for the point of origin. The night sky was illuminated by the flashes of guns as well and together they provided enough light to navigate around wreckage. He was concentrating on getting the sculling right, so that they maintained the correct course, so it took a while before he realised that the guns sounded differently to the *Warley*'s. More of a *chuff* than a *boom*.

"That sounds like a carronade."

Freyja moved to the bow and peered ahead at the ship.

"It has only five guns on the side."

Tom laughed. "It must be the *Aurora*!"

He redoubled his efforts as more rockets were fired and the carronades ceased firing.

"Ahoy, the *Aurora*!" he bellowed in his best quarterdeck voice that could be heard above a gale.

"Who's that?" someone yelled back.

"Captain Batrick of the *Warley*."

A gun fired on the other side of the ship and a rocket soared up to illuminate them.

"What the hell are you doing out there?" Edward Westcliff's voice came back.

"Can we come aboard?"

The *Aurora* changed course and closed slowly with them. Rockets fired from the bow kept them lit. She hove-to twenty yards away and Tom brought them alongside. Ropes were lowered and they climbed up.

"Well, this is a rum do," Edward said as he shook Tom's hand.

Whampoa and Home

Once the adrenalin wore off, Tom practically fainted as the wound on his shoulder blade made itself known. Freyja turned from death angel to nurse in a heartbeat as she realised he was hurt. She demanded—and got—raw alcohol and rum, gently took off his jacket and shirt and had him sit on a bollard facing outboard, leaning with his arms crossed on the rail. A crewman held a lantern so she could see what she was doing.

"I am going to clean it, then stitch it," she told him.

Tom took a big swig of rum.

"Christ on a crutch," he groaned through gritted teeth as she poured raw alcohol over the cut.

"Don't be a baby," she said.

From a pouch on her belt, Freyja took a selection of needles and a roll of catgut, which she moistened with the alcohol. She threaded a medium-sized needle.

"Hold still."

The needle went in through and out ten times. Then the wound was cleaned again, and sulphur powder was sprinkled on it before she had him sit up and be bandaged.

"There, all done," she said.

Tom noticed that the only clean part of her were her hands. He stood with her and Edward's help.

"Where did you learn to do that?"

"A warrior should know these things," she said, enigmatically.

The *Aurora* caught up with the *Warley* later that morning, went alongside and transferred the passengers aboard.

"We thought you lost!" Graham said.

"Only mislaid," Tom replied with a grin. His arm was in a sling. "Seems that the *Aurora* was on patrol and saw the gun flashes."

"She arrived in the nick of time, just after you got the junk out from under our bow," Graham said. "I dared not stop."

"You did the right thing," Tom said, and patted his shoulder.

Barnes insisted on examining the wound and was full of praise for the quality of the stitching. "Very neat work; you have a talent, my dear," he said to Freyja, who blushed at the praise.

That evening, dinner was a celebration and Peter outdid himself. Freyja seated herself on Tom's left and cut up his food for him. She had ordered a bucket of boiled fresh water be delivered to her cabin and emerged some time later, clean and dressed like a woman. When Tom commented, she said that she had cleaned and oiled her leathers and they needed to dry.

The sultan joined them for dinner and sat at the opposite end of the table to Tom, his interpreter sitting behind him. He wanted to know what had happened during the fight, and Tom gave an edited account taking the sultan's sensibilities into account.

"Did you lose many men?" the sultan asked.

"Four dead, seven wounded—of which only one is unlikely to recover."

The sultan nodded as his man told him.

"Will they attack on the journey to England?"

"We will go the long way around Sumatra and avoid the strait."

They arrived in Whampoa on the thirtieth of January and left on the thirtieth of March. The sultan stayed aboard all that time, as he suspected the Chinese had backed his brother's coup. Meanwhile, Tom healed under Freyja's oversight. She had him perform exercises to keep the wound from stiffening his shoulder. The sultan and his family asked to be taught English and Tom filled in the time as their tutor. The wives stopped using veils and had Freyja show them how Western women dressed. The sultan was reluctant to allow it to start with, but the wives placed him under constant pressure until he relented. He complained to Tom that only having two wives was a problem, as they ganged up on him. Tom asked why he thought that more would be better.

"They spend more time competing with each other to be number one wife than nagging me," was the unexpected answer.

They took on the usual cargo of silk, porcelain and tea. Tom bought several bolts of silk to trade when he got home. They were destined for London, where he knew he could make a healthy profit.

During Tom's recovery, Freyja took to spending more time in his company, in a daughterly way. Not that Tom had any romantic desires in her direction—he was madly in love with Mary. But Tom and Freyja would often sit together on deck, and he learned more of her history.

"My mother gave me to the daughters when a raven landed on my cot. She said it was a sign from Odin."

"Is Odin still worshipped?"

"In some places, in the back country. Anyway, I was just a year old then."

"So, you never knew your parents?"

"Not really. I met my mother once after that." She paused at the memory. "The daughters taught me to fight, how to treat wounds, how to read and other things."

"When did you leave them?"

"When I was eighteen. I was promoted to journeyman and told to travel to gain experience."

"If I may, can I ask how old you are now?"

"You may, it is no secret: I am twenty-one."

Tom had taken the precaution of doubling the harbour watch, especially at night. His caution was justified when a boat came alongside in the dead of night, when there was no moon. Assassins boarded and a lookout managed to shout the alarm before they killed him.

Tom woke and, grabbing a sword and a pistol, ran out onto the deck where more of the watch were fighting the boarders. Tom shot in the back one of two men attacking a crewman, then stabbed the other. The crewman slashed the man's throat as he stiffened in agony from the thrust.

The clash of arms was heard from below and Tom ran down the stairs to the passenger deck. Freyja and a soldier were battling three assassins. Tom charged them from behind. With his help, it was all over quickly.

"Did they get to the sultan?" he asked.

"No, we stopped them here," Freyja said—then giggled.

"What?" Tom said.

"I've never seen you in your nightshirt."

Tom looked down. He had been in such a hurry he had not pulled on any breeches, and his hairy legs and bare feet were sticking out from the bottom of the flannel shirt.

He laughed, and the soldier and Freyja joined him.

They sailed on time and Tom took them the long way around. South through the strait between Java and Sumatra and past the island of Krakatoa, which smoked quietly during the day. Then they turned west for the 8,000-mile journey to St Helena.

Propelled by the north-east monsoon, they made good time. However, the guns and impacts from attempted rammings had taken their toll. The *Warley* had become a wet ship. She was plagued with leaks, and they had to pump her for two hours a day.

"As soon as we plug one, another two appear," Frank said.

"And it will get worse if we hit heavier seas," Tom replied. "Get more men on the job and see if you can get ahead of them."

Frank left, calling out to men who were sitting around on deck.

"When we get to London I am insisting on a bloody refit!" Tom said to Graham.

"If we don't get one, she is likely to sink of her own accord the next time we sail." Graham frowned as the sound of hammers drifted up from below.

Tom decided that they needed to heave-to before negotiating the Cape of Good Hope. The pulled into a bay along the south coast of Africa and the whole crew went to work attempting to make her a dry ship.

The hammering went on all day, driving the passengers up onto the deck. Tom was asked to join the sultan.

"You are healed now?" the sultan asked.

"Yes, I am, thank you, your highness," Tom replied.

"I am very sad that more men have died to protect my life."

"They are gone, and it's their families I feel sorry for. They both had wives and children."

"Will they be provided for?"

"The Company will pay a pension, but it is not much."

"Will you do something for me?"

"If I can, your highness."

"I will give you some money for their families, will you make sure they get it?"

"That is extremely generous, your highness, and yes, I will."

St Helena was sighted on the ninth of July 1802, and they docked on the tenth. They reprovisioned, rewatered, refuelled and set sail for the coast of South America. They experienced more storms, and by the time they reached South Carolina were pumping four hours a day. They made the Downs on the fifth of September and tied up at India Dock on the ninth. The crew members were exhausted, and the ship had to be pumped even in the calm waters of the Thames.

Tom had just finished overseeing the unloading of the cargo when he was summoned to East India House. The note said *at his earliest convenience*, so he left straight away with a list of defects in his pocket.

On arrival, he was shown to the usual anteroom and waited for ten minutes before being shown in.

"Gentlemen." He bowed in greeting and took the proffered seat at the table. Francis Baring, Mr Darrell, Mr Hunter, Mr Lushington, Mr Mesurier and Mr Inglis were all present.

"Welcome home, Captain Batrick," Baring said. "We heard it was a rough trip."

Tom had sent in his report as soon as they docked. The sultan had been met by a representative of the Foreign Office and whisked away within hours of arrival.

"The report said it all," Tom said and was about to reach for his list when Hunter interjected.

"You did not say in the report that you were wounded."

How the hell did you find that out?

"Slightly, but I am fully healed."

"The sultan has praised your actions and skills to the foreign minister, who sent a message of thanks to us."

"My ship needs a refit," Tom said, trying to change the subject.

"And it will get one, the dock is booked," Baring said.

Hunter continued. "The sultan has asked that you and your crew are rewarded." He gestured to a servant, who stood by a side table. He served glasses of madeira and then placed a long and obviously heavy box in front of Hunter. "He sent this for you."

The servant picked it up and placed it in front of Tom, who looked at it, amazed. He looked up. "What is it?"

"Open it. We do not know."

Tom ran his hands over the lid. The box was made from the finest melunak wood; it was a soft yellow in colour and beautifully constructed. He flipped the three catches and lifted the lid.

He looked at the contents, which were nestled in silk, the central piece of which was an ornate dagger in what looked like a gold sheath. Tom lifted it out: it was heavy. He pulled the blade from the sheath, confirming for himself that the sheath carried most of the weight. The dagger blade was wavy, undulating like a snake. Sharp on both sides. The hilt was curved at the end and made of gold and ivory. He looked at the blade again and saw it was patterned, like Damascus steel. There was a folded letter underneath, in the space where the blade had rested. He read it; it was obviously written by an English hand and was from the sultan.

> *Apparently this is a keris knife and is one of a collection from the royal armoury. It is blessed and has magical properties that protect the owner.*

Tom looked back in the box. There were a pair of large rubies, another pair of sapphires and a bar of gold that probably weighed two pounds. He picked up a ruby and held it up to the light. Flawless, a beautiful colour and about ten carats. The board members all sighed, and one even whistled.

In a corner of the box was a pouch with gold coins in it. The letter said these were for the families of the dead men.

"You must have really impressed him," Hunter said. "We have a reward for you as well. A sterling silver dinner service, which to be honest fades a little in comparison with the sultan's generosity, and two hundred pounds. The crew will get a fighting bonus as well."

Tom mumbled his thanks, quite overcome by the generosity of the gifts, but Hunter hadn't finished. "Also, you will now carry the rank of commodore and command the first convoy to China. Yes, we have taken your advice and now a large convoy will sail from Whampoa once a year. This comes with an increase in your salary."

The dinner service was for eight place settings and included cutlery and serving dishes. It weighed a handsome amount and was worth a small fortune.

The money the sultan had provided for the widows was invested in a fund and Tom arranged for them to be paid a sum every month.

He visited them and broke the news personally. It was one of the hardest things he ever had to do.

The *Warley* went into dry dock at the place she was built, Blackwall. John Perry's company would take her apart and practically rebuild her before she sailed again. Tom took the next Company ship heading west and arrived in Poole on the second of October, along with his new-found riches. The first thing he did was to have a strongroom built in the cellar of his home. Three layers of stone and a four-inch-thick iron banded oak door secured the silver and gold. Freyja went with him.

The Fourth Voyage and the Battle of Pulo Aura, 1803–1804

War and Convoys

The news from the continent was bad. There had been peace for the last few years between Britain and France, since the Treaty of Amiens was signed in March 1802. However, Napoleon had consequently reordered Europe to exclude any British influence, which had mightily aggrieved the British government. The final straw came when Napoleon asserted control over Switzerland.

The *Warley* was due to sail on the sixth of May and Tom saw the writing on the wall: Britain would be declaring war on France again. His existing letter of marque had expired, so he applied to the High Court of the Admiralty for a new one. For this he was required to pay a bond of fifteen hundred pounds, which he did with a bank draft when presenting his application in person.

He collected his letter from the Admiralty. Now the *Warley* was an auxiliary to the British Royal Navy, and he had an improvement in mind. He had agreed with the Company that the *Warley* could have her armament improved after their experience in the strait, so he went to the Gun Wharf at Woolwich to talk to the representative of the Navy Board.

The main gates were impressive, with fouled-anchor motifs on the pillars. The guards were navy marines and asked whether he had an appointment. He did, and was granted entry—albeit escorted.

The escort took him to a large house with a clock tower. That clock tower had a very large weather vane mounted on its copper-covered copula and Tom noted the wind was coming from due west, perfect for manoeuvring downstream.

They climbed the steps to the entrance, and he was handed over to a clerk, who took him to an office on the first floor. Inside was a uniformed navy captain, who stood and clomped around to greet him. The clomp came from a peg leg.

"Commodore Batrick, good morning. Captain Sellers at your service."

"Good morning, Captain, thank you for seeing me."

They sat, and the good captain leaned forward attentively. "How can I help you?"

"I have a commission from the East India Company to upgrade the six-pounders on my ship to carronades and, as I am due to sail soon, cannot wait for the factory to deliver. I was wondering …"

"You have a letter of marque?"

"I do, issued but a week ago." Tom pulled it out and showed it to him. Sellers gave it back, pulled out a ledger and studied it.

"How long have you been here?" Tom asked, to fill the silence.

"Since '98. Lost me leg at St Vincent, the admiral was kind enough to get me onto the Navy Board. Aah, here we are. I have twenty twenty-four pounders and eighteen thirty-twos. What are you carrying now?"

"Thirty-four eighteens and twelve sixes."

Sellers pursed his lips and looked into space as he thought.

"I think a better balance between long- and short-range guns would be to swap out the sixes for twenty-fours and four of your eighteens for thirty-twos. That would keep you at around the same all up weight, while increasing your fire power by one hundred and sixty-four pounds."

"That would be perfect," Tom said. "What loads would you recommend?"

"Ball for smashing large ships and in your case, small ball and canister to counter boarding."

"That was my thinking as well." Tom pulled a purse from his jacket pocket; it gave a golden clink as he put it on the table. "When can we bring the *Warley* alongside to fit them?" He pushed the purse towards the good captain, while looking him in the eyes.

The purse was scooped up, weighed, and dropped into a desk drawer.

"When do you sail?"

"Friday the sixth of May."

"I will schedule you for the week before, on the Wednesday. Have your bankers draft for three hundred pounds with you. That includes carriages, shot and loading."

"Thank you, I appreciate your help."

Tom smiled and stood to leave. The ten guineas had been well spent.

The *Warley* wove her way to Woolwich to pick up her new guns. The eighteens had been offloaded at India Dock for the Company to reuse. The sixes would be left with the captain to scrap. Tom intended the forward pair of eighteens and those in his cabin to be replaced, as well as the sixes on the poop deck.

His cabin had to be opened to allow access and that entailed taking away the planking of the wall below the poop deck. The carpenters were busy, as not only did they have to take the wall away but they also had to change the gun mounts to suit carronades and reshape the gun ports as well. Tom was pleased: the footprint of the carronades was much less than the eighteens and he had more room in his cabin. They could take out the ring bolts, as well. Apart from the slight inconvenience of an iron strip set into the deck for the carronades pivot wheel to run on, it was a great improvement.

Once the refit was completed, they sailed back up to India Dock to start loading the cargo for the next trip.

The ship needed a slight retrim, but that was easily achieved by the distribution of cargo. Guns was very pleased with his new toys and spent hours retraining the gun crews. An added bonus, which Tom had not thought of, was the increased rate of fire the carronades gave them and the reduced number of gunners required. Each carronade only needed three men to operate, as opposed to the eight men for the eighteens and five for the sixes. On the Company's orders she had a new colour scheme as well; her gun ports were now painted light brown. They were no longer bait and, as they were to lead convoys, needed to be more conspicuous.

Tom did not beach any crew, rather he formed a flying squad of men who could replace wounded gunners or repel boarders under Freyja's command. Freyja, who had stayed with Tom and Mary in the interim, had welcomed that idea and started training the men in pike and sword work.

Mary and little Tom would come with Tom on this voyage. He had missed enough of his son growing up. He had bought him a pup for Christmas and that would be coming as well. The three-year-old was excited to be going on Daddy's big ship and the fox terrier, whose name was Sandy, picked up on that enthusiasm.

Tom, however, discovered that being a commodore was even busier than being a captain. The outbound convoy consisted of nineteen ships bound for India and China. Three of these would leave when they passed India, and make for Madras. He left the loading of the *Warley* to Graham and his mates and met with the five Company captains who would sail from London with him.

"Good afternoon, gentlemen," he said after they had seated themselves around the table in the boardroom of East India House. "We are the core of the convoy, being Company ships. The thirteen associate ships will join us at the Downs. In case of trouble, we will protect the convoy as a unit. You all have your letters of marque?"

The other captains nodded and grunted their approval. Their ships, while generally not as heavily armed as the *Warley*, by far outgunned the associate ships, which were privately owned.

Tom expounded on his tactics if they were confronted with pirates or, heaven forbid, a French squadron. The captains asked questions which he answered, and then he said, "Gentlemen, there are to be no independent actions. My instructions delivered by flag must be obeyed precisely and we will practise the manoeuvres while crossing the Atlantic. The *Warley* has a deserved reputation as a fighting East Indiaman, and I do not want to lose a single ship on this voyage."

Glasses of madeira were served, and he raised his in a toast. "To our success, may we sail safely and bring home prizes."

"Prizes!" The captains laughed and drained their glasses.

"How did it go?" Mary asked when he returned.

"It was hard, to start with. They are merchant captains and are independently-minded, but they saw the sense in what I told them in the end. The independent captains will be harder to manage."

"You will prevail, my love, you always do."

Sandy was excited that he was home and was bouncing up and down by his leg. Tom picked him up and the pup washed his chin. "Hello, little man, where is little Tom?"

"Having his afternoon nap," Mary said.

"This little fellow has adapted to ship life quickly."

"I am trying to train him to poop in a sand box on the deck. The crew are placing bets on it, I think."

"They will gamble on anything. Keeps them amused."

"Maybe, but they seem to have adopted Sandy as a mascot of sorts."

"Sailors love dogs and cats. That's a thought! How is he getting on with the ship's cats?" The *Warley* had several moggies to keep the rats under control.

"Competing with them. I found him chasing a rat this morning."

"Good for you!" Tom said to the pup.

Fully laden and with a full complement of passengers, the *Warley* led the embryonic convoy down the Thames. Tom had argued with the port authority that they only needed one pilot, however the authority had insisted that each ship carry one. Tom knew that this was the guild of pilots protecting the jobs of its members, since convoying could cut their income drastically. The same reasoning prevented the City from creating more bridges across the Thames. The watermen were a powerful guild and opposed anything that might reduce either the number of men, or their power, or both.

They got to the Downs to find only half the ships waiting. Tom sighed; they would have to wait, too. In the meantime, he invited all the captains present to dinner. As they were eating, another two ships sailed in and anchored. Tom invited their captains to join them.

Now he had nine of the thirteen in front of him, along with his five Company captains. Over the cheese and port, he introduced his tactics and what he expected from them.

"Gentlemen, if you doubt the seriousness of this, let me tell you that the French have installed a heavy squadron in the area. We do not know precisely what it consists of, or even where it is, but know that there is at least one ship of the line and a frigate or two. If they attack, our best defence is to confront them with the Company ships, our goal is to chase them off or make it too costly for them to proceed."

A round of "hear, hear!" went around the table. But one man spoke up.

"Captain Abrams, *City of Gloucester*. Why don't we have a naval escort?"

Tom patiently explained, wondering where the good captain had been the last few months. "The navy is overstretched at this time. To be honest, the politicians jumped on the peace premium far too quickly and put many good warships into ordinary. It takes time to recommission and man them. With the threat of invasion, they have to concentrate on keeping Napoleon on the other side of the Channel."

He looked around for any other comments or questions, then continued. "Now, if I was a French admiral, I wouldn't bother attacking convoys going to China. The best return would be to attack on the return trip. However, we need to be prepared in case our adversary is more interested in disrupting trade than making prize money. We will sail at two bells of the forenoon watch, whether the other ships are here or not."

He had a good night's sleep in the arms of Mary. Young Tom slept like a log, his pup curled up at his feet. Sea life seemed to suit him.

Tom rose at dawn and went up to the poop deck. Life was good, the weather fine with a favourable breeze that was building nicely. Two more ships had joined them overnight, so they were only missing two. The ships were all pointing south-west, turned by the incoming tide.

They were approaching slack water and at one bell he hoisted the preparatory. Thirty minutes later, as the tide eased to a stop, he signalled "execute". The ships came up to their anchors and set sail. As soon as the *Warley* broke free, she executed a neat pirouette under pressure from her jibs and spanker and headed south out into the channel. The other ships performed the manoeuvre at varying levels of competence, with one making him wince at the rare hash they made of it. He could hear the skipper bellowing at his crew and shook his head. A badly trained crew was still a badly trained crew, no matter how much he shouted.

On the trip down the south coast of England, the two missing ships joined, and another tagged on as they passed Portsmouth. This would become common as independents sought the security of convoys. Tom's biggest headache was keeping them all together, since some captains seemed incapable of sailing in formation.

"Signal the *Anna-Marie* to close up," he told the signal boy for the third time that morning.

As a former privateer, Tom knew that any stragglers or ships that dropped out of formation would be the first target for privateers and pirates. He had made good money picking off those ships in the past and knew they were invariably the oldest and poorest-manned ships in the convoy. He even suspected that some were sent out to be taken, so the owners could claim the insurance. He wished he had a brig or a sloop which he could task as sheepdog.

That would save him the trouble of dropping back and berating the errant captains for being laggard.

After the fifth day, he had to admit being a convoy commodore was almost more trouble than it was worth. They travelled slowly, only as fast as the slowest ship would allow, and hove-to every night to avoid getting scattered.

The only good thing was that during the evenings, being hove-to allowed him and the passengers to visit the other ships. Parties were thrown and one might think each ship was a country house, the way the richer passengers treated them. Tom and Mary had dinner on a different ship every night.

The trip south, once they had made enough westing, was rougher and they barely missed a storm that would have carried many of the convoy into the Bay of Biscay. Tom kept them moving at night during bad weather, as it helped steady the ships and make things more comfortable. Even at their reduced rate of progress and with every ship burning lights, they still had some wander off during the hours of darkness, who had to reform every morning.

They called in at Cape Verde to re-water and provision, and while they were there, a married couple who had no servants with them bought a slave. She was a pretty teenage girl, fresh out of Africa, with mahogany-coloured skin. They said they would train her as a house maid and teach her English. She followed them everywhere they went, dressed in a pretty dress that she had been given by the woman. They seemed to treat her well, so Tom left them to it. After all, slavery was legal and even supported by the church—although Tom himself didn't particularly approve of it. He had been somewhat saddened by the sight of so many slaves for sale in Cape Verde.

Freyja spent most of her spare time with Mary, learning things the daughters had never taught her, like needlepoint and crochet. She also set up fencing classes for those who wanted them. One of the crew, who had newly joined in London, turned out to be an artist and he captured Freyja's likeness in two contexts: one when she was exercising the soldiers and the second when she was relaxed. Freyja got to hear about the sketches and demanded to see them. She liked the first—it was martial, and she looked fierce. The second surprised her. She looked soft and pretty, even a little vulnerable.

"Do I look like this?" she asked Mary as she showed her the drawing.

"When you are relaxed and not thinking about being a warrior, yes," Mary answered truthfully.

Freyja looked thoughtful, but said no more.

Whampoa

They arrived, eventually, in Whampoa on the twelfth of November. It had been a slow, tedious and boring crossing from the sailing perspective. Life got more interesting with a visit from Bill Trafford.

"Good day to you, Bill. How is the security business?" Tom asked once they were alone.

"Interesting. We have discovered that the Dutch are feeding the French information about our shipping and our old friend Farrington, or Crémant, or whatever you want to call him, is still active."

"What about the rumour that there is a French squadron in the area?"

"That's true. Admiral the Comte de Linois has a squadron of five ships. A two-deck ship of the line, two frigates, a corvette and a brig."

"Quite a force," Tom said, thinking of the weight of broadside they could deliver.

"Yes, he can keep the bigger ships in a convoy busy while his two smaller ships cut out individual prizes."

"Is he getting information on the composition of the convoys?"

"And their cargoes," Bill answered.

"What about our idea of feeding him false information?"

"That is what I wanted to talk about. I see you have changed your paint scheme."

"Yes, the Company want us to look more like warships."

"Well, I want you to change it again. You see, the Admiralty, in its infinite wisdom, has issued an order that all ships be painted black and yellow. That is to say, a yellow stripe along the gun deck with the ports painted black."

"Are any of the captains taking any notice of that?"

"Some. One in particular is Admiral Nelson."

"Really? That is interesting. I will get the men on it," said Tom. "I will ask the other Company ships in the convoy to do the same."

Crémant, aka Farrington, sat at his desk and transcribed the current list of ships for the annual convoy. The final list would be very large; fifteen merchantmen were listed so far but he thought that the eventual tally would probably be thirty or more. As for cargo, they carried a fortune in tea, silk and porcelain that was brought from all over the Far East to convoy home. It amounted to cargo worth almost eight million pounds sterling.

Crémant made a copy of the list and annotated it with the cargoes the ships were carrying. When he had finished this work, he left the list at a dead drop for his contact to pick up. He was always careful and made sure he was not followed. However, he did not know that the dead drop was compromised, or that Bill's team were watching it.

Bill knew when Crémant was passing information and what that information was. And so Bill started manipulating him. The British had a powerful squadron in the Indian Ocean, and he made sure that false rumours of where that squadron was reached Crémant. The rumours were mostly commonly known but one or two were whispered as "insider knowledge" and had much greater credibility.

Crémant dutifully passed on all the information to his contact, who passed it to an agent who got it to Batavia and the admiral. Bill had the whole line in his pocket.

Tom was on deck when the *Earl Camden* came into anchor from the Thirteen Warehouses. She was a sister ship to the *Warley*, launched in 1802 and carrying thirty-six eighteen-pounders. She had arrived in China on the second of October and this was her first voyage. Her skipper was Nathaniel Dance, an extremely experienced man with forty plus years as part of the Company—he too carried the rank of commodore.

Tom went across to the *Earl Camden* to meet Commodore Dance.

"Call me Nat," Dance said as soon as they met.

"Tom."

Nat complimented Tom: "You have been quite the successful pirate hunter."

"We have had some success in thinning their numbers, but with the convoy system now in place I don't think we need to pretend anymore."

"Yes, a large convoy that stays together is far more than even the Chinese pirates will take on. Well, that's the theory anyway."

"Did you hear the French have a liner in their squadron?" Tom asked.

"Do they?"

"Yes, a seventy-four by all accounts. They are based in Batavia."

"Hmm, the bloody Dutch, sorry *Batavians* now that Bonaparte has them, are everywhere around here."

Two days later, Tom was told that Dance would command the convoy with Tom as second in command. They were due to sail on the second of February. Lascar troops were brought aboard and armed with boarding pikes. Freyja took them in hand and started forging them into a unified fighting force along with her soldiers.

Their cargo was loaded and stowed. It was the richest he had ever carried and worth close to a quarter of a million pounds. If this didn't entice the French, nothing would. A brig, the HEICS *Ganges*, came in and anchored next to the growing convoy. She would escort them through the strait.

"Is that all they have got?" Graham asked.

"They've only just heard we are at war again, they aren't prepared. The French got the jump on us by sending that squadron out during the peace."

"And the French know we are coming?"

"Yes, the Dutch and their spies will have given them the convoy size, cargo and time of departure by now."

"But—"

"Look, we have started rumours that the convoy will be escorted by British ships of the line. The *Warley*, *Royal George*, *Earl Camden*, *Hope*, *Exeter*, *Bombay Castle*, *Dorsetshire* and *Abergavenny* can all pass for them at a distance."

"*Pfft*. Let's hope the French are short-sighted, then."

In fact, Bill had done more than that: he had Crémant understate the size of the convoy by those eight ships. Admiral Linois thought he was facing twenty-three poorly armed merchant ships. He would be in for a surprise.

The ships came in from all corners of Indochina. Some were well-armed, others sported old, practically useless guns that were more of a danger to the gun crews than to any enemy. Some even had wooden dummy guns to give the appearance of being better armed than they were. Tom wondered at the greed of some ship owners, who put cargo tonnage over the safety of their crews.

As soon as the news that the war had started again became common knowledge, Bill purged the Pearl River of anybody who could be either a French or Dutch spy. All except, that is, the ones he already knew about.

Nobody accused the Dutch of being friendly with France. They were an occupied nation, after all. However, when it came to trade the Dutch were protective of their Indochinese holdings and informing the French of British movements was one way of levelling the playing field, in their eyes. After all, profit came before friendship and the French paid well for information.

The sight of all those ships was magnificent and more would join when they got to Penang and India. The sea would be covered in white—and rather grubby yellow/brown—sails. Tom smiled at the thought that most landlubbers imagined that all ships had pristine white sails, whereas the reality was that after only a year at sea they turned a dirty yellow due to the effects of the salt and sun.

Gradually, all the Company ships assembled: fourteen in all. They were joined by the *Cumberland*, *Henry Addington*, *Alfred*, *Ocean*, *Warren Hastings*, *Coutts* and *Wexford*. These were all well-armed, but there was a snag. This was pointed out by Captain Farquharson of the *Alfred* at a meeting of the Company captains, called by the HEIC Select Committee in Canton.

"We may have guns," Captain Farquharson said, "but our men have had no training to use them. They are not good enough to fight the French, even if we all join together. We should wait for a naval escort."

Tom stood up and asked to be heard. The chairman gave him the floor.

"The *Warley* is, I know, unusual in that she was commissioned as a pirate hunter and my gunners are trained. I would happily loan out my master gunner to train other ships."

"Is he navy?" Nat asked.

"Former master gunner on the *Ajax*, lost his leg and was invalided out."

"How long to train them?" another captain asked.

"He could knock them into shape in a day so that they know what they are doing, and I can let you each have an experienced man to act as gunner on each of the country ships." That would use up his reserve, but Tom calculated that he was better off having ships around him that could fire a broadside.

Captain Merton of the *Exeter* stood. He had captured a frigate during an action on the fourth of August 1800, where a similar convoy had fooled the French that the East Indiamen were liners.

"I believe we have a big enough and strong enough convoy to dissuade anyone from attacking us as we stand. Add to that the training offered by Captain Batrick, and I believe we could put on a show to fool anyone."

The argument swung back and forth, but in the end the committee decided to stick to the planned departure date.

Silas spent a day with each of the ships, after which one of the experienced gunners from the *Warley* joined and continued the training.

"Will we get them back?" Graham asked.

Tom shook his head.

"Probably not. Once they see what a bit of dumb show practice can achieve under the command of someone who knows what he is doing, they will want to hang on to them. We don't need the extra men anyway."

Tom received a letter from the committee.

Well, that settles that! he thought as he read it.

"Graham, can you join me?" he shouted up through the skylight.

"What's up, skipper?" Graham asked as he stepped through the door.

Tom flapped the letter at him.

"We are instructed to reduce our crew to one hundred and forty men and return the ship to being a regular East Indiaman."

"That's it?"

"Well, they go on about how we forged the way the fleet is following and so on, but yes, that's about it."

"What do we do with the men?"

"Distribute them around the other Company ships."

"Oh, I see. If one can make a difference, more can make more of one."

"That was almost poetic, but yes that's their thinking."

Graham laughed. "I'll draw up a list, we'll keep the best."

Given the tactics that Nat and he had worked out, only being able to man one side was not a disadvantage. Tom calculated the pay the men were due for the trip out, and handed each man his pay as he shook his hand and said goodbye. January came and went in a flurry of loading and preparation as they reordered the watches. February the first was on them before they knew it. Were they ready? Time would tell.

The Battle of Pulo Aura

The "execute" signal flew from the *Earl Camden* and the echo of orders being bellowed to get the fleet sailing echoed around the bay. Thirty-one ships departed in strict order and crossed the second bar on the second of February 1804. *Warley* was the seventh ship to leave, behind the *Royal George*, *Dorsetshire*, *Ganges*, *Earl Camden*, *Cumberland* and *Henry Addington*. Once clear of the river, the convoy would form three columns of ten with the *Camden* out ahead. The *Royal George*, *Warley* and *Dorsetshire* would lead the columns.

It took a day to get every ship out and into formation with the *Ganges* zipping up and down shepherding and cajoling the merchantmen into position. They hove-to for the night off the island of Hong Kong, ready for an early start the next day. Only, come the morning, the lines were muddled as ships had drifted off station.

"I wouldn't want to be the skipper of that brig," Graham said as they watched her chase another errant ship into place.

"They will run out of powder, the number of times he's firing that signal cannon," Tom said, and laughed.

They were making way, slowly, with the *Camden* leading at about five knots. Tom looked back down their column.

"I think the *Chester* just ran into the back of the *Sorley*."

Graham peered through a telescope.

"Just missed him by swerving out of line, I think."

The column was over a mile long with each ship, supposedly, a cable behind the one in front.

"Look lively, the *Camden* is setting more sail," Tom said.

This was the difficult part. The *Camden* was 200 yards ahead of the *Warley*, which headed up the centre column. They were expected to maintain that gap at all times.

"Set the mains. Ready the gallants."

The effect of the increase in speed was like a long, coiled spring. The column extended as each ship took time to react to the increase in speed of the one in front, then contracted as they tried to resume their position and invariably overshot. After a few bounces and stalls, they settled down. Tom decided then and there he hated convoys.

"What are we making?"

"Ten knots at the last throw of the log," Graham said.

Tom looked to the heavens. *Lord, give me patience.*

A scant seventy miles was made on the second day before they hove-to again for the night. The next morning was not so bad, and they were making ten knots after only an hour of faffing around. The commodore edged it up to fourteen knots for a while, but it was soon apparent that the older ships could not maintain that, so they dropped back to twelve.

Despite the slow speed, the crews were constantly trimming the sails to maintain the cable's gap between them and the *Camden*. Tired men slept well at night, which was the only advantage of heaving-to as far as Tom could see.

That evening, Tom and Mary were invited to the *Camden* for dinner. They were rowed across and found themselves in the presence of the good and the great. Nat had invited the most senior of the passengers from all of the Company ships. Tom sat with an earl, a viscount, a baronet and two knights of the realm.

Nat tinged his glass with a knife to get their attention once they had assembled for pre-dinner drinks.

"May I introduce Commodore Thomas Batrick of the *Warley* and his good lady wife, Mary. Tom is my second in command."

Then Tom and Mary were introduced to each guest in turn.

"Tom, may I introduce the Earl of Erroll and his daughter Lady Dulcibella." The girl was nine years old and was blossoming into the beauty she would later become.

"Did you enjoy India and China, milady?" Mary asked her.

"Oh yes, the people are so interesting, don't you think?" the girl replied brightly. The two would be seated near each other and chat over dinner.

Next was Viscount Standish of Guillamore and his wife Lady Katherine; then Sir Henry Mainwaring, baronet, and his wife Jane; Sir Theodore Kingsley and his wife Annette; and finally, Sir Martin Theakston and his wife Arabella. All three sirs were shareholders in the East India Company.

The dinner was sumptuous and long, and Tom was asked to regale them with tales of his battles with pirates—which he did, in as dramatic a way as possible to make what he considered quite mundane events more interesting. After dinner, two of the ladies entertained them with songs, accompanied by Sir Theodore on the violin. They made a pretty good fist of it.

The fourteenth day of sailing saw them 100 miles north by north-east of the eastern entrance to the Strait of Malacca, with the island of

Pulo Aura clear on the port bow to the south-west. Tom considered this to be the start of the danger zone, as any attacking ships would be able to conceal themselves behind the island and have plenty of sea room to make an attack.

"*Royal George* is signalling," Simon Seldon, the signal boy, said.

Tom picked up a small telescope to look, but let the boy read it.

"Strange sails to the south-west. Three ships."

He looked to the *Camden* and saw her signal the *Alfred*, *Ganges*, *Royal George*, *Bombay Castle* and *Hope* to investigate. The ships turned out of line and headed towards the strange sails. They didn't have to travel far to bring them hull up over the horizon.

Tom decided to have a look-see for himself and, changing his small telescope for a big bring-'em-near, he climbed the main mast rigging.

"How come you didn't see them?" he barked at the lookout as he scanned the horizon. There were three distinct sets of topsails coming over the horizon. *French cut, first could be a liner, the other two frigates.* Then, as he was about to put the telescope away, another sail appeared. *And that is the corvette. Now, where is the brig?* He waited patiently. *Oh, there she is, tagging along at the back.* He took a stay to the deck.

The *Royal George* fired a gun and signalled "enemy in sight". Tom scanned the line behind him. There were signs that they were starting to bunch up. "Signal the line to maintain their spacing," he barked, then watched as the signal was repeated down the line. A semblance of order was restored and he noted that the other lines had followed suit.

At midday, the commodore raised the signal to form line of battle.

"Get the lookouts down, they are doing no good up there," Tom said.

"Aye, aye, skipper," Graham said. "Do you want us to go to quarters?"

"No, not yet. There's no point in having the men stand around waiting." Tom turned to the wheel. "Helm, take us out of line to port and get us behind the *Camden*. Raise the blue ensign. Signal the line to maintain position."

By one o'clock the line of battle was formed to port of the convoy. The *Royal George* led followed by the *Ganges*, *Camden*, *Warley*, *Hope*, *Alfred*, *Bombay Castle*, *Coutts* and *Wexford*. The rest of the fleet was behind them to leeward. It was a smartly performed manoeuvre that would have done the navy proud. The captains and first mates put on coats that resembled naval officers' uniforms. Then the *Camden* signalled "quarters".

"Here we go!" Graham grinned and shouted the orders.

On the *Marengo*, Admiral Linois watched the manoeuvre.

"How many ships are there?" he asked his flag captain, Pierre Silvain.

"Lookout, give me a count of the ships."

They waited.

"I count thirty-one," came the reply. "I did it twice."

"That is very odd. Our informant told us there were twenty-three ships in the convoy, and all merchantmen. Those ships are not behaving like merchantmen. Look, they have run out."

"The brig is a Company Marine ship, for certain," Silvain said. "The rest fly the blue ensign of the Royal Navy."

"But are they really navy, or is it a bluff?"

"We need to get closer to tell." Silvain sighed. His admiral was a cautious man.

The admiral scanned the line of ships again. They looked like warships with their black and yellow painted, chequerboard pattern. He paced up and down.

They were three kilometres off when he looked again. He scanned down the line and stopped as his glass passed over the fourth ship in line. She was positioned perfectly for him to see her entire deck. He focused on her quarterdeck. "Carronades. She is armed with carronades. Merchant ships do not carry them."

He was wrong. The Company had been fitting them to their ships in the last year and any ship commissioned recently would have them.

"What are they doing?" Graham asked. "Why aren't they attacking?"

"I don't really know. I would, just to see what kind of firepower I would be up against, if nothing else," Tom said.

"Maybe he is frightened of us," Graham joked.

"Yes, shaking in his shoes no doubt." Tom looked down to the main deck where the men were looking at him. "Do you see that, lads? The Frenchy is shaking in his shoes at the sight of us!"

A roar of laughter echoed across the waves to the *Camden* ahead of them.

"Batrick has his men in good humour," Dance said to Farrell, his first mate.

"They are more battle hardened than ours, skipper; she's been hunting pirates for years."

The *Warley* crew members who had been sent aboard to bolster their gunnery looked back at the sound. "Hear that, lads? The *Warley* lads are having a party!" one shouted, setting off a round of cheering that spread throughout the ship.

Most didn't know what they were cheering *for*, but it eased tension and raised spirits.

On the *Marengo*, Admiral Linois couldn't hear the cheering as he was upwind, but he had finally decided what to do. He looked at his watch: it was only a few hours until dark.

"If we attack now, the convoy will scatter and we will lose them in the dark. They will heave-to if we leave them alone. Drop in a kilometre behind their line of battle. We will attack at first light."

Dance watched the French swing around behind them.

"He has decided to attack, from the looks of things. I anticipate that he will run up our lines on the windward side dealing at least one broadside per ship."

"You don't think he will try and sink us one by one?" Farrell asked.

"Not when he realises we are nought but merchant ships."

But the attack never came, and the sun set over a tense but peaceful ocean. The convoy hove-to rather than scatter and provide easy pickings in the morning. Dance sent the *Ganges* to shepherd everyone into position and had the merchantmen send men over to the Indiamen to augment their crews. The valuable passengers were temporarily transferred to other ships.

Come first light, Dance surveyed his charges. Amazingly, they were all where they should be—or thereabouts.

"Isn't it astonishing how the threat of capture instils discipline in the most errant of captains?" he said, and laughed.

The French stayed where they were and showed no signs of moving.

"Signal the convoy to make sail," Dance ordered.

The signal flew up the mast and the sea blossomed with sails as the convoy made way.

"Deck there," the lookout on the *Marengo* lookout cried. "The convoy is making sail."

Linois did not need to be told, he could see it for himself. What he could also see was that the convoy had rearranged itself overnight. Now they stretched out to leeward of the nine guard ships in rows rather than columns. He couldn't attack them without giving up the wind gauge. He decided to wait, and observe how they manoeuvred.

Tom watched from the mizzen boom. *My word he's cautious, I would have gone at first light.* At that time of year, that was a little before seven thirty. It was now well past eight o'clock and Tom anticipated that the first bell of the forenoon watch would be rung soon. He returned to the deck.

"Have the gunners pull their loads and reload. They may have got damp overnight," he ordered.

Freyja came to stand beside him. "Why are they waiting?" she asked, a hint of scorn in her voice.

"I honestly do not know."

"Is he a coward?"

"Who? The French admiral? I don't think so. He is just unsure of what he is facing."

She huffed and then asked, "Where are Mary and little Tom?"

"Down with the surgeon on the orlop deck."

"Good, she will be safe there. It's not good that we are going to battle—given her condition."

Tom took a moment for that to register.

"Her *condition*?"

Freyja looked at him in surprise, then looked embarrassed. "She hasn't told you?"

Tom ground his teeth in annoyance. "Told … me … what?" he said slowly.

"She is pregnant. Haven't you noticed?" she said to his back as he raced below.

Mary sat with the surgeon, with little Tom on her lap.

"Hello love," she said when he walked in. Then she saw the look on his face. "Aah, you *know*. Freyja must have told you."

"I do, and how do you know it was Freyja?"

"Because she is a woman and we know these things, unlike men who have to see a bump or have it told to them."

"So, it's true?" he said.

She handed little Tom to Barnes, who was showing signs of wanting to be somewhere else, and stood up. Then she stepped into his arms and kissed him.

"I didn't want to worry you until we were safe." She laid her head on his shoulder and he slowly relaxed.

He started to chuckle, and the chuckle turned into a laugh.

"What's so funny?" she asked, a little miffed.

"I suddenly had a thought … that we might have to name him Pierre, if this all goes wrong."

"*Phtt*, there isn't any way the French are going to take us. Freyja would never allow it."

The bell was struck twice and still Linois waited, sure that at least some of the ships in the line must be Royal Navy. Dance had a chance, and he took it. Signalling the merchant ships to go back into convoy formation, he increased speed to get into the strait before the French.

With the ships back in formation, they presented a much less intimidating target than before and Linois was spurred into action, albeit slowly.

"Increase speed, let us catch up with them."

They approached the rear of the convoy slowly, almost like a cat stalking a rat that it's not sure it can take.

By one in the afternoon, it was clear that the French ships were threatening to isolate the ships at the rear of the convoy. Dance ordered the lead ships of his line to tack and come about to cross the bows of the French squadron.

The *Royal George* led, under the command of John Fam Timmins; she was followed by *Ganges*, *Earl Camden*, *Warley*, *Hope* and the *Alfred*.

"Ready the starboard battery," Tom ordered. "Clew up the mains."

The *Marengo* opened fire as the *Royal George* came up on her beam. Tom checked his watch; it was a quarter after one, they would be in firing position soon.

"Fire as you bear!" Graham roared.

Freyja stood beside Tom on the quarterdeck. There was no indication she would get her swords wet, the way the French were behaving. She suddenly laughed.

"I think the *Ganges* just shot at the *George* by mistake."

Tom was about to say something when there was a crash and he staggered as the ship shook.

"What the hell?"

He spun around. The *Hope* had run into them and their rigging was entangled with the *Warley*'s.

"Pendergrass, what the hell are you playing at?" Tom roared across at the other ship.

"Get that rigging clear! *Move*, you lubbers!" Graham was shouting.

Men ran to cut them free and Pendergrass came forward to where the two ships locked together.

"Sorry, old chap. We misjudged our speed a little."

Fucking moron! Tom fumed. "Just get us untangled!" he bellowed back.

The sound of axes chopping lines and the grinding of the hulls carried on for twenty minutes before the ships parted. Tom shook his fist at the *Hope*, then shouted encouragement to the men repairing the damage.

They rejoined the line. The French had dropped back, and the two forces were running on parallel courses. Broadsides roared out, the *Warley* among them. Tom kept his ship opposite the French and was pleased that his men managed two broadside every three and a half minutes. The fact they were served so efficiently convinced Linois that he did indeed face a British squadron. He hauled his wind and started to sail eastwards. *Camden*, *Warley*, *Alfred*, *Royal George* and *Ganges* were the only ships to actually engage the enemy: the others never fired a shot.

"The commodore is signalling 'pursue'," Tom's signal boy said.

"Good, we should chase that bastard all the way back to Batavia," Tom snarled, still angry at the *Hope.*

The *Hope*, in a rash of enthusiasm and to make up for her mistake, went after the brig, *Adventure*. Tom shook his head; they had a bat's chance in hell of catching them, since none of the merchantmen could match the French for speed and the brig was especially quick. The French gradually drew away and after two hours Dance signalled "return to the convoy", emphasised by two guns. The chase was over and by eight o'clock they had anchored in the entrance to the strait with the rest of the fleet. The passengers returned to their ships.

Dance had them wait. First, he wanted to see if Linois returned. Second, he had news from a Company cutter out of Penang, that HMS *Sceptre* and *Albion* would be joining them to escort them to St Helena.

Tom treated his men to a slap-up dinner. They slaughtered a bullock, and it was roasted nice and rare near the bone, just as they liked it. The passengers got roast rib and fresh fish. The wine was supplied by them from their personal stores and a jolly time was had by all.

On the twenty-eighth of February, two seventy-four gun, two-deck warships flying the blue ensign sailed up. Now they could go home—but first the captains had to be entertained. Captain Dickenson of the *Sceptre* and John Ferrier of the *Albion* enjoyed royal hospitality aboard the *Camden* with the officers of the Company ships. The party lasted most of the night.

Homeward Bound

With the two liners sailing to windward and the *Ganges* acting as sheepdog to a growing flock of ships, they set sail at first light. Most of the Company ships were commanded by their first mates as their captains slept off hangovers. Graham smiled as he stood on the poop deck and watched the sun creeping over the horizon. For once, they would pass through the strait without fear of pirates.

Tom eventually got on deck for the afternoon watch, still a little grey around the gills but able to command.

"Must have been a good party," Graham quipped, and laughed as he saw his skipper climb the steps.

"Mary says you had to carry me up the side."

"Fisher did. Slung you over his shoulder and climbed up like an ape."

Tom groaned. "My head feels like there are a pair of dwarven smiths pounding on anvils in there."

"The evils of alcohol. Here, this will make you feel better." Graham handed over a flask. Tom sniffed it then took a swig.

"The hair of the dog that bit me?"

"Best French brandy."

Tom shook himself as the spirit hit home.

"You," he barked at a boy. "Have my steward bring up coffee."

He looked around. They were back at the head of the central column with the *Royal George* to port. When he looked back, Graham had gone below.

A sailor stuck his head up from the steps. "Skipper, there are some passengers who want to talk to you."

Now? He groaned inwardly but let them come up. It was a delegation of five who had not been at the dinner.

"Captain Batrick," Clifford Ferndale, Esquire, said. "We have come up to congratulate you on the victory over the French. A magnificent action!"

Ferndale's uncle was a shareholder in the Company and a member of Parliament, while his wife was an active member of the anti-slavery movement. He made a speech full of praise for the gallant sailors and their officers and the delegation gave a round of applause.

He will be following in his uncle's footsteps. Tom knew he had to make a reply.

"Thank you all. It was a fleet action, and we were just one element. Now, with our escort, we can comfortably and safely return home."

The passengers returned to the main deck, happily chatting. The ladies walked the deck with parasols to protect them from the sun, the men wore broad-brimmed hats. They had all been safely below during the action and only heard the rumble of the guns being rolled back and forth and the roar as they went off. Many stopped and chatted to sailors, asking what had happened, and Tom knew the story would get bigger with every telling.

They cleared the strait and stopped at Penang on the first of March, where they picked up another couple of ships. The warships were frustrated by the slow progress, which Tom heard about when he was invited to dinner one evening on the *Albion* after they anchored.

"Of course, we understand the rationale behind heaving-to at night, conditions permitting," Captain Dickenson of the *Sceptre* said. "But it does make the journey longer than it need be."

"I know," Tom replied. "I was in a privateer before joining the Company and it frustrated the hell out of me having to slow up or stop every night. But the passengers expect it, especially in fair weather and low seas. They like their parties and boasting about how much money they are carrying home."

Dickenson snorted at that.

"Is it true you Company captains make a fortune out of carrying your own trade goods home?"

"We are permitted to carry small items," Tom replied, modestly.

"Such as?" Ferrier asked.

"A case of silk, or porcelain, maybe some gemstones." Tom withheld the real extent of his personal cargo.

"Well, we have to rely on prize money, and we won't be getting any for this trip," Ferrier said.

"We also carry private cargo for other people," Tom said with a wink.

"Do you? Bedamned!" Dickenson said, looking interested.

"If you buy well, when ashore, goods that are popular in Britain, a captain will carry them back for you for a small consideration," Tom told them this *sotto voce*, as if sharing a deep secret.

Both captains nodded, wise looks on their faces.

"Then let us hope we can get to St Helena as quickly as possible." Tom grinned. "We will pray for a heavier sea so we can at least keep sailing during the night."

"Amen to that!" the captains cried and drained their glasses to heeltaps.

Dickenson got his wish. Halfway across the Indian Ocean the weather deteriorated, and a storm blew up, pushing the convoy relentlessly west for four days. They covered a thousand miles. Passengers were seasick and the physician was busy with minor injuries. They lost a man overboard—he was reefing the top sail when he lost his grip and fell into the sea, there was nothing they could do to save him. Tom performed a short ceremony of remembrance.

The convoy had managed to stay together in the main, albeit out of formation. Within a day of the storm ending, the ships that had become separated returned to the fold.

"They are a bit like sheep," Tom observed to Mary.

"How is that?"

"They like to be together in a herd and if they get separated, they worry and try to get back to the herd as fast as possible. There is safety in numbers."

The storm had blown them west, and Ceylon was visible on the horizon to the north as they turned south-west. Another ship joined, the captain thanking the gods of the sea that the convoy was that far north. Commodore Dance decided that from then on, they would heave-to for dinner, but at midnight they would proceed under reduced sail. They were making 200 miles a day.

Their shortest route would have taken them close to the Maldives and the Isle de France, but as that was where the French called home in those parts, Dance decided they would steer more to the west and take the Madagascar Channel. With such a big fleet and so many armed ships the pirates should leave them alone.

They entered the channel at midday and the lookouts immediately started spotting sails on the horizon shadowing them. The number steadily increased during the day.

"Signal from the *Camden*, 'maintain sail'," the signal boy reported.

"Nat does not want to give those heathens the chance to cut one of the smaller ships out," Tom said.

"Heaving-to would make it easy for them," Graham agreed.

Tom informed the passengers, who complained even though stopping would increase the danger. *I really cannot fathom their thinking. They would rather put themselves in peril rather than give up on a party.*

During the night a constant stream of rockets went up from around the convoy as lookouts spotted—or thought they spotted—pirate ships between the lines. The *Ganges* was kept busy running up and down chasing dhows away and even firing on some.

Come the morning, they were 180 miles further along with another 900 to go to get out of the channel.

"I really must protest," one overly entitled passenger told Tom over breakfast. "I could hardly sleep a wink with all the banging going on."

"My apologies, Mrs Merton. You see, we had a visit from some uninvited guests last night and we had to make it clear they were not welcome," Tom said.

"Whatever does he mean?" she said to the man next to her at the table.

The man, a lieutenant of the Marine travelling back to England to collect a ship replied, "They had to repel pirates." He winked at Tom. "They are particularly fond of ravishing European women, I hear. What say you, Captain?"

"It's true. I have heard that an entire crew will take it in turns," Tom said, absolutely straight-faced.

"My word!" she said and blushed furiously.

"Some they keep, for their harems. They do not get ravished but are taken to their palaces, dressed in scanty silks and become the playthings of the sultans," Tom added devilishly.

Mary kicked his ankle and whispered. "Tom! Behave."

Tom relented. "However, if we keep moving at night and are vigilant, we should be clear of them in two days."

Mary's pregnancy was proceeding normally. She was a strong woman and not prone to morning sickness. She started to show, but did not slow down at all and started inviting the female passengers to sit with her under a shade rigged above the deck. There they would crochet, knit or do needlepoint.

This turned into a regular ladies' club with tea and cakes. The ladies gossiped about the passengers on the other ships that they knew, and Mary would amuse Tom with such gossip when they were together. A reading group formed out of this gathering, and soon one or the other of the ladies could often be heard reading out loud to the others. Tom was not surprised that off-duty members of the crew would gather within earshot and listen to the readings.

The reading group seemed to particularly like the novels by Samuel Richardson. *Pamela* and *Virtue Rewarded* were favourites. These were romantic dramas, which one would hardly think sailors would be interested in. But the number of listeners suggested otherwise and the soppy looks on some of their faces … Well, Tom could hardly believe it.

Tom, like many captains, kept a journal. In it, he would mark down his observations of passengers and events and include comments. Some of these were downright rude and others pithy. One such entry said:

Miss Armitage has taken a lover, it seems; the steward reported seeing Mr Billings leaving her cabin. Mrs Billings was engaged on deck with the ladies' club which Miss Armitage had foregone on the excuse that she was feeling unwell. This evening at dinner she had a rosy glow in her cheeks and a healthy appetite. Billings must have the cure.

They arrived at St Helena on the ninth of June, and the warships returned to the Indian Ocean after replenishing. They were replaced by HMS *Plantagenet*, the only large seventy-four in the fleet with twenty-four-pound cannon on her upper deck. It took time to replenish such a large fleet and they practically emptied the island of fresh meat and vegetables. Dinner with the governor was mandatory, and stuffy. Tom was happy when they departed on the twentieth.

They were joined at St Helena by five whalers and the Indiaman *Carmarthen*, which was sailing from Bencoolen India. The *Blackhouse*, sailing from Guinea, joined them at sea.

Mary went into labour on the ninth and gave birth on the tenth of July. Freyja acted as midwife, with Barnes and Shayla in attendance. The baby girl was a healthy seven and a half pounds, and they named her Anne Florence after their mothers. Mother and baby recovered from the trauma of birthing well, but stayed abed. The crew, overjoyed at the event, all declared themselves uncles. Little Anne would never want for a toy or a playmate on this ship.

They arrived at the Downs on the eighth of August. The Thames was busy, and they had to wait for a pilot until the morning of the fourteenth. Dance sent his report ahead, and when they arrived it was to cheers from the dock workers, who lined up to see them in.

* * *

The news that the fleet had chased off a strong French squadron spread like wildfire and featured on the front pages of every newspaper in England. The captains were named and became heroes for a day. Their action had saved both the EIC and Lloyds from financial ruin.

Mary and the children went to Poole on the first available transport, to get away from all the hubbub surrounding the fleet. Once the ship was unloaded, Tom was paraded with the other captains in front of an enthusiastic and noisy public on the steps of Westminster Abbey. He never had to pay for a drink again.

The honours did not end there. Nathaniel Dance was particularly rewarded when King George III made him a Knight Batchelor. He was awarded £5,000 by the Bombay Insurance Company and a further £500 a year for life by the EIC. He retired from sailing straight afterwards, and lived in Enfield town. He never claimed sole credit for the action, saying in a written reply to the Bombay Insurance Company:

> *Placed, by the adventitious circumstances of seniority of service and absence of convoy, in the chief command of the fleet intrusted to my care, it has been my good fortune to have been enabled, by the firmness of those by whom I was supported, to perform my trust not only with fidelity, but without loss to my employers. Public opinion and public rewards have already far outrun my deserts; and I cannot but be sensible that the liberal spirit of my generous countrymen has measured what they are pleased to term their grateful sense of my conduct, rather by the particular utility of the exploit, than by any individual merit I can claim.*

Tom, along with the other captains, was rewarded by the Lloyds Patriotic Fund with a sum of 500 guineas and a piece of plate worth fifty guineas. The profits from the sale of his private cargo far exceeded that.

Linois continued to raid around the Indian Ocean and South China Sea, but failed to press home the attack at least two more times against superior numbers. His rationale being that he was far from any repair bases and could not risk his ships. Ironically, he was captured after mistaking a squadron of British warships for a merchant convoy in the mid-Atlantic. Napoleon was particularly scathing in his criticism, in a letter to the French minister of marine.

> *All the enterprises at sea which have been undertaken since I became the head of the government have missed fire because my admirals see double and have discovered, I know not how or where, that war can be made without running risks … Tell Linois that he has shown want of courage of mind, that kind of courage which I consider the highest quality in a leader.*

Tom returned to Poole as a local hero. The great and the good visited the house to shake his hand and congratulate him, and the local gentry put together a fund to gift him a packet of land that extended his holdings from a single acre to ten.

His mother asked, "Will you stay at home now?"

Tom pondered for a long moment before answering.

"I think I will have one more voyage. I should be able to make enough to live out my years in comfort from that."

The Last Voyage, 1805–1806

Outward Bound

The *Warley* sailed from Portsmouth on the twenty-fourth of April 1805 with a cargo of artillery destined to join the army in Madras. This was accompanied by a large number of commissioned and non-commissioned officers. Mary did not accompany Tom this time, preferring to stay at home for his swansong. Freyja decided she would return home, but promised to visit once she had become a shield maiden.

The *Warley*'s forward hold was converted into a makeshift barracks for the NCOs, with their field pieces broken down and stowed in the mid and aft holds. The commissioned officers took cabins, with their major and his servants having the state cabin. Tom's dining room became the senior officers' mess.

He learned that they were to form a regiment of horse artillery consisting of five batteries, which meant there were five captains, twenty lieutenants, one first sergeant, one company quartermaster sergeant, thirty sergeants and sixty corporals. The gunners would be natives recruited in Madras. Thankfully, only the major and his captains dined with Tom. Graham had the pleasure of entertaining the lieutenants. The NCOs looked after themselves.

The major ran the dinners like he would at the officers' mess at their headquarters at Woolwich Common. Full mess dress uniforms were mandatory, and all sat resplendent in their black jackets with gold facings and scarlet waist sash. No one was allowed to leave the table until the dinner was over, and they had been dismissed.

During their first dinner, Charles Foxton, the major, cautioned his captains with the words: "Gentlemen, please bear in mind we are the guests of the captain so please do not bore him with endless chatter about artillery."

Captain (Lord) Felix Radnor spoke up. "Sir, I do believe that the honourable captain has extensive combat experience."

"Is that so?" Foxton said, looking at Tom. He had rejoined the regiment just before sailing after a tour on the peninsula and was not up to date on current affairs.

"The *Warley* has been in several engagements with both pirates and the French," Tom admitted.

"You are too modest, Captain," Radnor said. "I believe you and your ship were at Pulo Aura."

Tom had to admit he was, and had to give a first-hand account of the action—which was a little less sensational than the one in the papers.

"How much cargo was the fleet carrying?" Foxton asked.

"I believe it amounted to some eight million pounds."

"Good Lord! That is a fortune!"

"The annual fleet brings that back every time—and that doesn't include the wealth the passengers bring home with them."

"A heavy responsibility, then," Foxton said. "That explains why you carry such heavy guns."

"Indeed." Tom smiled. "We can throw almost seven-hundred and fifty pounds of iron a broadside."

Several of the officers whistled; their own six-inch howitzers fired a one-pound ball or a sixty-ball canister.

"That is a lot of iron. How much powder are you carrying?" Captain Robin Haswell asked.

"This trip, ten tons."

"I take my comment back, Captain," Foxton said.

"No need. Those not familiar with the East India Company and its ships do not realise we have to be heavily armed merchantmen. Madagascar, the Bay of Bengal and the Strait of Malacca are rife with pirates, and we often have to defend ourselves. Now we also have the threat of French privateers and country ships, which is why we have one large convoy to bring ships back from China every year."

"Why can't the ships come back at any time?" Captain Angus McNally asked, with a gentle Aberdeenshire brogue.

"That is all to do with the wind, Captain. The monsoon winds from November to April are from the north-east and from April to November from the south-west. That means that on our outward leg we need to get there between April and November, and we must come back after November but before April," Tom explained.

They did not understand, so he asked the steward to bring him a sheet of paper and a piece of charcoal from his desk. He drew a ship and showed how the sails worked, in simple terms, then applied that to a sketch of the Malacca Strait.

"Do you see now?"

"Aye, I do," McNally said. "It makes it easy to predict when you will set sail, though."

"It does indeed. Add to that French and Dutch spies and you see the difficulty."

The first difficulty was a spring storm coming in off the Atlantic after they had turned south. It wasn't a particularly strong one, but the soldiers did not have their sea legs and suffered badly from seasickness.

The stench rising up from the forward hold was disgusting and they ran out of buckets. Every available bucket was emptied and put into service along with bowls and cooking pots from their own stores. The sailors steered well clear of the hold until the storm abated.

"Tell your men to clear their gear from the hold and bring up their hammocks. We are going to sluice the hold," Tom said to Foxton.

Foxton barked orders to a captain, who called over the first sergeant.

"Sergeant, would you be so kind as to get the men to clear the hold? The ship's captain wants to sluice it out," he said to the sergeant, who stood rigidly at attention.

"Sah!" the sergeant barked. Then boots crashed on the deck as he did an about-face and marched to the stairs to the hold. In a voice that could be heard all over the ship he bellowed, "Get your kit bags and hammocks on deck now!"

With a clatter of feet, the NCOs came on deck with their kit bags and hammocks, which were screwed up into balls. Tom took one look and stepped up beside the first sergeant. "Don't your men know how to roll a hammock?"

"Sah?"

"They have screwed their hammocks up into balls, but they should be rolled up tightly to keep them dry when they bring them on deck."

The captain had wandered up and heard what Tom said.

"Do you have someone who can show them the right way, Captain?"

Tom beckoned to a pair of mates who stood grinning as they watched from the side. "Stan, Reg will you show these men how to roll a hammock, please."

Stan cast an eye over the pile of screwed-up canvas and rolled his eyes. "Lord above, what a shambles. Aye, aye, skipper."

Major Foxton joined Tom on the poop deck. "Thank you, Captain. We don't normally use hammocks, you know."

"I know, I should have thought about it before. This is the first time we have carried troops."

"Not your fault, not at all," the good major consoled him.

The soldiers got their sea legs and life settled down as they made the turn across the Atlantic with the trade wind on their quarter. The soldiers exercised daily, to the amusement of the crew to start with, but the novelty soon wore off. Life settled down to the comfortable routine only found at sea.

Another storm hit them, with less disastrous effects. Some of the soldiers even enjoyed it, finding it exhilarating. Even so, they were glad to reach Rio, where they reprovisioned and watered.

"Next stop Madras," Tom told them over dinner.

The soldiers were expert observers during gun practice, which Tom started again as they approached the Cape of Good Hope. Whether the major was impressed or not he was polite in his appreciation of their skills. The sea soldiers and lascars exercised with their pikes as if Freyja was still there. Tom missed her and hoped she would be successful in her ambition to become a shield maiden. Again, the land soldiers observed with critical eyes but could find no fault in their technique.

The Cape came and went, Tabletop Mountain passing down their port side.

"We will be passing through a region where there is a chance of pirates and French country ship activity. We will sail under full sail day and night, as speed is our best defence," Tom told them.

"How do the pirates attack?" Captain McNally asked.

"They will try and damage our rigging to slow us down, then attempt to board us with overwhelming numbers. They want the cargo and the hull."

"Ha! They will get more than they bargain for if they try and take *this* cargo," Foxton barked, making everyone laugh.

"They will indeed," Tom agreed.

They sailed west with the circumpolar wind on their stern. Under full sail, the *Warley* fairly flew along.

"Fourteen knots and a fathom," Graham reported.

"Excellent, ten days should see us bear north."

The major visited the poop deck and looked at the chart over Tom's shoulder. "That looks to be the long way around."

"In distance yes, but in time, no." Tom took a pencil. "These are the prevailing winds." He sketched in the circumpolar and south equatorial winds, then drew a circle in the middle of the Indian Ocean that touched Madagascar to the west and the middle of the ocean just below the tip of India to the east. He then added a line pointing south down the Madagascar Channel, and one pointing east below the tip of India. Their route was marked in red.

"You see, the fastest route to Madras is to follow the winds. If we tried to go north up the Madagascar Channel, we would have to tack against the wind and current, making fifty sea miles for every land mile we advanced. Here, where the wind rotates around a cyclone, we can use it to go north and then west before catching this wind that takes us north then east. Do you see?"

The major saw the light and smiled.

"Damn me, but there is a lot more to this sailing business than I thought."

Just then, the sound of distant rumbling came across the ocean.

The *Dorsetshire*

"That is cannon fire," the major said, looking out to sea.

"It certainly sounds like it," Tom replied, as another rumble reached them. He looked up the main mast and hailed the lookout.

"Any sign of ships on the northern horizon?"

"Aye, there be sails to the north-east, and smoke."

Tom frowned.

"Someone is in trouble, that's halfway between here and Madagascar. Helm, steer a course for the north-east."

Graham appeared when he felt the change of course.

"Trouble, skipper?"

"For someone." The guns rumbled again. "Set all sail and go to quarters, we will want to send a message."

The log showed fourteen knots and a fathom and the conflict was at least twenty miles away. Tom feared they wouldn't make it in time, but as the ships came hull up over the horizon, he could see it was a Company ship in warm company with a xebec and a brig.

"Pirates, for sure," Graham said.

Major Foxton asked permission to come up on the poop deck.

"Can you see what's going on?"

Tom handed him a telescope.

"Aah, I see two against one. Will we get there in time?"

"They are holding them off at the moment—we will let them know we are on our way," Tom said, and signalled to Graham who was down on the main deck supervising the fitting of preventer stays and chains for the yards. "Fire a broadside. Let them know we are coming."

The port guns ran out and as soon as all the captains had raised their arms, he bellowed, "*Fire*!"

The thunder of the guns was immense, and his crews were working furiously to reload. They could only fight the centre four guns on each side because of the limited crew but they were doing just enough to hold off the pirates. Captain Robert (Bob) Hunter Brown wondered how long they could hold out. Then, in one of those quiet moments between broadsides, he heard the rumble of another ship's guns.

"Get a lookout up and see who that is," he barked at his first mate.

A very brave man climbed the rigging until he could see the approaching ship. "It's a Company ship, one of the new ones," he reported.

"Keep it up lads. Help is on the way!"

A cheer went up and the tired men redoubled their efforts. Just then, a ball from the brig smashed the rail behind him and a splinter spun wickedly towards him. He collapsed in agony as the eight-inch-long shard of teak hit his thigh, embedding itself behind the bone and protruding on the inside.

Major Foxton watched the gunners work, then turned to Tom.

"Would it be better of you could fight both sides?"

"Yes, but I don't have the men," Tom said from where he was studying the pirate xebec through his telescope.

"Yes, you do. All my men are trained gunners."

Tom lowered the telescope and turned to him.

"Trained in land artillery, not naval."

Foxton was not to be put off.

"They have watched your men practise They know what to do."

Tom looked at him for a long moment and sighed. It certainly gave him more options if he could fight both sides.

"All right, but any injuries are your responsibility not the Company's. Tell them to keep their feet clear of the wheels."

Foxton bellowed orders to his captains, who bellowed orders to his lieutenants, who bellowed at the NCOs. The starboard battery was manned in fairly short order. The rest of the soldiers lined up in two ranks on the centre line with muskets at the preparatory.

They had closed to a mile and Tom made up his mind. The xebec was more heavily armed and would be his first target. He called Graham to him.

"Aim low at her waterline, we do not want the shot passing right through and hitting our ship. Load the mains with double shot and the carronades with smashers."

"Aye, aye, skipper."

"Helm, I want to pass that xebec a cable to port."

They were just in time. The xebec was starting to close with the Company ship, which he could see was the *Dorsetshire.*

They swung into line and as they approached the xebec from behind Tom ordered, "Take in the mains and topsails." He wanted to pass match the xebec's speed.

He waited and watched the xebec run out her starboard guns. As they came up on her stern he ordered, "*Run out*!"

The port battery ran out. He could see the skipper of the xebec standing on his quarterdeck, his eyes wide as he saw the eighteen pounder's gaping maws rumble forward. As they ran down her side, the xebec's guns fired high at his rigging. Tom waited until they were level.

"*Fire*!"

The broadside rippled down the hull and the gunners were busy reloading. As the smoke cleared, he could see a row of star-shaped shot holes on or near the xebec's waterline.

"Give them another then load with chain and take down her rigging."

A soldier fell as a nine-pound ball cut him in half. His mates didn't flinch but raised their rifles and started volley firing into the men crowding the xebec's deck.

The second broadside hit home.

On the *Dorsetshire*, Captain Brown was propped up by the mizzen, his deck strewn with pieces of rigging and blocks. He was in pain but still able to command. "Concentrate on the brig, Terry," he told his first mate.

The gunners moved from the starboard side to man the full broadside of eight guns on the port. The brig was in for a surprise. The gunners—sensing victory and angry at the damage done to their ship—went to it with a will.

The xebec was taking in water after the second broadside. The smashers had done most damage, their large slow-moving balls wreaking havoc on the light hull of the xebec. The third broadside was due and her captain ordered more sail set. He couldn't win this fight, so he would run and live to fight another day.

Graham had all his guns elevated to the maximum. The chain should rip through the rigging at mid-mast height at this range. He looked across and saw sails blossom. He grinned.

"*Fire!*"

The howl of chain shot was one of the most distinctive sounds to be heard on the water, and the xebec's skipper knew what was coming just before it ripped across his deck. The main top mast was smashed just above the point where it was joined, and toppled to the deck taking more rigging with it. The fore mast after stays on the starboard side were severed. The ship acquired a list and slowed.

"Make sail, we will wear across her stern. Major, have your gunners fire high at her rigging as they bear," Tom bellowed. "Graham, have them load with chain."

Gunners from the port battery ran to help the soldiers load chain and then returned to their own guns. The *Warley* sailed ahead and reversed direction, bringing her starboard battery into play. The soldiers waited until they were sure of their aim and the broadside rippled from forward to aft.

"Not bad, not bad at all," Tom said to the good major, who stood proudly watching his men work.

They swung across the xebec's stern at fifty yards and raked her from one end to the other. Her scuppers were bleeding. Tom reduced sail and hove-to between the xebec and the *Dorsetshire*.

"Sink her," was all he said.

The brig had run away when confronted by two ships, the xebec was sinking, the sharks feasted. Tom took a boat across to the *Dorsetshire*. He climbed the battens and looked around the deck. Exhausted men staggered around, trying to return some sort of order to the mess of rigging and damaged timber.

He was met by the first mate, who shook his hand.

"Thank you, Captain Batrick. You were just in time."

"You are welcome." Tom looked around the deck. "Where is Bob?"

"Wounded: a splinter through the thigh. He is down in his cabin with the surgeon."

Tom went to the side. "Tell Graham to bring the *Warley* alongside and have the doctor join me. Then have our crew help the *Dorsetshire*'s men fix their rigging."

He found Bob laid face down on his dining room table, the surgeon hovering over his leg. The man was obviously concerned. He took Tom to one side once Bob and Tom had greeted each other.

"I might have to take it off." The doctor was sweating.

"Can't you cut it out?"

"I've never done that before."

Just then the door opened, and Barnes Redford stepped in, followed by Shyla and a crewman carrying his medical box.

"What have we here?" he said, and inspected the wound.

"Who are you?" Bob growled.

"This is Barnes, our physician," Tom said.

"A proper doctor, not a bloody sawbones?"

"I am," Barnes said, as he gently felt around the wound. "Shyla, please cut off the good captain's breeches."

"What?" Bob yelped.

Barnes had a quiet word with the surgeon, who left to take care of the crew. He carefully measured twenty drops from a pipette into a glass and added brandy.

"Drink this, it's laudanum in brandy."

"Will that make me sleep?" Bob asked before downing it.

"Probably not, but it will make you relaxed."

Bob downed it in one.

"Bite on this." Barnes slipped a strip of thick leather between his teeth. "Now, let's get this ready."

Shyla washed the wound area with neat spirit, which made Bob grunt as it hit the open wound. Then she laid clean linen cloths around it. Barnes took off his jacket, rolled up his sleeves, donned an apron. Then, influenced by Freyja's treatment of wounds, he poured some of the spirit into a bowl and washed his hands up to his elbows.

"We are ready. Tom, could you lay across the good captains' shoulders to stop him moving, please." He turned to a steward who was hovering nearby. "You, lie across his feet."

Once secured and sure that the laudanum had taken affect, he took up a scalpel and started to cut. His touch was light and exact, his strokes precise. He started to expose the splinter.

"Nasty, jagged little bugger."

As he cut, Shyla stood by to mop his brow and to mop up blood. He asked for clamps, and she passed them to him from a bowl where they lay. Finally, he asked for forceps. He lifted the splinter clear and held it up so the others could see it. Eight inches long, two and a half at the widest, it was a formidable chunk of timber to have embedded anywhere in your anatomy.

"It missed his femoral artery by less than an inch. He is lucky."

He stitched the wound in layers, making sure each muscle group in turn was secured with gut sutures that the body would absorb over time. He finished it with a neat row of stitches on the outside.

"There, done. He will be as good as new in about twenty days."

Shyla giggled and the men looked at her.

"Look!" she said and pointed to where Bob's buttocks were exposed.

"Well, that's not something you see every day," Tom said as he looked closely at the tattoo of a dragon.

Bob, who had passed out and was blissfully unaware, snored.

The *Warley* stayed with the *Dorsetshire* until they made Madras and before they got there, Bob had recovered enough to sit at the head of the table and have Tom, Barnes and the major over for dinner.

Tom sat opposite Bob at the far end of the table and the major sat midway opposite Barnes, with the teenage daughters of Lord Frobisher seated on either side of him. To Tom's right sat Lady Elanor Frobisher, and to his left sat the Right Honourable Sylvester Adams.

They had to retell the action and then Bob had Tom retell the battle of Pulo Aura. At the end, the youngest Frobisher girl asked Tom, "Did you not save any of those men on the xebec?"

"No, they all had the honour of going down with their ship," Tom said.

"But surely you could have?"

Tom looked her in the eye. "You see, my lady, pirates are given no mercy for their crimes and so even if we had pulled a few out of the sea, they would have been hanging from a yard arm not soon after."

Tears filled her eyes and Tom took pity on her.

"It seems hard, I know, but the crimes they commit against those they capture, especially the women, are too horrid to even talk about. They were better off in the sea. There they had a choice of how to die."

She did not understand and spent the rest of the meal quietly.

"Mother says that the pirates do unspeakable things to women," she said to Tom as he prepared to go back to the *Warley*. He could see she was still troubled.

"There are several things that can happen to a woman captured by the pirates. If she is young and pretty they will sell her at the slave markets to some man who will use her as his concubine. You know what a concubine is?"

She nodded.

"If she is attached to a rich family, they may hold her for ransom."

He looked at her, judging how far he should go. She looked boldly back at him.

"If she is neither pretty or rich, she will be thrown to the crew for their amusement. Women who suffer this often die or take their own lives afterwards."

"You mean they ..."

"Rape her? Yes."

Her hand went to her mouth.

"Pirates do not live by the standards we set ourselves. They are only interested in profit and to them, life is cheap."

"Have you killed many?"

"Any that have crossed my path, and my conscience is clear."

Madras, Penang and Malacca

They anchored off Fort St George on the twenty-eighth of August and were eventually guided to a dock, where they unloaded the guns. The carriages were reassembled, and barrels mounted by the NCOs, before teams of horses were brought up to take them into the fortified Black Town where the regimental barracks lay. Tom and the crew said their fare-thee-wells and waited for the Company agent. Tom would be due a reward for rescuing the *Dorsetshire*.

He decided to go into the town and see what he could find to take home, and took a pair of soldiers and Peter with him.

There were several silversmiths who had unusual wares, but that was not what he was looking for. Indian silver did not fetch high prices in Britain. After an hour he was wondering whether he was wasting his time, as all he had bought were personal provisions so far.

They then came to a marketplace with lines of people sitting on blankets with their wares surrounding them. The scent of spices was strong, along with the delicious smells of street food. Tom realised he was hungry and looked at the wares on offer.

One in particular caught his eye. The vendor had a large skillet, heated over charcoal, onto which he poured a batter to make what looked like a pancake. It was rolled around a filling of paneer cheese coated in spices and served on a leaf with chutneys.

"What is this called?" Tom asked the vendor.

"Why, this is dosa, *sahib*. Very tasty."

"We will take four."

They cost practically nothing and were indeed flavoursome snacks. To quench their thirst, the men bought glasses of chai—strong black tea mixed with sweetened milk and cardamom. The seller mixed it by pouring it from a height, from one tin cup to another. That was a spectacle in itself.

Refreshed and fortified, they continued their search. Eventually, out of desperation, Tom stopped a European couple and asked if they knew of any gem merchants.

"I would suggest you try the village of Ryapooram, outside the north wall. There is a Tamil enclave there which brings stuff up from Ceylon," said the man—who turned out to work for the Company.

Tom thanked him and the four men walked the short distance to the gate. The village was directly in front of them. It was small, with a dozen or so houses, but tidy. Street urchins ran and played. They walked through until they came to a house with an open front like a shop, but this was different. A pair of burly guards sat either side of the opening, watching alertly. The sound of grinding came from within.

Tom bade his men stay outside and entered. Inside it was gloomy, except for one patch of sunlight that came down through an opening in the roof. Within it sat a small man at a wheel, carefully grinding facets on a ruby. He stopped when he became aware of Tom's presence.

"What can I do for you, *sahib*?"

"Are you a gem merchant?"

"A merchant, cutter and polisher."

"I am interested in buying good quality stones."

"Quality I have. What types of stones is the *sahib* interested in?"

"Sapphires and emeralds are all the rage in London at the moment, but rubies and garnets never seem to go out of fashion."

"I have some sapphires from Ceylon. Very nice colour and very few flaws."

He went to a large strongbox that looked to be made of mahogany and iron, and lifted the lid. He took out a pair of pouches and a piece of black velvet, which he laid on the worktable.

The contents of the pouch tumbled out onto the velvet; glistening blues scintillated in the light. Tom picked up a cut stone of a deep blue colour. He took out his loupe and examined it in the sunlight.

"Nice colour, one very small inclusion, well cut and about four carats." He put it to the side and selected another that had been cut into a drop. "Now that is a beautiful stone, lighter blue. Untreated?"

"I do not heat my stones, *sahib*." Sapphires were often heated to make their colour deeper and more even. Untreated stones fetched higher prices.

"Only very minor inclusions, about six carats."

The third was a rare, natural star sapphire which had been polished in a button or round mogul cut. The six-pointed star lay white within it. Tom said nothing and put it aside. He selected two more stones from the pile and said, "These I will take, what else do you have?"

Emeralds followed, ranging in colour from green to blue-green. Again, he selected the best. The man had a selection of rubies and garnets as well.

"*Sahib* has extremely good taste."

"What do you want for all these?"

The man took out an abacus and started flicking beads up and down. Tom waited patiently; he knew what he wanted to pay and was interested to see what the man came up with.

"The stones will cost one hundred and twenty golden guineas."

Tom was surprised, then realised the man had calculated the weight of gold and converted it into guineas as they were a trusted currency. However, it was more than he wanted to pay.

"I only want to pay eighty."

"*Sahib*, you are robbing me. I have five children and a fat wife to feed. I can do no less than one hundred and ten."

"Your fat wife can lose some weight by eating less. Ninety."

"But my children, *sahib*. One hundred and five."

"At your age *they* should be feeding *you*. One hundred."

The price was agreed. Tom took out several pouches from different pockets and placed them on the table. "One hundred golden guineas."

The man opened them and tipped them out. "I am sorry, *sahib*, but my wife will beat me if I do not count them."

Tom laughed and let him get on with it. While he was counting, a slender woman with a very pretty face stepped out from the back. She bowed with her hands palm to palm in front of her. "*Madhiya vanakkam, sahib*," she said.

Tom looked at the man with a questioning expression.

"She said good afternoon, sahib."

Tom responded in kind.

"Your fat wife?"

Tom was happy with his purchases and decided that the drop sapphire would be made into something for Mary when he got home, maybe with the diamond he had bought earlier. The rest he would sell for three times what he had paid.

Their cargo turned out to be nutmeg, mace and cinnamon from Ceylon and pepper, coriander and cumin from India. The smell from the holds was wonderful and much better than the stink of soldiers' farts and sweat. Tom bought a keg of nutmeg to trade. Genuine nutmeg sold for a fortune in London and there was a growing market in fake nutmeg as a result.

He was ashore, looking for some last-minute bargains, when he noticed that he was being followed. He was not carrying a large amount of money, so had not brought an escort. However, he was armed.

He identified his follower as a European man, probably down on his luck or a deserter, as he was dirty and shabbily dressed. The man stayed about twenty feet behind Tom as he made his way through the market. Tom led him up and down the rows of pitches and spotted him signal to someone.

A casual glance around, as if looking over the pitches, revealed a second man on the edge of the market square. Tom decided he would see what they wanted. He reversed course and passed by the first man who was making a show of looking at some fruit. He bumped into him.

"Terribly sorry, old chap," he said and continued on his way to the outside edge of the market. He followed it around until he came to an alley, then walked into it and stopped in the shadows about ten feet in.

He pulled his pistol from his pocket.

The two men were suddenly silhouetted against the entrance. The one who had followed him reached for something on his belt and looked confused when he couldn't find it.

"Looking for this?" Tom said, and held up a nasty curve-bladed knife in his left hand. It was the man's dagger, which he had lifted when he bumped into him.

The man's companion pulled a long-bladed knife from under his jacket and the two charged. Tom shot the one with the knife in the belly and he fell to the ground. The other came on.

Tom twisted his body and, as the man surged past, brought the gun down on his head while slashing with the knife. The man didn't get up.

Tom whistled to himself as he checked them over. The one he'd clubbed had a gaping wound in his side. He was unconscious and had the beginnings of a large egg growing on his head.

The other was awake and holding his stomach. Tom crouched beside him and took his knife. He pulled his hand aside and looked at the hole in his stomach. Then he checked around the back to see if the ball had gone through. He sniffed; he didn't smell anything that made him think he had hit an intestine.

"Nasty wound, that. You might die," he told him. "But you will have company—I doubt your friend will see the day out."

The man groaned; he was obviously in a lot of pain.

"Army deserter?" The man nodded. "Find someone to treat that. I'll do you a favour and not report this. They would only hang you."

The real reason was that it would take too much time, as the authorities would want statements and the like. Tom patted him on the shoulder then stood up and walked away, whistling cheerfully.

That afternoon several passengers came aboard, among them a missionary and his sister who were bound for Malacca, a pair of Company men who had done their time and were returning home much wealthier and with Indian wives, and—most noticeable of all—an Anglo-Indian merchant with a very striking Englishwoman in tow.

Their next stop was Penang on the eighteenth of September. Dewi was there and he and Tom got reacquainted over a bottle of wine.

"I have a hot tip for something to take back that will net you a nice profit. They are growing cloves here now and you can get them for half the price of those from Indonesia."

"Interesting, that will piss off the Dutch."

"Won't it just?" Dewi laughed.

Tom bought more stones, cloves and pepper: his investment was large, but so was his expectation of profit.

The local authorities had dealt with the suspected French agents, who had been kicked off the island. Their likenesses had been circulated to all British holdings. A permanent patrol of the strait by the Royal Navy had been instituted: two ships of the line and a frigate were designated for the duty. Piracy was reduced but did not go away, the pirates just got sneakier.

More passengers came aboard. A couple who had been touring the East and were now heading home, and a young botanist, Robert Fortune, who was working for the Royal Society and investigating whether tea could be grown in India.

Malacca was their last stop before Whampoa. Seeing it on the route was a surprise, as it had been controlled by the Dutch until 1798 and had only been a protectorate of Britain since then. It didn't have much in the way of natural resources but when Tom looked at the map, he could see that it was ideally positioned to be a hub for the spice trade.

They loaded more cargo, spices from around the region. The trader approached Tom.

"Captain, may I have a word?"

"Certainly, Mr Edwards. What can I do for you?"

"Do you have a strongroom aboard?"

"We do."

"I have a chest coming aboard and would like it stowed securely. It is very valuable."

"We can put it in the strong room for you."

"Thank you ... there is another thing." He waited until Tom nodded for him to continue. "I do not wish the authorities in England to know that it is mine."

"Oh?" Tom replied with a raised eyebrow.

Edwards spoke quickly. "I am not asking you to smuggle them, just take them ashore under your name."

"Them?" Tom asked. "If I am to take *them* ashore, I need to know what is in the chest."

Just then, Edwards was hailed from the dock.

"With your permission?" he asked.

Tom nodded.

"Bring it aboard," Edwards shouted.

Two men clambered up the gangplank with a large chest.

"Can we take it somewhere private?" Edwards asked.

"My cabin." Tom led the way.

Inside the cabin, Edwards dismissed the men, who he said worked for him, and when they had gone he took a key from his pocket and unlocked the chest.

Tom watched as he opened the lid. Inside, the chest was lined with velvet and padded. Nestled in the velvet padding was a spectacular golden crown, either side of which lay golden diadems encrusted with rubies and sapphires. Tom whistled, leaned forward and gently picked up the crown. It was heavy. The detail on it was astonishing.

"Where do these come from?"

"Sumatra, the island of gold. They date from the 1100s."

Edwards gently lifted the diadems out and laid them on Tom's desk, then lifted out the velvet pad. Underneath were even more treasures.

"I am not only a trader but also an antiquarian. All of this was found in digs at an ancient temple ruin in Sumatra."

"And the Sumatran authorities don't know about it?"

Edwards shrugged. "I can make it worth your while to get these back to England."

Tom pursed his lips. "I will take them as part of my private cargo."

"Thank you."

"For a fee."

Tom looked at the artefacts, weighing up their value in gold and jewels. He picked up the crown again, estimating its weight, then weighed each artefact and assessed some of the jewels.

He estimated there was around forty-two-pounds of gold plus the jewels at three pounds, seventeen shillings and ten pence an ounce, which was the value the Royal Mint placed upon it.

"The gold alone is worth two thousand, six hundred and fifteen pounds. But these are worth far more than the value of the gold and jewels. Look, let's call my fee two thousand five hundred pounds and this lot will get ashore without being inspected."

Edwards looked relieved. "Agreed."

Whampoa

They dropped anchor in English Reach, between Danes Island and Whampoa Island, on the first of January. A new rule had been instituted that they had to offload their powder at Powder Island—that was between Blenheim Reach and French Reach. It made sense because now more and more Company ships were heavily armed and carried tons of powder, the risks were increasing.

It being New Year's Day, the crew wanted to celebrate. They had no goods for China, so nothing to offload. They would not be leaving until the end of February, so Tom gave permission. The passengers chipped into a party kitty and Peter acquired the means to prepare a celebratory dinner for the crew and the passengers.

The passengers and officers had their dinners in the captain's dining room of course and enjoyed:

A light and refreshing chicken soup with delicate rice noodles.
Pearl river prawns cooked in butter, garlic and herbs.
Roast suckling pig, stir fried Chinese vegetables and rice.
Spotted dick with raspberry jam.
Nuts

The pork had skin so crispy, and flesh so tender, it was completely devoured. The wine came from Tom and the passengers' personal supplies.

Bill Trafford visited the day after.

"Hello Bill, how's the security business?" Tom greeted him in their established manner.

"Good, things have settled down now. We know who to watch and who needs to be moved on."

"What happened to … what was his name? The chap who was in the clerks' office?" Tom asked.

"Oh, he ended up being disappeared."

"Disappeared, is that spy speak for killed?"

"Something like that." Bill abruptly changed the subject. "I hear rumours that this is your last voyage."

"How the hell? Never mind. Yes, it is."

"The committee wants to thank you."

"What for? I only did my duty," Tom said humbly.

"Oh, come on, you did more than that. Anyway, they want you to attend a small get-together Saturday evening at Company House in Canton."

Tom shook his head. He wasn't into such things, but he didn't have a choice. So he said, "I will be there, what time?"

"Seven for cocktails—and wear a dinner suit."

Tom had not worn his dinner suit for years, and after Bill had left, he tried it on. It was, of course, too tight. Tom blew a sigh; that would not do. He took it ashore and searched out a tailor.

The little Chinese man looked at the suit and shook his head.

"No good, me make new one."

"I need it for Saturday."

"No problem," he said pronouncing problem as *pwoblem.* "It ready tomorrow."

He had Tom stand on a stool and measured him with a length of cord with knots in it. An apprentice marked the measurements down on a slate. He took far more detailed measurements than his tailor in Poole did.

"You want shirt as well? Best silk," he asked.

"Yes, two please," Tom replied.

The next day, in the late afternoon, he went back to the shop. The tailor greeted him warmly and handed him his suit and shirts. The suit was divine, made of a medium-weight black silk, it fitted him like a glove—as did the shirts.

"This is wonderful, what do I owe you?"

"Two yuan."

That was ridiculously cheap. Tom handed over two silver coins. The little man beamed at him as he left.

Saturday night saw Tom suited and booted and being rowed upriver to the Thirteen Docks. He had completed his outfit with his top hat, a white silk cravat and a scarlet silk cummerbund. His shoes had silver buckles and were highly polished. He carried a cane in his right hand and a pair of silk gloves in his left.

Bill met him at the dock. Tom didn't ask how he had known when he would arrive.

"Perfectly timed, it is a ten-minute walk to the house."

Bill also wore a suit and top hat. The pair looked like a couple of dandies as they walked up the hill.

"Who is your tailor?" Bill asked.

"A little Chinese fellow in Whampoa town."

"Mr Xing, he is mine as well. He has made a point of learning how Western clothes are made. He works in wool as well, you know."

"Then I will get some suits made to take home; he is far cheaper than my tailor in Poole."

They got to the entrance where two Marine guards stood. "Mr Trafford," one said.

"This is our guest of honour, Captain Batrick," Bill said.

"Go ahead, sirs."

They entered a high-ceilinged, cool hallway adorned with pictures of committee members and worthies. There was a picture of the king in the most prominent position.

"It's all offices down here and on the first floor. We need to go up to the second floor," Bill said, and led the way up an ornate staircase.

The whole building exuded power. As they climbed, the sound of music drifted down. A quartet, if Tom wasn't mistaken. Then he began to hear the sounds of chatter.

"How many people are at this get-together?" he said suspiciously.

"Oh, not many, just the great and the good." Bill grinned as if it was a big joke.

Tom rolled his eyes.

They came to a large open set of double doors. A herald stood at the entrance. Through the doors Tom could see gaily dressed men and women standing around, talking.

"Are we the last?"

"Of course, they all wanted to be here to greet you."

The herald signalled to the quartet, who stopped playing. He took a deep breath and announced, "My lords, ladies and gentlemen. Commodore Batrick."

The crowd separated, leaving a clear path to the chairman of the committee. Tom realised that he should follow that path, as Bill gave him a light push to get him moving.

The gathered worthies applauded as he walked. He nodded to the few he knew. He then reached the chairman, Mr Philias Cummings-Wilson, who shook his hand and then turned Tom slightly, so he faced the crowd.

"Ladies and gentlemen, we are here this evening to honour one of our bravest captains. He has fought pirates and the French and helped our security people immensely during his time as captain of the *Warley*. He has now announced to the Company that he will retire from sailing after this voyage."

Another round of applause, which the chairman let die away.

"In recognition of his service, the Canton Committee has decided that he should receive the gift of a gold commemorative plaque, and a pension of two hundred pounds a year for life."

The plaque was brought forward and handed over. It was engraved:

To Commodore Batrick
In Recognition of his Sterling Service and Bravery
A Grateful and Thankful
East India Company, Canton Committee
In the Year of Our Lord 1806

Tom did not know what to say, so just shook the chairman's hand and smiled at the applause.

"You will also command the convoy on the way home," the chairman said in his ear.

The servant relieved Tom of his burden and the evening passed in a whirl of dancing, eating and drinking. He made some very useful contacts, among whom were committee members, traders and merchants.

All in all, he enjoyed himself and returned to his ship a little worse for wear—but happy.

A surprise cargo was brought aboard covertly that night. The young tea grower brought up several crates with holes drilled in the top. Tom sniffed one, and detected an earthy smell. They were stowed out of sight at the top of a stack of crates in the middle hold. Two barrels of rainwater were also brought aboard.

"What is it?" Tom asked.

"Tea bush saplings. If the Chinese find out I have them, they will murder me."

"And impound my ship."

Robert Fortune winced. "I have the backing of the East India Company. It is an experiment; we will plant them in different locations to see how they do. If we find soils and a climate that they like, we will expand to full plantations."

"How long will that take?"

"Years, I am afraid."

In fact, it would take over forty years before the Company established a plantation in the mountain region around Darjeeling. But Robert Fortune was young and keen. This was the first of many forays he would make into China to steal tea plants.

Tom invested more money in silks and jasmine tea. His private cargo grew to be the largest it had ever been. The official cargo also grew; tea, porcelain and silk filled his holds to the brim. The official value was £322,519. The most valuable cargo the *Warley* had ever carried.

There were already fifteen ships at the anchorage that would form the convoy home and more joined every day. Some he knew: *Royal George*, *Dorsetshire*, *Earl Camden*, *Cumberland* and *Henry Addington* had all made the crossing. The *Camden* had a new captain, Leonard Cartwright, who introduced himself to Tom over dinner. He had twenty years' experience with affiliate ships and had come into the fold of Company captains at the board's request.

They were joined by *Coutts*, *Wexford*, *Bombay Castle*, *Ocean* and *Warren Hastings*, making twelve Company ships. The rest of the convoy was made up of another fifteen affiliate or private ships. They would be escorted by three Royal Navy ships of war, the *Sceptre*—which would escort them all the way to England—the *Albion* and the frigate *Diana*.

Tom organised the convoy into the usual three columns led by *Royal George*, *Cumberland* and *Henry Addington*. The *Warley* would lead from the front.

Just before they left, the *Aurora* came into the anchorage and tied up alongside the *Warley*.

"Permission to come aboard," Edward called from the rail.

"Permission granted," Tom called back with a wave.

Edward jumped across to the deck and greeted Tom with a hearty handshake.

"Hoped to catch you before you left. We will be patrolling the Philippines."

"Still pirate hunting, then?" Tom smiled, pleased to see his friend.

"I hear you are retiring. You're a bit young for that."

"Good grief! Does everyone know?"

"My friend. When a captain such as you calls it a day, it makes the gossips happy."

Tom was amazed. "Why?"

"Oh, they are speculating as to why. You are still relatively young."

"I have a family, who I want to see grow up, and I have made enough to live the life of a gentleman landowner."

"*Pfft*. You will be telling me you are a magistrate next."

"Now that's a thought. I could slap errant sloop captains in gaol."

They both laughed at the thought. Then Tom asked, "Can you join me for dinner tonight?"

"Surely. We will sail after we have finished provisioning tomorrow."

Dinner was more of a party. Bill joined in, as did the captains of the warships and those that had fought at Pulo Aura. A merry time was had by all. Peter outdid himself with a five-course meal that would have graced the best tables in England. Much wine and port was drunk and tales told and retold. Tom slept content and sated, he dreamed of Mary and the children and woke with a hangover.

They set sail on the twenty-eighth of February. The convoy was one of the largest ever formed at Whampoa, with twenty-seven ships and three escorts. As they sailed out into the South China Sea they were joined by two more.

Malacca, Penang and St Helena

The schedule set by the Company required them to stop and collect more ships on their way. The already prodigious fleet made its way to the eastern entrance to the Malacca Strait, past the site of the battle. Tom ordered a single cannon fired in salute of the one man killed. The ships that had been there, dipped their flags.

"Deck there, sails a point for'ad of the port beam. Look like junks."

The escort had seen them, and the *Diana* went to investigate, her bow throwing up a fine wave.

"She's like a greyhound," Graham said.

"Aye, she sails beautifully."

The lookout reported that the sails disappeared as soon as the *Diana* got close.

"Probably Chinese pirates," Tom speculated.

At Malacca they picked up another passenger and put ashore the young botanist and his plants. He would take another ship to Chattogram. The new passenger was a striking young woman who radiated an air of independence and confidence.

She wore a French-style top hat set jauntily on her thick auburn hair, a long black skirt and jacket over a fancy blouse with a cravat. She had a Malay girl with her, who Tom assumed was a servant.

"Charlene Adams." She introduced herself and shook hands with a firm grip. "Call me Charlie." Her voice was deep and velvety, her accent clipped and educated. "This is Farah, my companion."

She put an emphasis on the word "companion" that caused Tom to do a double take. He realised the girl had a somewhat androgynous look that could be either male or female. He recovered and said, "Pleased to meet you, Miss Adams," then ducked a bow. "You are returning to England, I see."

"Yes, Father has expired, and I get the estate. Old bugger was seventy-eight and still chasing the fillies. Died after shagging the maid, I believe."

Tom was somewhat taken aback by her bluntness and mumbled some pointless condolences, which she ignored.

"Feel sorry for the girl, myself," Charlie concluded.

Edwards' lovely companion turned out to be the widow of an army captain, who had died of the fever while on campaign along the Afghan border. She joined them for dinner beautifully dressed and sporting an impressive set of jewels. Her name was Madelaine Griffon.

"Given to me by the Maharaja of Mysore," she said when asked where the jewels had come from. Tom's expert eye calculated that she could live comfortably for the rest of her life if she were to sell them. He also saw in her an iron core, that was wrapped around with a beauty she wore like a cloak. Her make-up was perfect, her hair arranged artfully, the dress cut low enough to entice without being scandalous. She was the perfect consort. Her conversation with Charlie Adams was mainly about horses, which seemed to be a common passion. Did Tom detect a flicker of annoyance on the face of Farah?

* * *

Penang was next. Several ships got new passengers and three more joined; one Company ship and two weather-beaten independents. They did not go ashore. A fleet of that size could not anchor in the bay and Tom did not want to spend a day getting them formed up again. He, however, did go ashore and found Dewi.

"I have a proposition for you."

"Really? What is that?"

"I want … no, I *need* someone over here who can continue finding the best quality stones for me and act as my buyer. Will you do it?"

"I work for the Company."

"And you can continue doing that, I don't believe there is anything in their employment contract that prohibits you doing something else as well."

"True … how will it work?"

"I intend to form a company in England to import and trade gems. It is the perfect time, as the war has cut off the supply from Holland. I have a man who I have been working with for the last few years who knows all the jewellers in London and beyond. He will be my partner." Tom didn't mention that he hadn't talked to Goldsmith about this yet.

Dewi looked thoughtful. "Will I be a shareholder?"

"Twenty per cent," Tom said immediately.

Dewi looked surprised then held out his hand. They shook, the deal was sealed. The two of them went shopping for stones.

After Tom had returned to the ship and just before they sailed, a package arrived. In it was a note and a gold cravat pin with a diamond head. It was from Dewi. All it said was, *Thanks, partner.*

Tom shook his head.

* * *

Miss Adams was a marvel. She was pithy, astute in her observations and had a scathing wit. None of the other passengers escaped her notice. Tom had a hard time not laughing out loud over dinner sometimes. She revealed that her family home was in Kent and her family were hop growers. They owned a five-hundred-acre farm that grew hops and barley, a brewery in the town of Gillingham and a shipping company. The brewery supplied the dockyard at Chatham, where they owned the pubs as well.

"Father never drank, apart from testing the brew occasionally. Said he never liked the small beer they sold for ships. We make gallons of the stuff. Costs practically nothing to make as it's from the third brewing of the wort," she told Tom one morning as she took a stroll around the deck.

Tom could see how the family had become rich. Supplying the navy with beer for their ships must be a licence to print money.

Charlie, in her turn, liked Tom. She was not *attracted* to him in any way of course, as she much preferred women, but he was intelligent and a good conversationalist, which made him good company. He also did not judge her, which was unusual. She saw him on the poop deck as she took her walk.

"Good morning, Captain!" she called up.

"Good morning, Charlie, you are up early. Come up here and look at this." He beckoned her up to his hallowed ground.

"My, this is a privilege."

"Don't tell anyone or they will all want to come up."

She laughed.

"Look at that," he said, and swept his arm from one quarter to the other. Spread out behind them were the three columns of ships. Two cables between columns and each ship a cable behind the one ahead, they covered 330 acres of sea.

"That is indeed an impressive sight," she said. "What are those ships doing over there?" She pointed to the escorts out to windward.

"Those are our escorts. They stay out to windward as that gives them the best opportunity to intercept any ships that get too close."

She looked at him out the corner of her eye.

"Pirates, you mean?"

Tom smiled, there was no softness there.

"Did you expect me to faint or something?"

"Not at all. I expect you have several guns and a sword ready to repel boarders," Tom said with a laugh.

"No sword but a sharp knife or two and a brace of pistols."

"There you are, then."

"Where is he going?" she said and pointed to the *Diana*.

"One of the ships at the end of the column is probably out of position." Tom took up a telescope and scanned the columns. "Aah, yes. The *Abergavenny* has dropped back."

Flags flew up the frigate's mast and a gun fired. The *boom* reached them moments later.

"The *Diana* has the hardest job. She is the sheepdog that keeps the flock together."

"She is beautiful."

Edwards came on deck with Mrs Griffon.

"There's Madelaine—will you excuse me, Captain?" Charlie said.

"Certainly," Tom replied.

As she reached the top of the steps, Charlie turned and grinned. "Look at her rosy cheeks. She was earning her keep last night!"

* * *

The trip across the Bay of Bengal was made interesting by a couple of storms that came down from the north and kept the convoy moving at night. Tom didn't mind at all as they covered more sea that way and they reached the Madagascar Channel on the seventeenth of April. The crew were on high alert and the convoy maintained ten knots all the way through.

Even with the high risk of attack in that region, some captains still lacked either the skill or discipline to maintain position, especially at night. Blue alarm rockets flew up as lookouts saw—or thought they saw—threats. The *Diana* responded to all, but in the morning a ship was missing. The *Abergavenny* was nowhere to be seen.

Tom could not risk the entire convoy to look for them and he did not want to weaken their escort by allowing the *Diana* out of sight. So the best he could do was allow the *Diana* to drop back and scan the horizon. She returned having seen nothing.

The loss of a ship annoyed Tom. "Why can't they keep station? It's not so hard," he complained to Graham.

"The *Abergavenny* was under manned. I spoke to one of the other first mates who knew her when we were in Penang, and he said they only had twenty-five crew and most of them were lascars."

"That explains it, then." Tom blew out his cheeks. "Well, they will all be dead now and the cargo lost."

"Lloyds will cover it—if they were insured."

"Isn't that part of the problem? Owners underman ships and Lloyds still insure them. The owner cannot lose."

They made it through the channel with no more losses. The *Abergavenny* incident seemed to focus the minds of the errant captains.

The southern tip of Africa presented other problems. The trade wind was against them until they got around it and picked up the south-easterly winds. That meant the whole convoy had to tack in unison.

Long tacks were the order of the day and Tom soon learned the limits of his charges. Some of the private ships could not sail as close to the wind as the Company ships so Tom had to ease a little until he found the optimal angle.

He anchored in bays overnight when he could, to rest the passengers and the lighter crews. They sailed over 1,200 sea miles to progress 850, rounded the corner and passed Cape Town. It was 2,000 miles to St Helena.

They reached St Helena on the second of July and Tom decided to stop for a week at James Town to replenish and give the crews a chance to stretch their legs ashore. There were a couple of whalers in port, who would tag along when they left, but apart from that the convoy and a couple of warships were all that were there.

The *Diana* and *Albion* would leave them, so he treated their officers to a farewell dinner. Captains and lieutenants attended. The predominantly rocky island had a couple of valleys to support agriculture, so fresh beef and vegetables were available. That enabled Peter to provide a sumptuous roast beef rib with all the trimmings.

There was not much to see on St Helena, but the walks were pretty for those who stuck to the fertile valleys. The exercise cleared Tom's mind and allowed him to forget his responsibilities for a day.

Epilogue

The ship tied up in India Dock on the seventh of September. The passengers debarked and cargo was unloaded. Tom's friendly customs officer was there, and he turned a blind eye to his personal cargo for a consideration. Tom took rooms in London and sent messages to Edwards and Goldsmith. The tea he sold to Twinings as usual.

Edwards arrived with Madelaine.

"Your chest," Tom said.

Edwards opened it and checked the contents. "Thank you, Captain." He handed over a banker's draft from Barings Bank. "I believe we have the same banker."

"We do, indeed."

Edwards shook his hand. "If I can be of any service to you in the future, please just contact me. The bank knows where to find me."

Two burly coachmen, both carrying guns, came in and carried the chest to the waiting landau.

Madelaine kissed him on the cheek. "Thank you for looking after us during the voyage, and I hope you enjoy your retirement."

Goldsmith turned up the following day. Tom laid out the gems for him to check.

"My boy, you have become expert in selecting the best. These are all outstanding stones. It is a real pity you are not sailing anymore."

"Don't you worry, they will keep coming. I have a man in Penang who will keep finding stones for us."

"For *us*?"

"Yes, I want to go into business with you. I have the connections overseas and I know enough about gems to be the buyer and importer. You have the connections to distribute them. My man in Penang gets a twenty per cent stake in the new venture."

Goldsmith pondered that. It was true, he had contacts throughout London, especially in the growing Hatton Garden district, and this would cut out the Dutch. Tom had capital to invest; it sounded like a good deal.

"I agree, we will start a new company. What should we call it?"

"We should keep it nondescript. How about Fortune Trading?"

Goldsmith laughed. "That will do very nicely."

They registered the company the next day. The gems Tom had brought back were their first offerings and they started to trade immediately.

Tom wrote to Dewi, enclosing his share certificates and a bank draft to buy more gems. The next home convoy would bring a wealth of new products of the best quality.

The last thing he needed to do was hand the *Warley* over to her new captain. He met William Augustus Montague as he walked up the gangplank.

"Good afternoon, Captain Montague, welcome to the *Warley*," Tom said and held out his hand.

"Commodore Batrick," Montague said stiffly.

The handshake was brief and not very firm.

Tom showed him his quarters. "I have no need of the furniture, you can have it if you want, or I can have it removed and sold off," Tom said.

"I have my own," Montague said looking at it a little disdainfully.

Not good enough for you, then. So Tom offered to introduce him to Graham and the mates.

"I will be bringing my own men aboard; please inform the crew they are dismissed."

Tom was horrified.

"But these men know this ship and are a well-trained crew."

"So I am told, and they are fiercely loyal to you as my men are to me. There are plenty of new ships looking for men, they will not suffer."

And that was that. Tom paid off the crew and shook each man's hand as they left the ship. Peter waited until last.

"I want to thank you, sir. By working for you I have gained knowledge of many different cuisines. I am going to open an eating house in London."

"That's excellent. Do you have enough money?"

"I have saved my pay and prize money. I have enough and more."

"Well, I wish you all the best. Write to me with the address and next time I am in London, I will come and eat there."

Last, but not least, he visited East India House. He was welcomed by the committee and thanked for his service. A special award was made for the rescue of the *Dorsetshire*, with Bob in attendance. Five hundred pounds was more than welcome and would be invested in the future.

With everything done, Tom could go home.

Poole was wreathed in mizzle when he stepped ashore. A carriage sat on the dock with a handsome set of four matched greys. He did not recognise it, and ignored it until a familiar head poked out of the window.

"Hello sailor," Mary said. "Can I show you a good time?"

Tom burst out laughing and stepped into the coach to wrap her in his arms.

"You are all wet," she laughed.

"It's this wonderful English weather. Whose coach is this?"

"Ours, I bought it from Lord Fredrick, he wanted rid of it."

"Probably needed the money." Tom grinned.

The coach rocked as his baggage was loaded. A face appeared through the window. "All done, governor," it said. Tom passed him a couple of coins. "Thankee, squire." The man touched his forelock and disappeared.

On the way to the house, Tom told Mary of the new company and the rewards he had received.

"You will be staying at home now?"

"Apart from regular trips to London, yes."

"Perfect."

When they got to the house he was greeted enthusiastically by little Tom and a waddling Anne. His mother had resigned herself to a life of comfort and a nanny was in attendance. The next phase of Tom's life was beginning.

Historic Notes

It is widely believed that **the flag used by the East India Company** prior to 1801 inspired the 1775 Grand Union Flag, which was the first national flag of the United States. Indeed, Benjamin Franklin is known to have publicly supported the use of the design in this way. Use of the East India Company's signifier was perhaps a means of indicating both support for the Crown and the ambitions of the nascent United States to be—like the EIC—independent, powerful and entrepreneurial. Furthermore, during this time some Americans hoped for support from the EIC during the American War of Independence, not least due to a shared dislike of British tax policies.

All this being said, there is little *written* evidence of a direct link between the flags.

Georgian Christmas Games

Games were a common feature of Christmas celebrations in Georgian times, and included:

- Questions and Commands: This was effectively a form of today's Truth or Dare. Players were asked a question or received a command and if any player answered their question incorrectly or did not complete their task, they had to take a drink.
- Nip Nose: Players sat in circles, one within the other and ideally with each man facing a woman. The guest on the inner circle had to "nip" the nose of the person facing them, and ask them silly questions or behave in daft ways to make the "nipped" person laugh. If the "nipped" person showed any sign of amusement, even a smirk, they had to complete a forfeit.
- Fly Feather Fly: Players huddled together and a very light object—often a feather—was thrown into the air above them. All players had to blow upwards to keep the feather airborne and if it fell and landed on somebody's face, that person had to complete a forfeit.

Indian City Names

1797/8	**2023**
Bombay	Mumbai
Tellicherry	Thalassery
Cochin	Kochi
Anjengo	Anchuthengu

Chinese City Names

1797/8	2023
Whampoa	Pazhou

Indonesian City Names

1797/8	2023
Batavia	Jakarta

The Swedish Christmas song *Jul, jul, strålande jul* translates as follows:

Christmas, Christmas, radiant Christmas, splendour over white forests,
the crowns of heaven with sparkling light.
gleaming arches in all the houses of God,
hymn, which is sung from time to time,
Eternal longing for light and peace!
Christmas, Christmas, radiant Christmas: Glory over the white forests!
Come, come, sign Christmas! Lower your white wings
over the blood and noise of battles,
over all the sighing of human bosom,
over the generations that go to rest,
over the nest of the young!
Come, come, blessed Christmas, lower your white wings

Letters of marque were issued by the High Court of Admiralty. Generally, the privateer had to pay a very substantial deposit (often more than £1,000) to guarantee his good behaviour at sea, and was required to record the details of his ship, crew and weapons, with ownership often split into shares. All gains the privateer made were valued, and the profits distributed in agreed proportions between stakeholders. These included the government, ship owners, captain and crew.

Batavia, now called Jakarta, was the capital of the Dutch East Indies. In eighteenth- and nineteenth-century contexts, Batavia can refer to the city itself, and/or to its suburbs and substantially beyond, areas that are now the Indonesian provinces of Jakarta, Banten and West Java.

Glossary of Sailing Terms Used in This Book

Beam – The beam of a ship is its width at its widest point.

Bowsprit – A spar projecting from the bow of a vessel, especially a sailing vessel, used to carry the headstay as far forward as possible.

Cable – A cable length or length of cable is a nautical unit of measure, equal to one tenth of a nautical mile or approximately 100 fathoms. Owing to anachronisms and varying techniques of measurement, a cable length can be anywhere from 169 to 220 metres, depending on the standard used. In this book, we assume 200 yards.

Cay – A low bank or reef of coral, rock or sand—especially one on the islands of Spanish America.

Futtock shrouds – Rope, wire or chain links in the rigging of a traditional square-rigged ship. They run from the outer edges of a top, downwards and inwards to a point on the **mast** or lower shrouds, and carry the load of the shrouds that rise from the edge of the top. This prevents any tendency of the top itself to tilt relative to the mast.

Gripe – A tendency to come up into the wind in spite of the helm.

Ketch – A two-masted sailing vessel, fore-and-aft rigged with a tall mainmast and a mizzen stepped forward of the rudderpost.

Knee – A naturally-occurring or cut, curved piece of wood. Knees, sometimes called ship's knees, are a common form of bracing in boatbuilding.

Knot – The measure of speed at sea. One knot = 1.11 miles.

Leeway – The leeward drift of a ship is with the wind towards the lee side.

Loblolly boys – Surgeons' assistants.

Lugger – A sailing vessel defined by its rig using the lug sail on all of its one or several masts. They were widely used as working craft, particularly off the coast. Luggers varied extensively in size and design. Many were undecked, open boats, others were fully decked.

Mizzen – (1) The after mast on a yawl, ketch or dandy. Or (2) the third mast from the bow on a vessel with three or more masts.

Nippers – Ships' boys who "nipped" the anchor cable to the never-ending messenger cable, attached to the capstan, with ropes so the anchor could be raised.

Pawls – A catch that drops into the teeth of a capstan, to stop it being pulled in reverse.

In ordinary – Vessels that are out of service for repair or maintenance, a meaning coming over time to cover a reserve fleet or "mothballed" ships.

Ratlines – Lengths of thin line tied between the shrouds of a sailing ship to form a ladder. Found on all square-rigged ships, whose crews must go aloft to stow the square sails, they also appear on larger fore-and-aft rigged vessels to aid in repairs aloft or conduct a lookout from above.

Rib – A thin strip of pliable timber laid athwarts inside a hull from inwale to inwale at regular close intervals to reinforce its planking. Ribs differ from frames or futtocks in being far smaller dimensions and bent in place compared to frames or futtocks, which are normally sawn to shape, or natural crooks that are shaped to fit with an adze, axe or chisel.

Sea anchor – Any device, such as a bucket or canvas funnel, dragged in the water to keep a vessel heading into the wind or reduce drifting.

Shrouds – On a sailing boat, the shrouds are pieces of standing rigging, which hold the mast up from side to side. There is frequently more than one shroud on each side of the boat. Usually, a shroud will connect at the top of the mast, and additional shrouds might connect partway down the mast, depending on the design of the boat. Shrouds terminate at their bottom ends at the chain plates, which are tied into the hull. They are sometimes held outboard by channels, a ledge that keeps the shrouds clear of the gunwales.

Stay – Part of the standing rigging, used to support the weight of a mast. It is a large strong rope extending from the upper end of each mast.

Sweeps – Another name for oars.

Tack – If a sailing ship is tacking or if the people in it tack it, it is sailing towards a particular point in a series of lateral movements rather than in a direct line.

Tumblehome – A hull which grows narrower above the waterline than its beam.

Wear ship – To change the tack of a sailing vessel, especially a square-rigger, by coming about so that the wind passes astern.

Weather Gauge – Sometimes spelled *weather gage* is the advantageous position of a fighting sailing vessel relative to another. It is also known as a *nautical gauge*, as it is related to the seashore.

Printed in Dunstable, United Kingdom

80913456R00170